BLURB

My name is Rev.
I like long walks on the beach.
A neat scotch.
And I like stealing from rich losers who have no idea the
town's Big Bad Wolf screwed their wives six ways to
Sunday.
Such a scandal, indeed.
I have one end goal-to get out of this town.
I'm a loner. And that's by choice.
People aren't really my thing. That is...until I meet her. The
little firecracker who sets more than my soul on fire.
No one has ever stuck around.
But Darcie is different. She seems to be as broken as me,
and when our worlds collide, nothing but trouble looms.
Watch out, baby...down the rabbit hole we go.

REV AND DARCIE

International Bestselling Author

MONICA JAMES
MICHELLE LANCASTER

CRYBABY

OTHER BOOKS BY MONICA JAMES

THE I SURRENDER SERIES

I Surrender

Surrender to Me

Surrendered

White

SOMETHING LIKE NORMAL SERIES

Something like Normal

Something like Redemption

Something like Love

A HARD LOVE ROMANCE

Dirty Dix

Wicked Dix

The Hunt

MEMORIES FROM YESTERDAY

Forgetting You, Forgetting Me

Forgetting You, Remembering Me

SINS OF THE HEART

Absinthe of the Heart

Defiance of the Heart

ALL THE PRETTY THINGS TRILOGY

Bad Saint

Fallen Saint

Forever My Saint

The Devil's Crown-Part One (Spin-Off)

The Devil's Crown-Part Two (Spin-Off)

THE MONSTERS WITHIN DUET

Bullseye

Blowback

DELIVER US FROM EVIL TRILOGY

Thy Kingdom Come

Into Temptation

Deliver Us From Evil

IN LOVE AND WAR

North of the Stars

Fall of the Stars

Set Fire to the Stars

REVENGE IS SWEET SERIES

Crybaby

HEART MEMORY TRANSFER DUET

Heart Sick

Love Sick

KISS OR KILL DUET

Bad For You

Kill For You

LOVE HARD

Love Hard

Love Harder

STANDALONE

Mr. Write

Chase the Butterflies

Beyond the Roses

Someone Else's Shadow

Like a Boss

AUTHORS NOTE

CRYBABY is a **DARK ROMANCE** containing mature themes that might make some readers uncomfortable. It contains strong violence, sexual assault, murder, accidental death, attempted murder, profanity, drug use, theft, criminal activity, pyromania, blood gore, and some dark and disturbing scenes. In no way, shape, or form are we glorifying any of the situations or circumstances in this book.
There is no cruelty to animals.
This twisted tale is not intended for the fainthearted. So, if you're game...follow us down the rabbit hole, baby.

Prologue

After

There's something about the force of a kick to the head that lets you know you're human. The blood rushing in your ears, pulsing to the beat of your heart. Everything sounds like it's underwater. Like the water in my brain sloshing around, realigning synapses.

I was reborn that night.

In the dirt, in the grass, amongst smelly teens with their cheap aftershave and wet cocks. Their voices barely broken and cheering as if it's a homecoming game to egg each other on.

"Fuck her harder."

"Hold her down."

Words that will forever echo in the deep recesses of my mind.

I was dragged by my arms across a football field...as if I'm not light enough to carry.

The floodlights blinded my eyes as they rolled back into my head, which hit the edge of the bleachers at one point. I still have the scar on my scalp.

War wounds.

I thought God would save me and just let me pass out. My parents taught me that God was our Savior and Heavenly Father. But life is cruel, and survival instincts made me stay awake to watch and witness every moment.

Did they know they were creating a monster that night when they used my body like a fun park? Deflowering me as my naked ass kissed the night sky.

I broke my fingernails clawing at the dirt just trying to dig my own grave.

They tore at my clothes and used me like a fuck toy for their own amusement. Was it power, lust, or revenge? I'll never know, and I don't care.

I found something within me that night, with every thrust and beating...I got a taste for havoc. I knew then that I'd be back for him, and him...and him too.

A wrath so bittersweet...I could taste it mixed with the blood in my mouth as I screamed silently into the night... *Forgive me, Father, for I will sin.*

CHAPTER ONE

Rev

Before

Three days.

72 hours.

4,320 minutes.

259,200 seconds.

That's how long the average human can survive without water.

However, food is an entirely different ball game.

One to three months is the ballpark figure, but as I stuff my cheeks full of this Reuben sandwich on rye, it's evident whoever came up with this cookie-cutter number was never a thief.

I don't know what it is about stolen goods, though. They just seem to feel, smell...taste better. This sandwich is no exception. However, I suppose, technically, I didn't steal it.

I fucked Maree Vanderbilt six ways to Sunday and made her come, and in return, as she lies in her post-orgasmic bliss, chasing her Oxy with an expensive scotch, I'll experience my own high as I help myself to the contents of her fridge...and the priceless artwork that hangs on Maree's kitchen wall—the real reason I'm here.

Red.

Yellow.

Pink.

Green.

A kaleidoscope of colors is before me, but all I can focus on is black.

How the stroke of a single black line can transform something so picturesque, so colorful, into something else.

How, in the end, the darkness...it always wins.

As I appreciate the splashes of color, I wonder what Maree thinks when she looks at it. Will she, too, see that beauty can be found hidden amongst the darkness?

But women like Maree—bored socialites—don't concern themselves with shit like this. I'm sure the only reason this Floyd Brassard—a local artist who made it big and moved to Germany before cutting off his cock to use as his favorite paintbrush—piece hangs in Maree's mansion is because she thought it matched her feature wall.

We walk, talk, function like we're alive, but the truth is, we're all waiting...waiting for something more.

And when you have it all, you're always chasing a bigger, better ending, never satisfied with the riches you possess, which is why I can do what I do...and not feel a fucking thing.

With elbows resting on the marbled counter, I chew my sandwich leisurely. I'm in no hurry. Ballsy, I know. Helping myself to Pierre Vanderbilt's prized corned beef after desecrating his marital bed.

Looking at the stolen gold Rolex on my wrist, courtesy of Pierre, I see he'll be home any second. Maree said he was working out at the gym, but I'm sure he didn't break a sweat doing cardio. Doing a pretty blonde at the gym is the most probable scenario.

Most would make haste, but I'm not most.

I wipe the spilled sauerkraut from the corner of my mouth with my thumb, sucking it with a pop. The fridge door is ajar, and the light inside is the beacon I need. My scuffed black Converse squeak on the linoleum as I walk toward the painting.

I stand in front of it, my reflection staring back at me from the polished glass frame.

"You could be a model," Maree said as she lay spread out on her king-sized bed, nestled in Persian silk. *"With those piercing, come fuck me golden eyes, dark, tousled hair, and a jawline that goes on for days, you must have all the young girls wrapped around your little finger. Your mere presence commands attention, and you're not even aware of it."*

I've heard this before, but I don't really understand it. Sure, I fucking love being in control, but I don't really look the part of Prince Charming. But it doesn't seem to matter.

"Why would I waste my time with young girls when I can fuck a real woman?" I confessed, leisurely winding the red silk tie—the one Maree insisted I use—around my wrist as I stood at the foot of the bed. *"There was a reason we met at the farmers' market."*

She didn't know the real reason was because I scouted that farmers' market for women like her—rich, powerful women who are my meal ticket—no pun intended—out of here.

Our meeting wasn't fate. It was an opportunity, and I took it, just like I've done for a long time.

Pilfering has helped me survive. It gave life to the demons inside my head, but the demons, they linger, and sooner or later, they'll consume me for good, which is why I need to get my mom and me out of here.

It's just us. I don't know who my father is. And I'm okay with that fact.

He promised her the world, but what he left her with

was a void so big, she has tried to fill it with any booze or drugs she can find.

She dresses in her best clothes, looking out the window, believing today is the day he comes to save us from hell. But no one's coming. There never will be. We can only save ourselves.

"Are you going to fuck me now?" Maree purred into my ear as I fastened her wrists to the headboard.

"Yes, Maree, I am," I stated with confidence.

Regardless of the fact that I was using her and she me, I appreciate beauty whenever, wherever I see it, and I won't forget the image of Maree Vanderbilt tied to her four-poster bed as I fucked her senseless anytime soon.

As I carefully remove the glass frame from the wall and unlatch the backing, I softly rest the frame on the wooden kitchen table. When I lay my hands on the parchment, a sharp intake of breath leaves me.

This is what gets me hard.

Cautiously removing the painting, I delicately roll it up and retrieve a Polaroid of my cock from my backpack. I lick the back of it and slap it so it sits dead center in the frame with a lovely amount of negative space around it.

Once it's on the wall, I take a step back, cocking my head to the side with a lopsided smirk.

Chef's kiss.

Not sure if Maree will appreciate the memorabilia, however. But I'd kill to see her explain her way out of this one. I, on the other hand, would have no issues explaining why there's a cock hanging on the kitchen wall.

It's all about thinking outside the box—pun totally intended.

I'm good at what I do because I pay attention. Most people listen, waiting for when it's their turn to talk, but not me. I listen and learn, as a smart predator should. It's the only way I know how to survive.

The women I fuck and steal from use me just as much as I use them. I'm their dirty little secret they replay in their minds when they get fucked from behind by Mr. Viagra's small cock. They like to reminisce about how they had dirty sex with a high school student.

But I'm far from a kid.

I grew up quick as I was more a parent to my mom than she was to me.

I've lost count of how many times I've thrown her drunk ass into the shower to sober her up. Or shoved my fingers down her throat to force the concoction of prescription pills back up.

But I don't complain.

This taught me early on that to survive in this world, you've got to stop hitching a ride and grab life by the balls. If there's an opportunity, take it. Hesitating will only end in regret, and I won't live a day wondering what-if.

That's why I do what I do with a smile, and I don't regret a single thing.

Guys my age will be talking about pussy and getting drunk, but I don't have time for that. I want more in life. I refuse to be a statistic. I'm leaving this fucking town, and I'm doing so on the wealth of the people I stole from.

It's poetic justice, really.

The roller door on the garage whines open, alerting me that it's time to bounce.

Shouldering my backpack, I go to the fridge and open Pierre's packed lunch for tomorrow and quickly defile it with my tongue...just like I did to Maree's pussy.

Seems only fair Pierre gets in on the action too.

My footsteps echo in the empty hall as I coolly make my

way toward the front door. I stroll. Don't run. Just as I exit the front, Pierre enters through the back. It's that easy.

Slipping on my hood, I walk through the manicured gardens and peek into the kitchen window.

Pierre tosses his car keys onto the counter, shaking his head when he sees the fridge door ajar. He closes it, but I know that Rueben sandwich has caught his eye. This fucker doesn't look like he's had a carb since 1984.

A temptation awaits him. What will he do?

Pierre stuffs the entire thing into his mouth but freezes mid-chew as his gaze becomes fixed on the wall in front of him.

And that's my cue to leave.

Walking across the plush front lawn, I ensure I leave muddy footprints. I'm about to disappear into the night but stop dead in my tracks when the full moon catches a flick of silver from across the street.

I don't know why I stop, but it's like my feet are suddenly rooted to the earth beneath them.

I feel her eyes before I see them. Like a cat in the night, they seem to glow.

A girl stands by the curb, a towering white oak tree obscuring her from the world.

I wonder if she's waiting for someone. She's barefooted, and in a white hooded bunny suit, so I doubt she's waiting for a ride. I wonder what she's doing out here so late at night.

I don't have time for anything, or anyone—period—but something about this girl, who doesn't give a fuck standing in the darkness, her white bunny outfit contrasting the night sky, intrigues me.

I've never seen her before. I would have remembered if I had.

Her long blonde hair is tied in two loose pigtails, which spill free from the bunny-eared hood she wears. The silver that caught my eye comes from the large silver crucifix around her neck. Out here, under the moonlight, dressed like a white bunny, she fucking takes my breath away.

I stare at her.

She stares at me.

I expect her to look away, but she doesn't.

She simply stands under the tree, watching me as closely as I'm watching her.

Her confidence as well as what the fuck she's doing out here dressed this way leaves me fascinated, and against my better judgment, I cross the street.

However, I stop in the middle, not wanting to crowd her. Needing to keep some space between us.

Digging my hands in the pockets of my ripped jeans, I wait for her to speak. Most girls would act coy and maybe bite their lip.

But not this girl.

Up close, she's even more captivating than she is from afar.

Her eyes light up her delicate face, though it also has an edge to it. She purses her red lips and raises her eyebrows, unimpressed that I'm invading her space. Not the usual response I receive from the opposite sex.

A dark-green leaf catches the cool breeze and detaches from the tree. It flips in the air before landing between her bunny ears. She leaves it perched on her head.

"It's called white oak because newly cut wood appears light in color and is almost white," I say nonchalantly.

I'm expecting a smile or maybe even a twitch of the lips, but I get nothing. Nada. Now would be the time to walk away, dignity intact, but I can't—the whole living life without regret thing.

I open my mouth, about to spew off another fact, but she folds her arms around her small frame. "You can use Google. Congratulations."

"Google is for lazy morons," I counter without thought. "I prefer the old way—actually reading a book. In a library. Away from people."

"You're not a people person?" she questions evenly, brushing the leaf from her head. "I can't see why not? Spurting all that fun, factual information must win you a load of friends."

"I don't know why you'd think I care. Friends are only good for long treks in the snow. Just ask Alfred Packer."

"Who's Alfred Packer?" Her interest has me wishing I used a different fact to prove my point. But I can't stop now.

"The Colorado Cannibal," I explain coolly, running a hand through my long bangs. "A prospector who got hungry during one of his quests and ate his crew during the winter of 1874."

I smile.

She does not.

I expect her to turn away, disgusted, as most would, but she doesn't.

"At least he didn't have to worry about refrigeration."

I open but soon close my mouth because, for once in my life, I'm caught off guard.

"How do you know all this stuff?"

And there is the question that has plagued me my entire life.

I always knew I was different. Since I can remember, I've been able to retain information and recite it without a problem. That seems like something most can do.

But when I explained to my mom how to change the spark plugs in her car, she knew I was special. I was five.

I overheard the mechanic at the local garage we walked by the week prior describe it to Mrs. Murphy, and it just stuck with me, as do most things. I don't know how I know. I just do...but being here with this strange girl is something I don't know.

And I don't like it.

I like to assert control in all aspects of my life, and standing here, in the middle of the street, under the full moon, I am not in control.

Reaching into my backpack for my pack of cigarettes, I casually light one, making a point to look at the crucifix around the girl's neck. I don't even know her name.

"So what's a good girl like you doing out here in the dark?"

Smoke plumes between us, and the nicotine is exactly what I need to calm this pulsating energy.

Her eyes linger on my lips, but I soon realize it's not my mouth she's transfixed by, but rather, the ember of my cigarette, which glows red.

Her gaze soon focuses on it, and I don't move when she steps forward and stands on her toes to steal the cigarette from between my lips.

She places it between hers, inhaling deeply.

I wait with bated breath.

"What makes you think I'm a good girl?"

I point at the crucifix around her throat.

A smile spreads across her cheeks, but the devil himself may as well be grinning at me, and when a red glow suddenly smolders from behind her, it just confirms the fact.

"Looks can be deceiving," she states, calmly blowing out a cloud of smoke.

The crimson glow suddenly gets bigger, brighter, and when I look over her head, I see that's because the prized red rose bush of the double-story house we stand in front of is on fire.

"Your rose bush is on fire," I say casually, and she laughs lightly. The sound fucking scares me for all the right reasons.

"I bet you say that to all the girls." Does she know what I was doing across the road?

Before I have a chance to reply, the porch light switches on. I suspect her parents are about to put out the fire, but when she tosses the cigarette to the ground and grabs my hand, it seems I've misread this entire thing.

"Run!" she cries, her excitement palpable as we break into a dead sprint away from her house. But the farther we run, the clearer it becomes that that isn't her home.

We run through the neighborhood, our footsteps pounding against the concrete in sync with our heavy breaths. Her amused giggles punch me low when we hear the anguished screams of whoever's rose bush she just set alight.

"Just another Sunday night for you then?" I quip while she turns to me, grinning.

We continue running away from the crime scene, hand in hand, and I can't help but feel it's us versus the world. A stupid thought to have as this girl is clearly a pyromaniac, and I'm a thief. But this is the most fun I've had in a while.

We turn a corner, and she suddenly lets go of my hand.

We stand still, breathless and facing one another with the world on fire around us. But I don't look away. I can't. And it seems she can't either.

With her bare feet and bunny suit, she fucking slays me because I want to know who she is. But I don't get the chance to ask as she suddenly runs down a driveway where she jumps over the fence, ignoring the German Shepherd that nips at her bunny tail.

"Who are you?" I say to myself in awe, staring toward where she disappeared into the darkness.

I don't believe in fate, but I can't shake the feeling the world as I know it is about to be set alight—in every possible way.

CHAPTER TWO
Darcie

I rarely look at myself in the mirror.

Mainly just at my hands as I button my shirt or shift my school tie—a prerequisite for the new school I'm attending today.

I'll look at my mouth, then skim over the details of my face and look at my hair as I tie it back so that it hangs like a pale horsetail down my back. I don't dare look into my own eyes. They are my mother's eyes...ones I'll never see again.

It was the summer of 2019, and we were driving down to our regular holiday cabin for the school break. It had just gone dark, and cars flashed past us from time to time, but most of the road ahead was just black.

We'd driven this way what felt like a million times before.

I sat in the back trying to get service on my iPhone and cursed under my breath about having to spend my break in the middle of nowhere with my parents. My father hated anything electronic and anything that took quality time away from the family. There wouldn't be any television.

Mom was the peacekeeper and often drove the car on these trips. I'm sure my father was just humoring her by giving her the wheel. He was very traditional with strict churchgoing values. Values he couldn't really impress upon me without an argument ensuing.

"If you spent less time on that device, you'd do yourself a great favor, Darcie!"

His voice was the same booming sound that carried over the pews in church. He always spoke to me like I was standing at the back of a room, amongst a crowd. He didn't even have to turn around in his seat for me to hear him.

"If I didn't have this device, I wouldn't have one friend since you always make me go on these holidays while everyone is out doing what kids my age are supposed to do!" I spat back at him.

"What children are supposed to do is experience the world as one should without their heads buried in utter garbage!"

"Garbage? How do you even know? You don't even know what Facebook is. You've never even seen the internet! This is 2019! Not 1960!" I shrieked, infuriated.

My mother sighed as she drove on, and I knew this argument was wearing thin on her. She asked me not to poke the bear, yet I found myself doing it every single time.

"As soon as we arrive, I'll be taking that from you so you can focus on what's important, Darcie! I'll hear no more about it. God did not intend for us to walk around with our heads attached to telephones!" he retorted firmly.

"*Telephones?*" I scoffed. "You don't even know what you're talking about!"

In my frustration, I threw my phone forward between the two front seats, and it hit the windshield. I immediately regretted it, of course, and my father spun around in his seat to reinforce his authority when, out of nowhere, I saw blinding lights block my vision.

In some evil twist of fate, a truck veered into our car. It felt like slow motion.

The details are blurry, and I often think about them

from the outside, as if I'm standing on the side of the road watching and not inside the car at all.

I never heard one word from either of my parents again. Only the sound of metal screeching and the loudest bang that made my ears ring. Everything went black, and I could feel warmth flowing all down my head and face.

Blood.

My parents' and my blood.

My knees were crushed beneath my seat. I saw my mother destroyed behind the wheel.

Broken.

I could smell the soap she used; it always comforted me.

Lying with her, I hoped I would die, and I closed my eyes, trying not to breathe. If I could just stop breathing, this nightmare would end.

My father would surely leave me behind at the pearly white gates and send me down to hell.

I deserved to go to hell and burn.

I killed my parents that night. And in a way, I killed myself too.

Only, I had to continue to walk the earth as the pissed-off empty shell that I am.

So I burn things. Letterboxes, fences, small bugs, my hair, and, more recently, my school gym.

I guess you'd call that a cry for help.

And now, I've been given one last chance to prove I can behave in society by being placed with my aunt and uncle, who are sending me to a new school where no one knows anything about my past.

The first day of school is like being put in a group assignment with a bunch of morons.

I've walked half an hour in new shoes to get here, so most of my anxiety has settled in my blistered feet. I'm an observer; I like to watch and remain passive unless someone rattles me, then my response is like a catfight on a fence.

I have my earbuds in, pretending to listen to music so I don't have to interact with anyone or make small talk. I'm watching people go by and giving them all a soundtrack to the way they move.

High school jock—blond, broad shoulders, square jaw—walks down the hall with his head turned to the side to see who is staring at him. His track is "Watermelon Sugar" by Harry Styles.

As he walks past the lockers, girls spin around to say "hi" every time the song hits watermelon sugar 'high.'

Then there are gangsters—pockets of guys who wish they were living in the hood but really go home to Daddy's mansion while their mom prepares their lunch for the next day. They push their uniform pants down super low and cock their ties to the side.

They walk like they're carrying a week of shopping in both pockets, and all I'm hearing is the song "Fuck Tha Police."

I start laughing, and I'm suddenly aware of a body standing way too close to me.

"Care to share?"

Turning, I don't know if this is fate or bad luck, but standing before me is the guy from last night. He looks different in a uniform, but I wouldn't forget those piercing eyes.

It takes a lot to shock me, but what the actual fuck?

Last night, I wasn't expecting to run into anyone, let alone a guy who looks like Zac Efron and Superman had a baby. Jet-black hair and golden eyes stab at my senses, but it's not just his good looks that get me. It's the fact that underneath all that, I sense something...more.

Our meeting was far from what most would call normal, but the moment between us, me standing in my bunny suit and him skulking in the shadows, was normal to us.

However, I have the best poker face you've ever seen. My walls are high, so good luck getting over them.

I can hear him clearly, but pretend my music is too loud.

"Huh?" I respond without taking my earbuds out.

A slanted smirk spreads from cheek to cheek, revealing he doesn't buy my story. Smart *and* attractive—it doesn't seem fair.

The bell rings, and I'm shuffled through the crowd toward my first class.

"Good morning, everyone. Take your seats! Take your seats!" shrieks a small woman wearing pumps and a cardigan draped over E cups.

Every schoolboy's wet dream, I'm sure.

I wonder if tall, dark, and annoying has paid her a visit yet. I'm sure he came out of a woman's house last night. He had pink lipstick on his neck and smelled of expensive perfume.

I take a seat next to the window and watch the teacher banging her hand on the table. The room smells like leather shoes and hairspray. I put my head down and pretend to be busy with something. The principal of the school enters the room and addresses the class.

"Students. Your regular teacher, Mrs. Jamieson, will be on leave due to a personal emergency involving a house fire. To quash any rumors that may arise, she is safe and in good health.

"Miss Knox will be taking over until further notice. Please give her your attention and respect. Over to you." He nods toward her breasts and leaves the room.

House fire? Please.

It was one fucking rose bush...and an ugly one at that.

My cheeks suddenly heat, and on instinct, I turn over my shoulder discreetly to see *him* slouched back in his seat, watching me with those insightful eyes. He doesn't shy away from openly staring at me from under his disheveled hair, which pisses me off. Even though he is privy to my secret, that doesn't mean we're going to bond.

Besides, I'm sure he has secrets of his own, like whoever's house he was creeping out of last night.

He is the epitome of a "bad boy," and I'm pretty sure all the girls at this school secretly have a crush on him. They would never admit it, though, because he's the arty weirdo who would leave dirty Polaroids in your locker just for fun.

He crosses his ankles and leans farther back in his chair, unfazed by anything, as Miss Knox hands out a pop quiz to the class. All the guys are ogling her indiscreetly but not him. He merely yawns when she places his quiz on his table, facedown, not interested as she all but shoves her E cups into his face.

I can't help but snicker as I turn back around, but it's too late as Miss Knox has caught me laughing at her expense.

"We have a new student, class," she says, drawing attention to me like the bitch she is. She places the quiz on my table and smiles sweetly. "How about you tell the class a little about yourself?"

"How about not," I mumble under my breath but stand reluctantly.

She gestures that I'm to stand in front of the class, like I'm giving a Noble Prize speech or something.

With a sigh, I hold my head high and pass the rows of pupils who look at the new girl with interest, distaste, and boredom.

I don't cower because, like sharks circling their prey, they will strike if they smell a wounded animal. And I don't intend on being anyone's prey.

"Hi," I start, refusing to look at the one familiar face that makes my body burn. "My name is Darcie. And I transferred to this shithole from Declan Valley High School."

Miss Knockers looks unimpressed with my introduction. "Class, does anyone have any questions for Darcie?"

I refrain from eyeballing the fuck out of her and instead look at the faces of my uninterested peers. A group of guys catches my eye, one in particular, and that's because he seems to be one of the only students remotely interested in what I have to say.

He is the quarterback, judging from the blue-and-yellow varsity jacket he wears over his uniform, and he looks how you'd expect every star athlete to look—blond and muscled with a jawline that could cut glass. His eyes are an icy blue.

The crowd he sits with looks like your typical meatheads, but this guy appears different. He watches me closely, and I'm suddenly feeling self-conscious.

"Miss, didn't a pupil get *expelled* for setting the gym on fire at Declan Valley?" asks a girl in a sickly sweet voice, instantly breaking the weird stare-off with the quarterback.

My attention shifts to her, and she grins smugly as she leans over her desk to whisper something into the quarterback's ear. She may as well cock her leg and mark her claim here, now. But I have no interest in her trophy.

He chuckles, looking directly at me, hinting whatever the girl said was about me.

"You're right, Giselle. I read it online," says a red-haired guy with freckles and a toothy smile. He pushes his silver-rimmed glasses up his slender nose. "Was it you, new girl, 'cause my pants are on fire?"

Seems he's the class clown.

The class erupts into laughter while I bunch my fists behind my back. A paper plane soars past my head, hitting the blackboard behind me.

"Yeah, *new girl*. I bet it was you." Folding her arms arrogantly across her chest, Giselle snickers, challenging me to take the bait. "Do we have to hide our lighters in case you'll set *our* gym on fire? What do you think, Carson? Do you think she's going to be trouble?"

The quarterback has a name—Carson.

"All right, Giselle, that's enough," Miss Knox snaps, deciding now is the time she should act the role of concerned teacher.

But I know what this is. If I don't bite back, if I surrender, they will see it as weakness.

Staring into Giselle's eyes, I reply blankly, "If anything were on fire, it would be your pussy from fucking the entire football team."

The boys around Carson fall into silence because perhaps I've hit the nail on the head. Carson shifts in his seat uncomfortably, clearly ruffled that his friends might be sticking their fingers in his honey pot.

Giselle's eyes narrow into slits, and I know I've just made an enemy.

"I don't know why you'd think I care. Friends are only good for long treks in the snow. Just ask Alfred Packer."

His comment from last night suddenly crosses my mind, and a grin spreads from cheek to cheek, merely infuriating Giselle further.

"You've made quite an impression for your first day, Darcie. Back to your seat."

I don't say anything and simply stroll back to my desk, unable to wipe my mischievous smile away. Before I sit, however, I meet *his* eyes. And all I see is nothing.

He doesn't shy away from looking at me, but I can't tell if he's curious or bored. And I like that. I like that he keeps me guessing.

I take a seat, refusing to acknowledge my classmates, who now look at me with something other than boredom reflected in their eyes.

"Turn over your pop quizzes."

The class groans but does what they're told.

This quiz may as well be written in Swahili because being a good student hasn't been a priority lately. But I try my best, chewing the end of my pen as I read over the questions.

Five minutes in, I hear Miss Knockers speak, but unlike when she spoke to me, this time, she seems like she's mid-orgasm. "Yes, Mr. Blackwood?"

"Can I please have a hall pass? I need to use the restroom."

And he has a name. Well, a surname, at least.

It takes all my willpower not to turn around. So instead, I look at Miss Knockers and how she's openly eye fucking Blackwood.

"You can go after you're finished with the quiz."

"I am finished," he counters coolly.

Three words filled with so much arrogance, but his arrogance isn't overbearing. It's subtle, where one doesn't know if he's being sarcastic or not.

Miss Knockers purses her lips but eventually gives in as she writes out the hall pass for Blackwood. The smooth slide of the chair across the floor and his unhurried footsteps announce he's getting closer.

I quickly focus on my quiz, but when he passes my desk, I peer up at him from under my lashes. I'm convinced this place is set to winter all year round 'cause all it's done is rain since I arrived, but a beam of sunshine breaks through the darkness, igniting Blackwood in a way that highlights how his white shirt clings to his broad back.

He's tall. I'd say six-four.

"Here you go, Mr. Blackwood," Miss Knox purrs, leaning over her desk to hand him the hall pass.

He slides it out of her hand nonchalantly. Even his subtle movements display confidence and control. "Thank you, miss."

There is so much promise to the word *miss*. I wonder how many Miss Knoxes he has on speed dial.

He makes his way to the door, but when he turns around, that sliver of sunlight catches the gold in his eyes, making them appear liquid amber. He walks out the door while I take a muted deep breath. My urge to follow him is almost uncontrollable.

I attempt to focus on the quiz, but I can't. I want to know where he's going, as the bathroom trip was clearly an excuse. So I raise my hand.

Miss Knox looks at me, an annoyed sigh slipping past her lips. "What is it, Darcie?"

I can't help but compare her response to the way she addressed Blackwood. So I decide to use his line and dare her to refuse me.

"Can I also have a hall pass? I need to use the bathroom too."

She replies just how I knew she would. "You can go after you're finished with the quiz."

It's multiple choice, so I quickly color in the dots in no particular order. It may as well be color by numbers. But I knew I'd fuck this quiz up, so it doesn't matter.

"I'm finished."

I don't give her time to refuse me and stand, making my way to her desk. I extend my palm with a smile. She makes clear she wishes I never transferred and slaps the hall pass into my hand.

"Thank you," I say sweetly.

She gestures for me to leave with a wave of her hand.

Once out in the empty corridor, I let out an elated giggle because that was fun.

Looking from left to right, I wonder which way Blackwood would have gone. I don't know how I know he's up to something. Maybe it's just a gut feeling. Or maybe I'm connected to him in some way, and I just have to know.

I think he's a thrill seeker like me, and I want to come along for the ride.

Muting my footsteps, I hear the unmissable sound of someone trying to break into a locker, and when I turn the corner, I see Blackwood with a brown paper bag in hand.

I cross my arms and shake my head slowly.

"What's that?" I ask, stopping a few feet away.

He doesn't even appear concerned he's been caught red-handed doing something he shouldn't.

"I don't know. What do you want it to be?" he counters with that annoying cocky smirk.

"Whose locker is that?"

"What makes you think it's not mine?" he poses, flick blade in hand as he jams it into the lock.

I realize our conversation has just been a series of questions, so I decide to watch and get the answers myself.

Blackwood isn't bothered and continues picking the lock until it finally snaps open with a satisfying click. He opens the door, and when I see a mirror attached to it with pink lipstick lips pressed to it, I roll my eyes.

"I stand corrected," I state. "That is clearly your locker cause what other narcissistic fuckass would kiss their reflection every time they look into that mirror? Mirror, mirror, on the wall, who's the most annoying guy in this school?"

Blackwood clutches his heart, faking hurt.

He places the brown paper bag into the locker and extends his hand.

I arch a brow, confused.

"Give me your lighter," he says, and before I can lie through my teeth, he shakes his head. "Don't tell me you don't have one. I know you packed it before you packed your lunch."

It's like he knows me already.

My curiosity gets the better of me, and I walk forward until we're standing mere inches apart.

He towers over me, but I don't feel dwarfed in his presence. I don't know what it is about him, but I loosen my tie and unfasten two buttons on my shirt. But he doesn't seem to notice. He continues looking at me as if deciphering the world's most fascinating puzzle.

I reach into my shirt and produce the lighter from where it's hidden in my bra. I don't know how he knew I'd have it. I guess the fact that I was standing in front of a flaming rose bush when we met is the reason.

The moment I come in contact with it, warmth and comfort embrace me tightly. It's the only time I ever feel safe.

Passing it to Blackwood, he shakes his head. "This is yours."

"My what?"

"Your turn."

"For?"

"For setting the world on fire," he replies, gently coaxing me toward the locker by placing a hand on the small of my back.

His touch has an unexpected reaction. He's bold, I'll give him that. I fucking love it, but I would never tell him that.

Without hesitation, I run my thumb along the spark wheel, and the moment I do, a shiver racks me. It's foreplay before the big climax. Suddenly, nothing else matters but setting that bag on fire.

The moment the flame sparks to life, I am transfixed by it and how fire can destroy in the blink of an eye. Something so beautiful can cause so much pain—like me, as my mom used to tell me I was the most beautiful girl in the world.

Thoughts of her, of her mangled body as she took her last breaths, has me extending my arm into the locker and setting fire to that bag. I wish it could burn away this anguish I feel, but it never does.

It goes up instantly, which means Blackwood used an accelerant.

We both stand by the door, watching the small bonfire spark to life. Anyone could come out at any moment, but neither of us seems to care.

As the flames grow higher, I casually redo my buttons and fasten my tie. "Do you have a name?"

"I do."

"And it is?"

"Rev." He slams the locker door shut on the fire.

"What kind of name is Rev?"

He leans in close, so close he steals my breath away. I fixate on the two nose rings he has—one hoop in each nostril. "It's a name."

When I remember to breathe again, I go to press him further, but he grabs my hand and whispers into my ear, "Run."

It sends a shiver through me.

Those words are very reminiscent of last night. Still, when he lifts his eyes to the ceiling, and the sprinklers go on two seconds later, I realize he means it in the literal sense.

We take off down the hallway, my shoes slipping on the wet floors as the sprinklers shower down around us. We are sopping wet, and maniacal laughter spills from me when I witness the bedlam we created. Students rush from their classrooms, screaming and crying with mascara running down their cheeks.

Rev drags me outside, where ironically, it's started to pour. But I don't notice the downpour. All I can focus on is standing in the rain with a delinquent who is as beautifully messed up as I am.

Our chests are rising and falling quickly as adrenaline bounces between us. My skin tingles, and it has nothing to do with the cold. He lets go of my hand but doesn't walk away.

His white shirt clings to his muscled body, and as he rolls up his sleeve, I see he has a tattoo on his wrist. It's a star in a circle with two half-moons on either side. I want to know what it means, but that will have to wait because the doors burst open, and a flurry of students swarms outside.

Rev runs his long fingers through his wet hair, emphasizing his flawless face. He licks a fallen raindrop from his full lips. I'm envious of it.

"What happened?" a girl asks her friend, wringing out her wet ponytail

"Donna Jo said Giselle's locker caught on fire!" her friend replies while I almost inhale my tongue. "Apparently, her term paper was in there, as well as her laptop. I hope she has a backup at home. Otherwise, the girl is screwed. It's due this week."

Rev doesn't react.

He simply smirks before pushing through the students and leaving me with a mouth full of nothing. Why did he do this? Did he do this for me? Maybe chivalry isn't dead, after all.

Peering up at the wooden crucifix nailed to the wall, I know there aren't enough Hail Marys to save my soul.

CHAPTER THREE

Rev

The moment I open the front door, I know things are about to go south.

"Mom?" I call out, tossing my keys into the porcelain bowl that sits with military precision on the hallway table.

My entire house is set out this way in case *he* ever decides to come back. My mom doesn't want a thing out of place in case the deadbeat who knocked her up, aka my dad, ever waltzes through the front door. She wants him to believe our perfect life has been put on pause for him as we awaited his return.

It'll never happen.

She knows it.

I know it.

But she clings to unrealistic hope that she'll get her happily ever after. That she somehow deserves it. But that's not how life works. We aren't owed anything. We work for shit to happen. We work to better our lives so we aren't waiting and pining for a useless fucker who couldn't give two shits about the family he never wanted to begin with.

The house is deadly quiet, which is never a good sign.

Checking the living room, I see she isn't sitting in her usual spot, by the window, in case he walks by.

Climbing the stairs two at a time, I race toward her bedroom. The door is ajar, and when I shoulder it open, I see an all too familiar sight—red and white pills strewn on the white carpet, an empty bottle of cheap scotch close by, and my mom's comatose body laid on top of her silk duvet.

"For fuck's sake," I curse under my breath, running toward her. "June! Wake the fuck up."

I gently slap her cheeks, trying to get a response.

She simply moans. At least she's alive.

Lifting her limp body in my arms, I carry her into the bathroom. Turning on the faucet, I dump her ass into the shower and let the cold water slap some sense into her.

I stand back, arms folded, waiting for her to come to. This is the third time this week, and it's only Wednesday.

Her eyes flutter open before the realization of her being drenched with cold water hits her. She screams and scrambles back, her back hitting the white-tiled wall.

"You ruined my dress," she slurs, attempting to stand, but she's not going anywhere. "Your father loved this dress."

"Oh, bull-fucking-shit," I counter, not interested in her theatrics. "He isn't coming, Mom. When are you going to accept that? He is a selfish fucking asshole who hasn't thought twice about us!"

"You know nothing!" she cries, brushing her soaked hair from her eyes. "He loves me. He told me he would look after me. Without him, I am nothing. I have nothing."

She lunges for my razor, fumbling to extract the blade.

Her actions prove what self-centered assholes both my parents are.

"Is this what you fucking want?" I scream, crouching in front of the shower and reaching in, fighting her for the razor.

The cold water drenches me, but I don't care. I can't feel anything anymore. I am numb.

"I want to die! Let me die!" she bellows, her tears mingling with the waterdrops falling around us.

Gripping her wrist, I force her to drop the razor. It skids along the shower floor.

"I will not let you ruin your life because of someone who doesn't give a fuck about us. You may not want to live, but I refuse to let that asshole fuck up both our lives."

Her eyes beg I help make the hurt go away. I withstand the pain for both of us, which is why I climb into the shower with her.

With water soaking us both, I hug her tight, offering her my strength because she has none. "I love you, Mom. And I wish you loved yourself."

She sobs into my shoulder, her tiny frame shuddering in my arms. I let her grieve for the life she wanted but never had.

"He loved me. He really did," she whispers, a broken record stuck on a loop. "You look just like him. He was so handsome. Popular. So smart, just like you. You're going to be someone. You're going to change the world."

Reaching overhead, I turn off the water but don't let go of my mom.

As much as I wish she'd stop being the victim, I love her nonetheless. She always tried her best when I was growing up. She tried to be a good mom.

But we never had enough.

I was the kid who wore hand-me-downs two sizes too big. The kid with the weird haircut because his mom cut his hair to save money.

When I was eleven, I realized life isn't what it's made out to be on TV. *The Brady Bunch* was not a representation of the ideal American family. Cindy and Bobby were making out in the doghouse when they were nine, Greg was fucking Carol, and Mr. Brady was a closet homosexual.

Life changed for me, and it had nothing to do with *The Brady Bunch* and everything to do with June having a breakdown. It was coming. The warning signs were there. But it was too late, and when she snapped, she snapped hard.

I found her unconscious on the bathroom floor as she had popped every one of her prescription pills and chased it down with a bottle of Jack. I called 911, who instructed me on how to bring my mom back to life.

That day changed me forever.

June was deemed an unfit mother, and because of that, I was thrown into a Catholic boys' home—Saint Paul's.

I hated every single fake smile, every single fake promise. They were going to provide what my mom couldn't, but I could smell their bullshit a mile away. All I was to them was another innocent boy they could harm for their own sick perversions.

Behind closed doors, it was clear that I was to eat, sleep, and breathe when the brothers told me to, and if I disobeyed, I would be punished, and by punished, I mean starved, beaten, and locked in the dark.

But being locked in the dark, away from society, wasn't such a bad thing—it was here I taught myself how to survive. I was forgotten, and because of this, I could slip undetected in and out of the shadows.

It was here I began to steal to better my life, as well as the lives of the other boys who were terrified of the dark. Not so much of the dark itself, but rather what lurks in the shadowy depths.

Reverend Franchot was the savior of Saint Paul's Boys' Home. He could do no wrong. He was seen as the town hero because he "saved" us boys who were discarded by most. But looks are deceiving because when the Rev came down those dark basement stairs, belt in hand, I knew it was the last time I'd allow anyone to hurt me again.

Rev was a pedophile. He liked the younger boys to call him daddy.

But there was no way I was calling him a name that was supposed to encompass protection and care, so that rainy November night, when he came down those stairs, I ripped that belt from his hand and showed him who was his daddy.

"On your knees, Rev," I said, stretching that thick belt between my hands.

"I'll have you locked away for good. You're nothing but a—"

Thwack!

A pained oof left the Reverend as I brought the belt down on his back.

"Are you a little hard of hearing, old man? I said...on... your...motherfucking knees."

He had no other choice but to surrender.

"Please don't hurt me." His pleas were sickening. He had no right to beg for clemency because he never delivered the same fate to those he defiled.

"I will bring down this house of lies if you ever touch any of the boys again. We clear?"

He interlaced his liver-spotted hands. "Please—"

Crack!

His head snapped back as I smacked him across the forehead with the edge of the belt. A trickle of blood dripped down his face. "What will the clergy say?"

I shrugged, not at all bothered by his pleas. "Tell them it's stigmata, seeing as you think you're a fucking god. But you know what you are?"

Smack!

The question was rhetorical because his time to talk was over.

"You are a predator."

Smack!

"A wolf in sheep's clothing."

Crack!

The Reverend was crawling on his hands and knees, desperate to flee, but he wasn't going anywhere. Each time he scampered away, I hit him—over and over again.

"You're going to leave. Tonight. If you don't, Sunday Mass just got a whole lot more interesting because I will broadcast the video of you and little Tommy playing leapfrog together—naked."

He knew I wasn't lying because that, in fact, had happened.

I would have stopped it if I had known. I set up the video camera I stole from the visual arts department because I thought the Reverend was fucking Sister Polly after hours, but I was wrong.

And that's why I put that motherfucker to his knees.

Us boys, we learned to survive in the shadows, and it's here where the Reverend's "favorites" emerged, inflicting their own revenge on the monster who stole their innocence.

From that day forward, the boys looked at me as their savior and officially crowned me their Reverend. The name stuck, and they called me Rev.

I knew how to survive. And I knew I couldn't rely on anyone but myself. I soon learned stealing from the rich is a great way to live, and it's what I've been doing ever since.

Most of them had no clue of the wealth they sat on. They bought their designer pieces because it was something to brag about over mimosas on Sunday brunch. And I exploited their ignorance for my gain.

I stole anything of wealth which helped me survive on my own. I sold it. Traded it. Used it for bribes. I could have bribed the guards at the state hospital they had my mom at. But I was able to easily sneak into there to see her in the dead of night.

She was a medicated zombie—drooling, tied to a bed, and staring vacantly into the darkness. I always wondered what she saw.

No one was looking for me. I was just another delinquent kid who fell through the cracks of the system, and that is why when I knew the boys were safe, I blew off Saint Paul's and went back home—*my* home—and made sure it was ready for when my mom came back.

I visited her every fucking night. I talked to her. I begged her to snap the fuck out of it and come home. At first, she didn't look at me; she looked through me. I thought she was lost to me. I brought photos of us, hoping to spark some sort of memory or recognition in her.

It didn't.

I then brought her favorite things—jewelry, perfumes, anything that made her June.

Nothing worked.

But I should have known the only thing which could drag her back from the depths of hell was the devil himself —the fucker who held her captive in the abyss from the very beginning.

My father.

My mother used to watch all the old movies—over and over—Marilyn Monroe, Al Pacino, and Marlon Brando. These were some of her favorites. And I have fond memories of watching these movies with her as it was the only time she appeared happy.

I thought that was because she was a movie enthusiast, but the truth was, my father loved these movies. He even took her to see one at the cinemas—just one, of course, because the bastard was too busy doing anything but the right thing.

So I knew the only way to get my mom back was to remind her what she was missing by being locked away. It wasn't being a mom to her eleven-year-old kid or even facing her demons for herself.

The only thing which gave her strength to go on was my father—the asshole who abandoned us. She persevered for *him*, in hopes that one day, he would come back to her. But if it meant she returned to me, I didn't care.

I downloaded the movies she loved onto a laptop I stole and watched them with her night after night. And piece by piece, she came back to me. Through the memories of my father, June returned.

And no matter how much I hate that fucker, I have a bittersweet relationship with those movies.

But I won't end up like June. I will fight with my last dying breath to better my life and hers.

"I'm tired."

Lifting her frail frame into my arms, I walk her into the bedroom and gently place her on the bed. She is wet from the shower, but she doesn't seem to mind as I pull the blankets over her.

She's asleep in minutes.

There is a knock on the front door, so I leave my mom sleeping peacefully and answer the door quietly.

It's Nonna.

Her name is Julia, but she insists everyone calls her Nonna.

I think it's because she wishes she was one, but she doesn't have any family of her own. It's just her and her ten cats.

I run my fingers through my wet hair, not explaining why I'm soaked. "Hey, Nonna. What's up?"

Her short gray hair is dyed violet. "I just wanted to check on your mom," she says, peering over my shoulder into the house. "I came by earlier, but she didn't answer."

Nonna is our next-door neighbor, and if it wasn't for her, ringing me countless times to let me know my mom wasn't answering the door or her calls, June would be dead. I owe Nonna everything, which is why I look after her.

I buy her groceries. And I make sure her cats get the organic cat food she insists they like. The money I make from stealing, I give to her to help pay her bills—even though she never wants to take it.

I do what I can to help because the truth is, she's helping me just as much as I'm helping her. I know one day, I will need to call on her. One day, when I can't be here, Nonna will be the only person who can be.

She knows where I keep my hidden stash. And I've told her, if anything were to happen to me, she is to take the money and look after my mom.

I don't have anyone else.

An eighty-year-old woman is my saving grace.

"She's all right," I reply, not wanting to worry her. "She's sleeping it off."

Nonna purses her lips. "I'll bring over a tuna casserole."

There's no point in arguing or reminding her that I fucking hate tuna because Nonna is a part of my fucked-up, dysfunctional family—and I wouldn't have it any other way.

CHAPTER FOUR
Darcie

I decide to cut through the forest on my way home from school. I've always felt safe feeling lost and surrounded by trees. When I was little, maybe five years old, I strayed from a camping site where my parents and I were staying for the holidays. I remember wandering into the thick trees and turning to watch their campfire get smaller and smaller in the distance.

Eventually, I turned to see blackness. Only the sky split into pieces through the trees lit my way, and I felt nurtured by being taken by the woods. Looking back now, I realize this wasn't a regular response because most kids would probably be screaming.

But I never felt more alive.

I was gone for eight hours as search parties looked for me, but it felt like only minutes as I was hypnotized by the sticks and creatures that crawled around my tiny steps.

So now, I find myself in familiar territory, walking through the woods. It's very cold and wet with a soft mist circling my movements. My breath is frosted in the air, and the only sounds are the steps I take and the birds crying out above, enjoying the sprinkle of rain.

I feel I'm in heaven until the serenity is broken by some laughter echoing in the distance and the sound of glass breaking. It pisses me off to think someone is destroying this beautiful place.

I head toward the sound and see some broken-down furniture arranged in a circle and a dirty space cleared in the center. A weak fire has been lit but is struggling to roar under the spits of rain.

Boys are goofing around under some kind of influence. I can see Foss, the dumb surfer with curly long hair from school who doesn't stop laughing all the time. Happy idiot. The big one, I don't know his name, but I heard them call him Buckets. I think they use him to mow down players on the football field. And lastly Blake, who is just sitting like a corpse on one of the chairs, looking like a fashion model in his blazer and slick black hair to match his black eyes.

I don't know about him. He doesn't fit the footballer mold, but I'm guessing he's athletic and perhaps strategic.

He's watching the fire while ignoring the other two.

I'm at quite a distance so as not to be seen. I begin to back away to conceal myself further behind a large tree trunk when my body hits some kind of wall.

"Little girls should never walk alone in the forest."

It's Carson, and the wall I hit is his big, muscled chest. I spin around to face him, and those icy-blue eyes leave me dumbfounded. His thick shock of blond hair falling down over his face is pure sex, if I'm honest.

"Darcie." He's amused by my stunned face as he stares down at me.

His jawline is perfection, with a light blond shadow dusted across it. I refuse to let myself become another chick who just falls for his appearance and status. That's not who I am, and it never will be. But damn, my body is making it hard for my brain to control the situation.

"Carson," I respond.

"Yes?" His charm is revolting, and I feel like I'm on fire.

"What are you doing here? And why are your boys fucking up the forest?"

"I'm hunting rabbits, baby."

"Rabbits?" I'm horrified, and I feel my blood begin to boil.

Just then, a wiry shirtless pale-skinned boy bursts through the clearing, squealing like a pig as he must have stepped through the fire in his haste to escape. He bounces headfirst into me, panting, and I swear his eyes are bloodshot as they plead with mine.

He grabs my shoulders with his bony white fingers and breathes cold air in my face. "Run!"

Carson looks at his watch as the boy staggers off, trying to lose himself in the woods, his back covered in lashings and dirt and his feet bare. I can't help but think something really bad is going on here.

"Don't worry, it's just a game," says Carson, turning my flushed cheeks to face him.

"A game?"

"Wanna play?" He smiles down at me, brushing my hair back from my face, which I shake away with irritation.

"I don't think I like your games."

"Oh, but you would," he says. He hoists me up like a little doll and pushes my legs around his waist. I'm pushed up against a tree while his lips brush against mine.

"It's a game I'd let you win, Darcie," he whispers against my mouth.

"Put me down."

"Yeah?"

I'm not struggling. I should be, but my brain is on a coffee break.

"Yes, please," I say to his mouth.

"Say it again," he says, smiling and bringing me in tighter.

"Please put me down, Carson." My heart is racing.

I hate this guy. I really do.

He gently places my feet back on the ground and straightens my skirt for me. "See me tonight?"

"I'm washing my hair."

"No, you're not."

"What are you doing to that boy?"

"Tonight, Darcie."

He whistles to his goons, who respond like well-trained dogs. "Time's up, boys! Hunt!" he yells, and the three boys rush off in different directions into the forest.

Carson turns his attention back to me. His eyes burn into my soul, seeing right through my attempts to resist him.

"I have some business to attend to here. I'll see you at eight on the edge of the clearing."

"No, you won't."

"I'll have a gift for you."

"I don't care. I won't be here."

"Till then," he says, kissing my cheek before racing off to join the game.

I hope that boy will be okay. I don't know if I should join in and search for him too, or just mind my own business and go home.

I feel pathetic, but I go home and pray I see that little thing at school tomorrow. Why do men have to be so cruel?

I should turn up at eight and cut his dick off. Why do I have these thoughts? Sometimes I don't think I'm quite right in the head.

I have a million sticks in my socks and go round the back to bang the dirt off my shoes on the porch.

"Why are you late?" My aunt stands at the back door with her apron tied around her ample belly and her portly arms crossed.

Without waiting for an answer, she whacks me over the top of the head with a spoon and huffs off.

I hardly felt it and wonder if I'm numb on the outside as well.

Walking inside while holding my shoes, I can smell freshly baked cake that we won't be eating. It will be for all the church folk who are worthy of it and not heathens like me who take shortcuts through the forest.

I'm glad I'm getting the silent treatment while baking trays smash against the sink. The last thing I want to talk about is my day.

I go upstairs to my room, designed by my aunt. It's covered in crucifixes. The bed is made, and my uncle is hunched over my underwear drawer, fishing around and muttering to himself. I should be creeped out, but I'm so desensitized to life that I merely clear my throat.

He stands upright. "Routine drug check, my girl."

I flop down on the bed, and he hands me a plastic jar for me to pee in. He awaits my response.

"Thanks, Uncle Ray. I'll have it for you soon."

"You'll do it now before you come down for dinner!" he says like a drill sergeant.

I don't know why burning a few things makes me a drug addict, but hey, whatever.

Home sweet home.

This is my life now. One day, they'll be claiming house insurance when this hellhole burns to the ground.

It's a win-win situation.

Why am I here?

I don't really know, but I find myself in this forest clearing with my classmates and a few stray party crashers who look like they probably graduated a decade ago.

Burning drums dotted around glow amber among the faces of everyone standing around them. I love the sounds of wood breaking and crackling as it burns. It soothes me into a state of calm. I'd burn the entire forest down if I could just to hear those sounds, but I couldn't stand destroying the homes of whatever wildlife lived there. I start wondering if rabbits can climb trees, then realize how ridiculous the thought is.

I'm stroking a lighter in my pocket, wondering who I could bum a cigarette from. I see Carson and some of his teammates standing by one of the burning drums and gently inch over to where they are. I know one of them would have something to inhale.

Giselle is staring at me like I just killed her sister, and I feel a giggling energy bubbling inside me. I check my phone to distract myself from laughing in her face.

"I haven't messaged you yet," says a familiar voice beside me. I know it's Carson. He stands so tall beside me with the faintest scent of aftershave mixed with wood-fire smoke.

"That's because you don't have my number," I reply, still staring at my phone.

"Yet," he says, laughing.

"Got a cigarette?" I say, peering up at him. His blond mop of hair lazily hangs over his chiseled face, and it's kind of adorable. He's smiling at me, and I feel a little leap in my belly.

"Foss!" he yells suddenly, and the crazy-looking, curly-haired surfer guy comes rushing over like an obedient lap dog.

The wind whips my hair around, along with little firefly ashes from the bonfire. I close my jacket around my body.

Foss stands to attention beside Carson and doesn't take his eyes off me with that overexcited wide grin of his.

"Whatcha need?" he says, winking at me.

"Give Darcie a cigarette," says Carson. "You know you shouldn't smoke that shit," he continues and looks down at me.

I roll my eyes. "Yeah, okay, Dad." Foss tries to place it in my mouth, but I jerk my head back and take it between my fingers.

I then proceed with the annoying process of trying to light it.

Carson opens his quarterback jacket and steps in close, shielding the wind for me, and I can feel his body heat from his broad chest radiating off him.

After failing miserably, he grabs it from me and lights it on the first go, cupping it with his big hands. He blows smoke up into the air with a few well-crafted smoke rings despite the wind interference.

"Thought you said I shouldn't smoke...you seem to know what you're doing," I say, watching the smoke rings dissipate into the night air.

"Old habit," he says with a shrug and hands the lit cigarette to me. He's smiling like he just washed my car or something.

"Thanks," I say, taking my first drag and feeling self-conscious as his eyes watch my mouth.

"I think you can thank me better than that," he jokes, watching me intently.

"Oh yeah?" I reply, taking a longer drag and looking around.

I see Rev in the distance.

He always seems to appear out of nowhere. I kinda like that.

His dark hair pushed back, overgrown on the top; he's beyond cool.

"A kiss," says Carson grabbing my attention again. "You won't regret it." He gulps down the rest of his beer and smiles.

He's cocky, and I'm sure this routine works on every girl he tries it with.

"Is that right?" I laugh and almost choke on my inhale.

I'm suddenly nervous, which really sucks. I'm not great at being cool and often just come off as being rude instead.

Foss has bounced off to his crew surrounding the fire. He's talking to another guy who's probably taller than Carson. Jet-black hair and well-groomed. Not the usual footballer type. I see him glance over at us.

"Try me," says Carson, moving closer, and he takes the cigarette from me to bum a drag.

"No tongue," I say, staring up at him and laughing.

"Where's the fun in that?"

"Where's the fun in any of this?"

Too harsh? But the words just spill out of my mouth like a busted gumball machine. I really suck at flirting; I think I've ruined the banter. I'm hoping he doesn't try to kiss me while Rev is watching because I kinda like him too.

"You think you'd have more fun with grease lightning over there?" he says, nodding toward Rev.

Okay, that was kinda funny.

"Well, he wouldn't ask me for a kiss. It's not polite."

"Polite doesn't make your head spin, Darcie."

"Confident, aren't you?" I say as my eyes dart around to see who's watching.

"Do you want to go for a walk?" he suggests, noticing my awkwardness.

"Why? So you can chop me up in the woods and throw me in the river?" I've watched too many crime shows.

He takes my hand gently in his big warm hands.

"I'm just trying to get to know you. Not all of us are dumb jocks y'know." He looks over at Foss playing a drinking game while a pack of guys chants, "Skull! Skull! Skull!"

I can see Rev watching us from a distance. He's an observer, and I feel like he's probably disappointed in me right now for falling for the charms of this football jock who's probably had every girl in the school so far.

I'm not that girl, Rev.

My mind is trying to send him telepathic messages. Not that I wouldn't kiss Carson—he's so damn good-looking and is currently appearing entirely sweet with that stroke of cheekiness that teases my wild side. Why can't I have them both?

I'm smiling like the cat that got the cream.

"You're thinking about it," says Carson, and he toys with a strand of my hair.

"It's nice in my mind, but that's where it's staying," I say, and his face creases with a frown. I don't think anyone has ever said no to him.

I step around him and begin to walk over to where Rev

is perched on a fallen tree stump flicking bottle caps into another burning drum.

I hear some of the boys laughing behind me, ribbing Carson for his epic fail.

"Crashed and burned, huh, Mav?" says one of them, borrowing a line from that old classic, *Top Gun*.

Rev

As much as I want to rip off Carson's face and shove it so far down his neck he can kiss his own ass, I am more amused by the fact that Darcie just owned the quarterback in front of his goons.

Damn, pretty sure I saw the moment his ego shattered into a million pieces when Darcie stepped around him, leaving him standing around, dick in hand.

What a fucking chump.

Girls like Darcie don't fall for guys like Carson with all their bullshit. She is a little firecracker and just looking at her walking in my direction makes me want to run and throw her over my shoulder and take her away from this shit-festival.

I don't know what it is about her. She is different, and she still intrigues me as she did the very first night I met her, standing in her bunny outfit, setting the neighborhood alight—literally.

But we've not spoken since the day Giselle's locker was set on fire...by us.

That was a week ago.

Filling my red cup with beer from the keg, I snort a humored chuckle when I see Giselle running after Carson who's clearly spat his big boy dummy.

Poor girl. She needs to get the hint—he's not interested. He's probably already had her one too many times.

Being the only son of Mr. Assface Beckett, Carson is never lacking attention from the opposite sex, which is why Darcie rejecting him, and doing it publicly, is the best fucking thing I've seen all day.

"Just fuck off, will you?" he barks at Giselle, who stops dead in her tracks, blinking in utter shock that he would speak to her in such a way. Seems like Prince Charming has left the building.

This night just keeps on getting better.

I wasn't planning on coming to this stupid bonfire because, well, it's fucking lame. But when I overheard Darcie say she was coming, it was a no-brainer.

My life is complicated enough. I mean, I'm hardly boyfriend material. I seduce rich women and give them what they want to get what I want, and that's to rob them blind. But Darcie isn't your typical teenage girl, I suppose... and that is why she intrigues me.

I watch with interest as Giselle storms over to her, yanking her by the arm to grab her attention. Darcie stands her ground, which just gets me hard.

"Stay away from Carson!" she exclaims, and just when I thought Darcie couldn't get any hotter, her full lips tip into an amused smirk.

"Trust me," she rebukes arrogantly. "I wouldn't fall for that lame performance. He's all yours!"

Just for good measure, she shudders her disgust at Carson's attempts with her.

She's said it loud enough for the others to hear, and when they do, they erupt into laughter, hollering at the expense of the cocky quarterback. Good to see the shoe is on the other foot for once because that motherfucker is a spoiled royal brat.

Giselle's mouth hangs open as Darcie has once again shown us who's running this freak show.

Our classmates look at her in a new light because she's so fucking fearless, and I am so fucking screwed. I bet Carson wants her even more now. It makes me laugh.

Darcie then steals the beer cup from Giselle's limp hand and turns around, walking away. I have no idea where she's going, but all I know is that I'm following.

Quickly downing my beer, I toss the cup into the fire and chase after her.

I don't call out, but simply follow as she enters the dense woods alone. She isn't Little Red Riding Hood—she's the fucking wolf. I don't mask my footsteps behind her, and she doesn't turn around to see who's following her in the dark.

Once she's finished throwing back her beer and tossing her cup onto the ground, she climbs the steep hill to get to the place the local kids call Jacob's Point. The lookout from here is really fucking beautiful. I come here often, late at night after I've fucked some woman into next week, to just get away from the noise.

I know the terrain well, so I keep back and allow Darcie to navigate at her own pace. She grips the ledge and pulls herself up, dusting off her hands once she gets to the top. Gripping the rocks, I scale the hill like a monkey and am behind her in seconds.

Her back is turned. Arms folded as she stares into the distance. From up here, you can see our entire miserable town. The moon is full, bouncing off the silver strands of blonde in her hair.

"What star is that?" she asks, pointing into the sky.

She knew I was the one behind her all along. At least she doesn't think I'm a serial killer and feels safe being alone with me. Or maybe she isn't bothered either way.

I follow her line of sight and peer into the heavens. "Sirius. It's part of the Canis Major."

I don't go heavy on the details because I don't want to bore her, but she cranes her neck to peer at the brightest star in the sky. "How do you know all this stuff?"

I could reply with a smart-ass response, but I get the sense she's asking a serious question.

"I don't know," I reply honestly. "I like to read, and I guess it just sticks."

And that's the God's honest truth.

"My mom said I take after my dad"—I can't keep the bitterness from my tone—"but I wouldn't know because I've never met him."

Her attention dithers from the night sky as she turns to look at me. "So it's just you and your mom?"

"Yes, but it may as well just be me because June is broken...and she ain't ever going to be fixed."

She arches an inquisitive brow, watching me in the darkness with those sharp eyes—like a predator watching her prey. "Sometimes, people don't want to be fixed."

Her statement catches me off guard. I don't speak. I let her continue.

"Sometimes, it's better when things are broken. People tend to leave you alone when you're unfixable."

"Is that what you want to be? Left alone?"

She lifts her shoulders in an apathetic shrug. "It doesn't

matter what I want. Every action has a consequence...and this is mine."

I have no idea what that means.

"Why did you set that rose bush on fire?"

"Why not?" she counters quickly. "Whose house were you sneaking out of?"

So busted...and her defiance just turns me the fuck on.

"If you're not prepared to answer a question, then don't expect others to answer yours." She folds her arms across her small frame, daring me to challenge her.

Challenge accepted.

With a sluggish pace, I step forward, bringing us close. I tower over her, but she peers up at me, jaw firm, those eyes setting me on fire with the need to eat me alive.

Bending low, I take great pleasure in hearing the hitch to her breath.

Our lips are mere inches apart, and her scent is a combination of ripened strawberries and the precise moment a thunderstorm lingers on the horizon, about to shatter your safety forever—she's dangerous, and I'm addicted to the taste.

"I wasn't sneaking," I state, relishing in the way her bottom lip quivers. "I calmly walked out of the house I just robbed."

Her mouth parts.

"Your turn."

She licks her lips, which sets me on fire.

Unable to stop myself, I run my thumb along her pouty bottom lip. "What's wrong? Cat got your tongue?"

She doesn't appreciate me insinuating she's weak, which is why I did it. She slaps my hand away, showing me the stubborn little rabbit I know lurks beneath the surface.

"I set it on fire because I don't play with fire unless I'm

willing to get burned. I set it on fire because I want to feel...
something."

"And did it work?" I ask softly, the mood soon shifting
from playful to somber.

Peering up at from under her long lashes, she shakes her
head. "Every action has a consequence...and this is mine,"
she repeats, never breaking eye contact with me. "I don't
want to feel anything because it's better not to. Being numb
stops the whispers, late at night—when everyone is tucked
safely into their beds—being numb stops the whispers that
remind you of everything you've done."

That visual hits hard as all I can think about is June
being bound to that bed, a medicated zombie.

"What have you done, little rabbit?"

She steals my breath away when she closes the small
space between us and presses her chest to mine. "Something very, very bad," she whispers, her sweet scent making
me weep. "And because of that, I'm forced to live with my
zealot aunt and uncle."

"Where are your parents?"

The air between us pricks with electricity—I can feel it
all the way to my toes.

Leaning in close, she presses her lips to mine and whispers, "Dead."

I'm the one to pull back...which is what the little rabbit
wanted. She just fucking owned my ass, and I am besotted
by whatever the fuck she's throwing down.

She smirks, and if I've ever seen a hotter sight, then I
don't remember it because it pales compared to this.

"Wanna go to prom?"

We both recoil because, what in the actual fuck?

I have no idea why the fuck I just said that because I
have no intention of *ever* attending this fucking stupid rite

of passage. But when Darcie seems to ponder on the idea, I wonder if my brief stint with insanity was a moment of ingenious madness.

"Okay."

"Okay," I repeat, wanting to kick my own ass for sounding like a fucking chump. "Not really sure what we're supposed to do. I'll watch *Carrie* to get up to speed."

She purses her lips before a magical laugh spills from her. "Good...and I want a corsage. White."

"Yes, ma'am."

Not sure how we went from talking about her dead parents to prom, but it's just another day in the office for both Darcie and me, it seems.

This can only lead to trouble...and I can't fucking wait.

CHAPTER FIVE

Rev

Showering with a bunch of jocks is far from my ideal Thursday afternoon, but the same can't be said for Coach Anderson. He's in cock heaven.

"Don't show weakness, boys! We have to dominate on and off the field!"

Not sure why this pep talk couldn't wait until we're not fucking naked, but whatever floats your boat.

The football team is standing under the showers, talking casually to one another while Coach Anderson peers at their junks subtly from behind his clipboard. Everyone knows he's a fucking pervert, but they overlook it because of the success he's had on the football field.

I'm not on the football team as I would rather cut off my own arm and beat myself to death with it, but I needed a shower before I paid Mrs. Kingston a visit. She has a limited-edition coin I saw her pick up from the jeweler when I was people watching for my next meal ticket on the weekend at the mall.

I gave her a smile, and within two minutes, she told me where she lived and when her husband would be at his weekly poker game. It's tonight, hence me using the school showers as I'm bouncing straight after school.

The guys are talking smack to one another, which has me quickly washing the suds off my body because I can feel my brain cells dying the longer I stay here. I have zero interest in their talk of football, pussy, and getting wasted.

I can't help but snicker when I hear Buckets talk about banging his latest conquest. With a face only a mother could love, I wouldn't be surprised if it actually is his mother he's speaking of because that's the only way he could get laid.

Reaching for my towel, I wrap it around my waist and head toward the changing area so I can dry off and dress. As I turn the corner, I groan because Carson is quickly slipping into a pair of jeans.

I fucking hate this guy. Hate is probably not a strong enough word. He hasn't worked for anything in his life, thanks to his father being a very powerful and influential man in our town. The entire Beckett family looks like they've been cut out of a *Forbes* magazine.

He's been a pain in my ass since I can remember, always flaunting what he has because I've never had a cookie-cutter family, and I never will—something he likes to remind me of often. I don't know why we don't like one another—we just wouldn't think twice if the other got bludgeoned to death with a snow globe.

"How's your mom?" Carson quips when I walk past him. "Still a pathetic junkie?"

I stop in my tracks and deadpan him because if he's trying to insult me, he better try a little harder.

"How's *your* mom?" I challenge, arching a smug brow. "Still a hot piece of ass?"

Carson grits his teeth together because I know how much it pisses him off that his mom is spank bank material for every one of his friends. Just to fuck with him and his asshole father, I fucked her a few months ago.

It really was too easy.

Carson's entourage arrives, ready to protect their leader in case he's about to cry. They're walking around, cocks in the wind, unlike Carson, who, come to think of it, always seems to be quite reserved when in the locker room.

However, when Coach Anderson rounds the corner, it seems Carson is reserved around *him.*

Carson's fists clench slightly by his sides when the coach slaps him on the back. "Good play out there, Beckett. You boys could learn a thing or two from our quarterback."

Usually, I would have zero interest in this roughhousing, but Carson is actually squirming, and I wonder why. His fists clench tighter.

Carson notices me watching him, and his discomfort twists to rage. "Watch out, boys," he quips, folding his arms across his broad chest. "I think Rev is checking out your cocks."

The brain-dead losers laugh and fight to gain dominance over the sound of the shower spray against the tiled walls. It's a cesspool of testosterone, ball sweat, and arrogance, but at the core is Carson's deflection. He wishes to redirect the attention off him, which just makes me all the more curious.

I don't entertain him, however.

"I think you're the only one who has penis envy around here, seeing as you're the one who is always dressed first," I state, never breaking eye contact with Carson. "Don't want your clones to see their big, brave leader has a runt dick?"

Foss's mouth falls open while Buckets stifles his chuckle behind his large hand.

I know what's going to happen, and I welcome it because if this fucker throws the first punch, he better make sure he knocks me the fuck out because I won't stop until I knock out every single one of his teeth.

He charges for me, shoving my back against the lockers. The meatheads holler, jumping up and down like wild monkeys in a jungle as they egg Carson on. He punches me in the mouth while I laugh hysterically. Blood trickles down my mouth and somersaults onto the floor.

"Is that the best you got, you limp dick motherfucker?" I taunt, wiping the spilled blood from my lip with the back of my hand. "No wonder Darcie laughed at you. You're a fucking chump."

I wanted to add that in there to add salt to the wounds and also to remind him that she will never be his.

He raises his fist again, but this time, I grip it in midair and twist it outward.

It's on.

Shoving against his chest, he stumbles backward, which I use to my advantage as I launch at him and headbutt him. One of the guys pushes him back into the fight when Carson falters once again.

I punch him in the jaw and nose, which cracks—music to my ears.

Lifting my chin to the ceiling, I inhale deeply. I love the smell of victory.

Carson advances for me, but I duck low and punch him in the ribs. Just as I'm about to deliver an uppercut, hands wrap around my middle and drag me away.

"That's enough!" It's Coach Anderson. "Both of you in my office. Now!"

I'm surprised he didn't step in earlier.

Coach Anderson drags me away while I smirk a bloody grin, flipping the bird to Carson, who is slumped against the lockers, attempting to catch his breath. Fucker can throw a punch, but I would cut out my tongue and eat it before I ever admitted that to him.

"Have fun in there," Carson says, spitting out a mouthful of blood. I wonder what that's supposed to mean.

Coach throws me into his office, slamming the door shut behind us. Looks like he's seeing us one at a time.

During the fight, my towel had fallen off, so I'm standing in Coach's office butt naked, and it's because of the fact that I stand taller.

"I should give you detention for the stunt you pulled!" he says, rounding his desk and taking a seat in his worn-out leather chair. "You could have broken Carson's arm."

"That was the plan," I counter smugly.

Coach Anderson's chair squeaks as he rocks backward and forward...backward and forward, his eyes scanning up and down my naked body. If this is some form of intimidation, he better try harder as he's not the first dude to look at me this way.

I'm tall, muscled yet lean, and the "I don't give a fuck attitude" seems to only entice them more.

Maybe they see me as a challenge, but in Coach's case, I think he sees me as someone who he thinks he can exploit. He's about to be sorely mistaken.

"I won't tell Principal Yates, but I expect something in return," he says, making what he wants very clear when he peers at my junk.

"Oh, is that right?" I question, eyeing him firmly. "And what exactly do you want? I doubt you want me to join your little barbaric football club, so tell me, Coach Anderson... What. Do. You. Want?"

The pause between each word seems to lure him further.

"I think you know what I want, Mr. Blackwood." He shifts in his seat.

"No, I really don't." If this fucker wants something from

me, he can stop speaking in innuendos and say it because when he does, I'm going to feed him his tongue.

"Has anyone ever told you your eyes are an unusual shade?"

"A lot of people, actually," I reply, folding my arms, unimpressed. "But I'm sure you didn't drag me in here to talk about my eyes."

Coach Anderson grins, but it's that of a predator.

He opens his drawer and places a stack of papers on his desk. He looks at me and then at them like I'm supposed to know what the fuck that means.

"That's the cheat sheet to the SATs," he explains like he's some god and I'm some inept peasant. "And it can be yours. A favor for a favor."

"And what favor would that be?"

I'm daring him to stop being a pussy and say it.

Instead, he leans back in his seat so I can see the bulge in the front of his short shorts.

If he's expecting some sort of a response, he'll be waiting a long time. "Why would I need that? I have a 5.0 GPA."

Coach Anderson's cocky smirk soon fades when I place my hands on the edge of his desk and lean forward. "So it appears *I* won't tell Principal Yates that you're propositioning one of your students to blow you."

The moment I have the balls to express what he didn't, the mood shifts because the coach realizes I'm not one of his brain-dead footballers who will jump to his every command.

He quickly stands, brushing the paperwork into his desk drawer, and slams it shut. "I was suggesting no such thing," he declares, faking horror. "I was talking about you washing and waxing my truck."

He lunges for his truck keys off the desk. A white rabbit foot is on his keychain, but his luck has run out.

"Pretty sure you wanted me to wax something else," I counter with a snicker. "Try to blackmail me again, and I swear to fuck, it'll be the last thing you do."

I hate men like Coach Anderson—I've been around enough of them. And I won't sit around and let slimeballs like him prey on kids.

"We clear, *Coach*?" I mock, using his title as a clear fuck you. "You stick to football and not trying to get your dick sucked."

I deadpan him, ensuring he knows I'm not playing.

When his head bobbles in a shaky nod, I smile.

"Fucking peachy."

I don't wait for him to reply because I've given this waste of space enough of my time.

I open the door and almost bump into Foss, who is standing by the coach's office. He quickly sidesteps, pretending he didn't have his ear pressed to the door. I ignore the jocks who are looking at me weirdly.

I walk to where my backpack is and get dressed. As I slip into my jeans, I meet Carson's eyes from across the locker room. He looks livid...and I suspect it has nothing to do with our fight and everything to do with the fact that I did something he couldn't—I told the coach to go fuck himself.

It seems I've just given Carson another reason to hate me, and as I kiss my middle finger and give it to him, I make clear that I don't fucking care.

I leave him and his bunch of lapdogs and make a quick trip to the library. Most would be returning books or to study, but for me, the quiet means a place where I can make a discreet exchange. I enter, and this is the one place in this hellhole that I actually don't mind.

I like the quiet, and I like books. Something about both allows you to reflect on life and all that philosophical shit. I understand why some people choose to live their lives as a recluse. Sometimes, the noise becomes deafening, and the only way to deal with the chaos is to seek utter solitude.

I wonder if that life is for me.

It seems a waste to continue doing what I do because I can live comfortably for a very long time with the money I've saved. But that's not the reason I do it. I do it because I want to give my mom the life she never gave to me.

"Rev," whispers someone, breaking the silence.

I see Ms. Perinton, our art teacher, peering at me through the gap in the shelves. She's hiding behind a modern history book. "Have you got it?"

Nodding, I subtly check down the narrow aisle to make sure we're alone.

We are, so I open my backpack and retrieve the painting I stole from Maree Vanderbilt and slide the tube through the shelf.

Ms. Perinton has been a great client of mine because she's got good taste and she also knows where to sell these stolen artworks. I don't ask questions. She pays, and I deliver. Being an art teacher at the local high school is a great cover because no one would ever suspect her of dabbling in criminal activities after school hours.

She doesn't even look inside. She trusts me because I've never double-crossed her in the past.

She slides a small white envelope to me, and by the feel of it, I know she's stuck true to her word and paid the ten grand I asked for.

"Let me know what you have next."

Nodding, I slip the envelope into my backpack and bounce. That's how easy it is.

I don't need a secret lair or special code word for shit to go down because I make shit happen on my terms. I exercise control in all aspects of my life, but when I shove open the door and see that asshole Carson talking to Darcie, I realize she is the one exception to my rule.

Instantly, jealousy stirs in my stomach. I want to punch out Carson's teeth, but instead, I watch because that's what a smart predator does. I have no idea what they're talking about, but it's apparent Darcie isn't totally repulsed by him.

No girl is, though.

I mean, he's tall, muscled, and smooth as shit, so I get why women would find him attractive. However, I want to throat punch him every time I see his fucking face. Images of doing just that flood my brain, and I inhale happily—my happy place is laced with violence and broken teeth.

I think back to the bonfire, and although Darcie rejected his advances, I could see it wasn't because she didn't find him attractive. She did it because maybe she wanted to kiss someone else, and that someone is me.

I have no idea when she got under my skin, but it's unknown territory for me. I don't like it. But I know it's a game I'm going to lose.

CHAPTER
SIX
Darcie

I've gone to bed early because sitting around with my aunt and uncle watching *Wheel of Fortune* is something I'd rather skip. It's nine o'clock, and I'm restless, scrolling through my phone and watching tarot readers on TikTok telling me something about mercury retrograde. The stars outside my window are super bright, and it's almost like the night is fighting with them to be dark.

My phone buzzes.

Wyd?

A message appears, and I roll my eyes at how slack the world has become. How hard is it to write What. Are. You. Doing?

I stare at it. I don't know who it's from.

Another message appears.

?

Oh, get fucked. I respond with a thumbs-up.

Darcie...

A third message appears.

Who is this?

I respond, but I should've written WIT.

Your future husband

says the rogue texter.

Unlikely

I text back.

I'm so bored that I'm figuring this is probably the most fun I'm going to have tonight.

Come out. We're at The Planet.

The Planet is a local diner where all the footballers go to celebrate their wins and drive all the patrons crazy with their sweaty bravado.

Carson…

I type back. Strangely, my heart is starting to race, and I hate myself for it.

Yes, darling?

I'm in bed…

I say, but I'm thinking about what I'm about to get dressed in and wondering if anyone would notice if I slipped out the window tonight.

Is that an invitation?

...

Seriously, come down and hang. Nothin'
weird, just wanna see your pretty face.

I shouldn't go, but since when do I follow the rules?

I get out of bed, throw some clothes on, and open my bedroom door a crack to see if I can locate where my jailers are. Pots and pans are clanging in the kitchen, and I think that's probably enough noise to conceal the sound of me hightailing it out the window.

I'm coming

I text to Carson, followed by,

shut up

Hahaha...cool.

Strangely, it's a warmer night during this cold snap, and I'm grateful for it. Like maybe five degrees instead of below zero. I never liked the cold, yet somehow, I'm perpetually living in it. Everything here is constantly dark and wet, which is why I think most people in this town are in a bad mood.

Lifting my bedroom window, it shudders because the house was made before oil was invented. I try to force it up quickly and end up getting splinters in my fingers. Sucking my knuckles, I squeeze my way out of the small gap I've created and find myself standing in my aunt's bed of roses outside.

I try to close the window again, but it's not budging. I

silently open my mouth and scream. Oh well, what can I do?

I check my phone maps to see how far The Planet is from my house. It's a twenty-minute walk. Not too bad.

Pulling my hoodie over my head, I slip away into the night. I'm not dressing up for these clowns. I'd rather be seen as one of the boys because anything with boobs turns them into hyenas.

The diner is lit up like a pink flamingo bar in Tahiti. Their attempts to conceal the morbid culture of this town are kind of hilarious really. But like moths to flames, it seems to attract a big crowd. Through the windows, I can see a crew of footballers in their sports jackets crowding over booths and playing some kind of beer pong game.

The Planet is licensed to serve alcohol, and despite them all being underage, the establishment makes exemptions for the big boys. Carson's dad is a big deal in this town, and if he gets what he wants, so do they. Like being open twenty-four hours when every other venue has a curfew of eight o'clock to stop the kids from running around the streets at night.

I enter the diner, and the bell rings, but no one pays attention. I can see the boys throwing dollars into plastic cups lined up along tables. Carson is nowhere to be seen, but I'm pretty sure I saw his car out front.

I walk up to a guy they call Magnus, who seems to hang with him often.

"Hey, have you seen Carson?" I tap him lightly on the shoulder, but I don't think he can feel it through the rock-hard shoulder muscle under his jacket.

Why do all these guys look like they bounced out of an *Abercrombie* campaign?

Magnus is a field favorite due to his trademark dance at

the end of every game. Sun-bleached hair from hell knows which sun because I feel like I haven't seen it in a decade. He looks down at me, still distracted by his game, but sporting the cheekiest grin. I swear these boys could get any girl they want just by flashing those grins.

"Hey, little one," he says. "Sup?"

He suddenly picks me up while a crowd of boys yells over someone doing an epic coin toss from across the room. I'm being shaken like a cheerleader's pom-pom as they all bellow, "EEYYYYYOOOO!"

Fuck my life. I really hate being part of any kind of excitement.

Putting me back on my feet, he grabs my face in two massive hands and plants a tight smooch on my lips. "Out back with Blake, tiny dancer!" He turns and throws a coin at someone's head.

Foss bounces up and yanks my hand. I really don't like Foss. I don't know why, but his happy demeanor makes me want to punch him square in the jaw.

"He's in the stalls," says Foss, laughing, and bangs open a door in the men's toilets to reveal Blake passed out on a toilet seat.

"I'm looking for Carson. What's wrong with him?" I ask, staring at Blake slumped so gracefully in some kind of coma.

"Snow probably," replies Foss, studying Blake with his head tilted.

He drapes his arm around my shoulders, then goes flying across the room as Carson appears in his place.

"There you are," I say, suddenly annoyed I'm even part of this now and wishing I'd just stayed in bed.

"Yeah, sorry, Blakey boy has done it again." He slaps

Blake hard in the face with a right hook, but he doesn't react.

"Is he okay?"

"Yeah, he's just passed out after overamping. Needs water. BLAKEY BOY!" he shouts in his face and drags him off the toilet seat.

Blake already looks like a beautiful undead vampire, but now, he's stepped up a level. He looks peaceful, but not coming to anytime soon. Carson launches his big body over a sink and turns the tap on hard. I kinda like watching Carson care for him. I'm seeing him in a different light. He covers Blake's face with running water but to no avail.

"Maybe we should call an ambulance?" I say 'cause he kinda looks dead.

"Nah, he's cool. Don't worry." Carson watches my face, enjoying my concern. His smile makes my stomach leap a little.

"C'mon, I'll buy you a milkshake. He just needs to sleep it off," he says and props Blake up in the corner of the men's bathroom.

I follow Carson back into the diner, where I meet those inquisitive eyes, eyes which set me on fire, and for someone who is a self-confessed pyromaniac, this can only lead to trouble.

Rev

What the fuck is she doing with those group of morons? And when Buckets appears, it seems the stupid just continues.

I'm here to pick up an apple pie for my mom. On the rare occasions when she eats, she always asks for apple pie, but it has to be from this shithole.

No doubt it's got to do with some memory she has of my father. She needs a fucking lobotomy. Or an exorcism.

Or both.

This fucking town can fuck off and blow me. I cannot wait to get out. I thought Darcie felt the same way, but seeing her with Carson and his posse of fuckheads has me thinking that maybe she's falling for their bullshit just like everyone else.

I know they can be charming and smooth and promise girls the world, but when they're done with them, they discard them like yesterday's trash. But as Carson whispers something into Darcie's ear, it does appear he has a sweet spot for her—as well as a hard dick, a dick I want to rip off and shove down his throat. But of course he does because who doesn't.

I wonder if she still wants to go to prom with me because it's every chick's dream to be on the arm of this dickhead jock. You just know he's the type of guy who positions a mirror in the bathroom in just the right way so he can see himself from every angle, including while he's taking a shit.

"Here ya go, Rev," says Connie, handing me the box containing my pie. She's wearing the retro blue waitress uniform with matching hat. Sometimes, she wears roller skates. Not today, though.

I slip her a twenty, which is way too much for some mushy-ass pie, but she deserves the tip having to deal with these primates. They all resemble a bunch of monkeys in the wild—jumping up and down and hollering loudly, fighting for food as they scavenge off each other's plates. The boys walk around with their chests and cocks out, wanting to impregnate any female they see.

Fuck, I hate this town.

Someone wolf whistles, but I don't respond because I'm no one's bitch. I turn to leave, but Buckets stands in the way. "What's in the box?"

"Something for your mom." I shove him out of the way, but roll my eyes when I see Carson standing by the door. Darcie is by his side.

"I would love to stay and chat..." I pause and appear like I'm mid-thought. "Actually, that's a lie. I would rather take a vow of silence and never speak again."

Darcie giggles, and I smile.

"Hey, baby. Doing your charity work hanging out with these assholes? Your aunt and her congregation would be so proud. Blessed be." And I do a sign of the cross.

"She's here 'cause I texted her," Carson says, riling me up.

"Oh, big boy, you know how to use a phone. Momma must be so proud." I slap him on the shoulder playfully.

Foss jumps to command while I chuckle. "Oh, calm down, monkey boy. I don't fight tweens."

I don't know why Darcie agreed to socialize with these clowns. I guess it beats being stuck at home with her zealot family. What I do know, however, is that these assholes are sweet on her. They like her, which is just the beginning of a shit show I don't want to watch.

Maybe they want to initiate her into their little lame gang?

All the girls are glaring at her, probably envisioning

cutting off all of that beautiful blonde hair. But I know they're wondering—what does she have that they don't?

Carson doesn't "date." So being seen in public with an actual girl has caused quite the stir. Maybe he wants her to be his queen...which has me thinking.

"I'll pick you up at seven."

Darcie smiles, and I want to eat that smile off her pretty face as I smash my lips to hers.

"For what?" Carson asks, looking back and forth between us in confusion.

"For none of your business, candy ass."

Buckets decides to play the hero and slams those big hands down onto my box of pie. But he really is too predictable. And also, he's really fucking stupid.

I elbow him in the nose, the box never wavering from my hands.

Our classmates eagerly look on, the air filled with excitement at the possibility of a fight. But I have better things to do.

"Bye, baby. Make sure you shower before bed. You don't know where these dogs have been."

"I'll be tucking her in," Carson says with a shit-eating grin, needing to get in the last word.

"We know that won't happen because your mom will be too busy tucking *you* in. Not that I would mind...'cause your mom." I bite my knuckle, closing my eyes, recollecting all the good times we've had. "Am I right, boys?"

The entire diner erupts into catcalls and brain-dead hollers at the expense of Carson and his hot mom. I leave him to deal with the lewd comments, and suddenly, apple pie has never tasted sweeter.

CHAPTER
SEVEN
Darcie

Picking a gown for prom is like forcing a screaming cat into a dress and making it pose for photos.

I hate traditions, and if I could, I'd probably just go in my bunny onesie. I'm secretly excited to go with Rev, though—I think he could be a good time.

I'm half expecting him to arrive in a skeleton suit just to be different.

I want to look sexy with a dash of fuck off. My inclination is to pick black, but I saw a dark green dress in the store that reminds me of the forest I've become accustomed to walking through after school. It's long but fitted through the bodice and sits off the shoulder. I want to rip the bottom off to make it shorter and wear some boots with it, but maybe that's a bit much.

I'll wear my boots under it, and no one will know, but at least I'll keep true to myself. My long blonde hair looks good with green, and it sets off my eyes.

I get dressed in front of the mirror and slip a lighter into my boots. There's not room for much else, so I'll have to take a clutch for my phone.

I can hear the rumbling of a deep engine coming down the street, and I wonder if it's Rev. I peer out the window and see a very old GT Mustang pull up. Weirdly, it's also dark green, and suddenly, I feel like ripping my dress off for something else. If he's wearing green as well, I'm outta here.

Grabbing my clutch, I race to the front door, not wanting my aunt and uncle to see the "delinquent" taking me to prom.

I open the door and need a moment because Rev stands before me wearing a black suit. His white shirt is unbuttoned, exposing an expanse of bronzed chest. His dark hair is long in the front, and strands fall down his face. I can see he tried to slick it back, but I don't think anything about him behaves.

It looks hot as hell, and I try everything I can not to smile like a complete goofball. He likes what he sees, and my breath hitches when a lopsided smile appears on his face.

"You ready, Miss Darcie?"

From behind me, I can hear my aunt's footsteps thundering out from the kitchen. This is exactly what I wanted to avoid.

"Where in Sam hell do you think you're going looking like that?" she bellows, wiping her hands on her apron. She's not wearing her glasses, so she's squinting like a day-old prune.

"Prom," I say, trying not to laugh at Rev, whose mouth hangs open while he takes in the beast behind me.

I quickly shove him back toward the street, and once again, I seem to be dragging him along and running. We're laughing as we launch ourselves into the car and speed off.

"What in Sam hell was that?" he says mid-cackle, bending over the steering wheel.

He drives super fast, like we are on the run even though my aunt couldn't chase a snail. I find myself gripping the sides of my seat.

A smirk creeps over his mouth. He likes the control.

"Got any gum?" I yell over the sound of the engine.

I pop open the glove box in front of me, and I'm immediately starry-eyed by what I see. "Did you rob a jewelry store?" I say, reaching for a diamond-encrusted bracelet.

"Gifts," he replies, eyes still fixed on the road.

"Gifts?"

It's women's jewelry. I slip a sapphire ring onto my middle finger, and it fits perfectly.

"For services rendered," he adds, laughing as he breaks eye contact with the road to look at me with nothing but cheek behind his gaze.

I don't want to ask any more questions.

Pulling into the parking lot of the school gym, I feel my nerves creeping up my neck. I'm wooden in my seat and stare ahead when I feel his hand cover mine. It squeezes, and at that moment, I take in a breath.

"You ready for this shit show?" he asks like he can read my mind.

"No. Yes," I say, looking at his stunning face and trying to seem at ease.

We enter the gym, and it's dark but covered in fairy lights, and the music is throbbing to the feeling in my chest. Familiar faces dance and weave into each other in an array of outfits that makes everyone look like someone else.

I can't believe this lame rite of passage is something kids my age actually look forward to.

A small giggle escapes me, and Rev peers down at me, eyebrow cocked.

"I don't see what the fuss is about," I explain, taking in our classmates. "I mean, it's just our gymnasium. Underneath the glittery lights and lame love songs, I can still smell armpits and see the outline of Coach Anderson's junk in his way too tight white gym shorts."

Rev continues looking at me with those inquisitive eyes

before an amused snort leaves him. "You're a tough crowd, firecracker," he says, surprising me with the nickname.

But that surprise turns into a startled breath caught in my throat as he wraps his hand around my waist and draws me against him.

He towers over me, and I like that I feel dainty in his arms. I would never tell him that, of course, but he is so alpha, and for some reason, I feel nothing but protected being entwined this way.

"How about we see what the fuss is about then?"

Now, I'm the one to cock my brow.

No words are spoken as he pulls me in even closer so that we are pressed front to front. I don't know what he's doing, but honestly, I don't care because when he reaches for my wrists to position them on his broad shoulders and wraps both his hands around my waist, I am lost to everything that Rev is.

He is arrogant, cocky, and so fucking alpha, and I find myself forgetting all the pain that makes it hard to breathe when I'm with him. He quells the noise. With him, it's... quiet.

But I know it's the calm before the storm.

He leads me into a slow dance as we sway to the music, and if I were there with anyone else, I would be rolling my eyes and snickering, but with Rev, everything just feels right.

I am well aware of our classmates staring at us, some whispering about my choice of footwear or that they never thought they'd see us here, seeing as we aren't really the conforming type, but I don't care.

I wrap my arms around Rev's neck, toying with the longer strands curling at his nape. He seems surprised that I'm openly touching him, and so am I.

Maybe something is magical about prom, after all.

We continue swaying, never breaking eye contact, and it's almost a challenge as to who will look away first. But neither of us will back down. We are just as stubborn as the other, and when a lopsided smirk touches Rev's lips, I know he can once again read my thoughts.

He bends down and whispers into my ear, "If I didn't know any better, I'd say you were having a good time."

His comment is dripping with humor, and I fight the urge to stomp on his foot to show him what my idea of a good time consists of.

"Don't be ridiculous," I scoff but can't mask my grin.

Rev wipes that grin from my face, and I mean that literally when he reaches down and runs his thumb along my bottom lip slowly. I watch in fascination as he brings his thumb toward his mouth and sucks it.

It pops free a moment later while I remind myself to swallow.

"I taste lies," he states while my heart threatens to rip free from my rib cage. "And I like the way you taste, little rabbit."

The air between us is filled with an electrical current, sure to shock me into oblivion, but I don't care.

I want the destruction.

I want the fire.

I want Rev...because he is my fire. He is my destruction. And I revel in the madness. It is here where I feel alive.

I want him to kiss me, and the way his eyes are zeroing in on my lips, I know he wants that too, but our perfect bubble is soon to be popped when I realize the music has stopped, and a bright spotlight beams down on us.

For a second, I think maybe my mind is playing tricks on me, but when I hear my name being called and notice everyone…and I mean *everyone* staring at me, I know that this hell on earth is really happening, and it's really happening to me…and Carson.

"Holyyyy fuck." Rev snickers in part horror, part humor, looking at Carson standing on stage wearing a tacky crown and high-fiving his moron friends who stand front row and center, cheering on their…prom king.

It's no surprise he's been crowned prom king, but what *is* surprising is who his queen is.

It's me.

"No," I say, shaking my head animatedly. "There's no fucking way."

I spin to look at Rev, who joins in with the clapping, laughing his ass off. "This is a joke, right?"

"No, your majesty. I believe your king awaits you."

I elbow him in the ribs, and he grunts under the force. But it doesn't wipe the amused smirk from his face. "Get me out of here. Now."

I suddenly am burning up.

Everyone is looking at me, just how everyone was looking at me when my parents died. Or when I set my school gymnasium on fire.

I'm sick of people looking at me…especially this asshole, Carson, who won't take no for an answer. If this is legit, then the only reason I'm prom queen and not Giselle is because Carson rigged it.

He thinks I won't embarrass him in front of the *entire* school and just suck it up because it's every girl's dream to be prom queen, right?

Well, he's shit out of luck because this girl has had enough. And I am not like anyone he's ever met before.

I launch forward but am snared back as Rev grips my

wrists and draws me toward him. My back is pressed to his front.

He leans down, his breath hot on my neck as he whispers into my ear, "Set the world on fire, firecracker."

"Let's burn this fucker to the ground." Those are my parting words as I march through my peers, head held high, intent on telling Carson what he can do with his crown and where he can shove it.

CHAPTER EIGHT

Rev

Darcie is a fucking firecracker, and I love it.

She just doesn't give a fuck about...anything, which makes her even hotter. But honestly, she is so fucking beautiful that it's been almost impossible to behave like a gentleman around her.

When I saw her standing before me in her green dress and caught a glimpse of her black boots underneath, I had to mentally slap myself to stop staring like a fucking creeper. Her fuck-off attitude combined with her looks are a deadly combination, and I find myself falling deeper and deeper under her spell.

But that's the thing about Darcie—she doesn't even realize how captivating she is. And it just makes me want her all the more.

I watch with a grin as she stands up on that stage, unapologetic for calling out Carson, who clearly rigged this poll so they would be crowned prom king and queen.

Poor chump.

Anyone with half a brain would have got the hint by now, but I suppose seeing as no isn't a word he hears often, he seems to have forgotten what it means. But the fact that Darcie keeps rejecting him is what I suspect is the reason he keeps coming in hard.

She's a challenge, and for someone like Carson, she is someone he wants to win; just another trophy to add to his collection. But someone like Darcie will never be owned—she is best wild and free.

My cell vibrates in my pocket, and pulling my attention away from the stage, I see it's a text from Mrs. Kingston.

Be here in ten minutes…

Mrs. Kingston lives about five minutes from school, so that time frame is totally doable. When I paid her a visit the other day and swiped the limited-edition coin I was after, I saw she also had some stamps that would rake me in a small fortune.

I really want them, especially after finding June passed out again before coming here tonight. She's just getting worse, and the truth is, I'm not sure how much longer her body can withstand the daily abuse, which is why I make the decision that I do.

I need to get her out of this town before I lose her for good.

I'm not proud of my actions, but Darcie will understand, and this won't take long.

Taking one last look at my little rabbit who is holding her own in front of the entire school, I discreetly slip away, not wanting her to know I've left. I hope to be back before she realizes I'm gone.

Shouldering open the gymnasium doors, I decide to walk to Justine's house so if Darcie comes looking for me, she'll see my car and know that I haven't bailed.

I know I'm a complete bastard for doing this, but I never claimed to be a hero in disguise. I do what I have to, to survive, and I take opportunities when they arise because I don't like wasting time. Time is something we can never get back.

I quicken my pace and get to Justine's in no time. The house is shrouded in darkness, and I know what this means. Justine Kingston is into role play and hinted the next time I was to pay her a visit, she wanted it to be under the pretense that I was breaking into her house.

I don't have time for this kinky shit, but when I think of June, I suck it up and think of the greater good.

I walk to the back door, which is unlocked, of course. But if Justine wants a fantasy, then I will give her one she'll never forget.

Reaching for a large rock in the garden bed, I smash it straight through a window panel on the door and reach inside to open the door. Totally unnecessary, seeing as the door was unlocked, but I like to make a mess.

I step into the kitchen, and it takes a moment for my eyes to adjust to the darkness, but once they do, I make my way through the house and take the stairs two at a time to get to Justine's bedroom upstairs.

I'm suddenly struck with a brilliant idea—for Justine to invite me back, she's oblivious that her coin is missing. So when I swipe her stamp collection, she will surely know it was me who robbed her, but will of course blame the "thief" who broke into her house late one night and stole from her.

I decide to also take the antique pistol I saw displayed in her husband's office because, why the fuck not?

She won't be able to tell the cops or her husband the truth because to do that, she'd have to confess to the atrocities I'm about to instill on her. Only she and I will be privy to the fact that she welcomed a thief into her home... and bed.

I mute my footsteps and softly push open the door.

Justine is lying on her stomach, and the light from the full moon spilling in through the parted curtains allows me to see her skimpy nightgown. It's riding high up her legs, stopping just under her ass.

I love all women—age, shape, size, it makes no difference to me. I see beauty in everything because I prefer to view the world this way.

Instantly, I'm hard, but truth be told, I've been turned on all night because being near Darcie does that to me. Everything about her turns me on—her smell, her looks, but most of all, her attitude. And although I wish it was her I'm about to fuck into a legless mess, she'll be my muse for what's to come.

I see a red tie sitting conveniently on the bedside dresser, but Justine needs to give me a little more credit.

She's doing a great job at faking sleep, and I half wish she was so I could get what I came here for and bounce. But I'm not going anywhere until I cough up the goods.

Standing at the foot of the bed, I take a moment to admire Justine Kingston. She's in her forties and in fucking fit shape. Her legs are long and shapely, and her ass is a perfect specimen of someone who does squats regularly. Any guy would be eager to fuck her senseless, but I can't stop thinking about Darcie.

And it's thoughts of her that have me crawling on top of Justine, pressing my full weight into her back.

A staged startled yelp leaves Justine, but I slap my hand over her mouth and thread my fingers through her hair, arching her neck back at a painful angle.

"Don't scream," I warn into her ear. "If you scream, I'll fucking kill you."

She nods shakily, hinting she won't scream, which we both know is a fucking lie because the moment I remove my hand, a cry for help escapes her.

Flipping her over roughly, I straddle her, pinning her flaying legs with my weight. "I told you not to scream."

"T-Take whatever you want," she cries, licking her glossy red lips.

I refrain from confessing that I plan to.

"Just don't hurt me."

Her nightgown is sheer at her chest, so I can see her nipples are hard.

Running my thumb down the middle of her lips, I push into her mouth. She hungrily tongues it, watching me with arousal.

I slip it out of her mouth and rub over her nipple with it. She hisses and attempts to arch her back but can't move because I'm sitting on top of her.

"What are you going to do to me?"

"Whatever the fuck I want," I reply with a slanted grin.

A moan leaves her because she likes being dominated. Her eyes dart to the tie on the dresser, hinting she wants to be tied up, but I'm feeling creative and instead gather the hem of her nightgown and glide it up her body.

Once it gathers at her wrists, I lean forward and fasten the silk garment around them, tying her to the headboard. She's lying naked before me, her heavy breasts rising and falling with her quickened breaths.

Gripping her chin between my fingers, I arch her head back and slip my thumb into her mouth.

"Suck," I order, and she happily complies.

She licks and suckles my thumb, and I instantly remember when it was my cock in her mouth when I was here last. I think of Darcie, and how I wish it was her naked body I was straddling right now. Just the thought of her has my dick aching with need.

Justine squirms beneath me. "I want—"

I don't let her finish as I reach for the tie on the dresser and shove it into her mouth.

"I don't give a fuck what you want."

Her hooded eyes hint at her excitement, and I know the rougher I am with her, the quicker and the harder she'll come.

"I'm going to take anything I want," I state, peering down at Justine. "And I mean anything."

I make my intentions clear when I cup her throat and squeeze lightly. I can feel her neck dip as she swallows beneath my grip. With my hand still around her throat, I reach around with the other and run them over her sex. No surprise, she's wet and hot.

She doesn't need a warm-up. I sink two fingers into her. A muffled moan escapes.

She can't move because I am still pinning her down with my weight. I use that to my advantage as I increase the tempo of my fingers. I'm relentless and don't let up until she's thrashing wildly, pleading around the gag in her mouth.

"I'm going to fuck you now," I declare, removing my fingers from Justine's pussy.

She watches breathlessly as I come to stand by the foot of the bed and kick off my boots and remove my pants. I leave my shirt on.

I don't move. I simply stand still, looking at Justine, who scissors her legs impatiently.

I like that she's impatient. But I can't help but think of Darcie and how she would make me work for it. She would rather suffer in silence than let me know how much she wanted it. And that thought is fucking hot.

It turns me on that being with her isn't easy. Half the time, I don't know what she's thinking. And I like that. I like that she's challenged me from the first moment we met. I can read most people with ease. I know it'll take a couple of minutes before I have Justine coming and coming hard.

But if this were Darcie, I don't know if she'd thank me or set me on fire—literally—for making her come.

She keeps me guessing, and I can't stop. I'm so fucking screwed.

Gripping my cock, I commence jerking myself off. My eyes are locked on Justine, and she watches my hand hungrily. I like that she can't speak. I like that I'm in control.

"Please," she begs from around the tie in her mouth.

"Did I give you permission to speak?" I continue working my dick, wishing it was Darcie's hand and not mine. Just the thought of that has me buckling and almost coming.

Justine arches her neck so she can get a better view. I like her watching me.

All I can think about is Darcie. The way her body felt pressed up to mine as we danced to some ridiculous song I would usually cringe at. But with her, everything feels exciting and new. I mean, I went to prom, for fuck's sake.

But I had no qualms doing so because it was with Darcie, and I have a feeling that's how I'd approach most situations involving her. Whatever she asked for...I don't think I can say no to her.

I would kill for her.

I don't know how or when I fell so deep, but I don't question it because in this lifetime, you only meet a handful of people you have that instant chemistry with. And those people are ones you grab onto with both hands and never let go of.

The thought of her alone at prom has me gripping Justine's ankles and roughly spreading her legs apart. I never go bareback, so I hunt for my wallet in my pants and grab a condom packet. Once I'm suited up, I kneel onto the edge of the bed, but it suddenly feels wrong to fuck Justine missionary.

I don't want to look at her because it's not her eyes, not her face I want to be looking at.

She has enough slack in her wrists as I haven't tied her tight, so I slap her ass after flipping her onto her stomach. Her arms are twisted, but she doesn't seem to mind as she arches her back, hinting at what she wants.

Positioning myself, I sink into her pussy in one hard stroke, her whimpers doing nothing to salve the burn for someone who isn't her. But no one ever will because I've never wanted anything, anyone, more than I want Darcie.

I commence fucking Justine without apology because this is the fantasy she wants—to be ravaged by a stranger here to defile and abuse her against her will. So I fulfill her fantasy, all the while wondering just how far I will go to fulfill my fantasy of getting the fuck out of this town.

Gripping her hips, I fuck her hard, loving the way her ass quivers with every brutal stroke. Her muffled screams and the slapping of flesh are amplified in the bedroom, and it pleases me that although Justine is a means to an end, she's enjoying herself. I'm not a total bastard.

She arches her back, offering me her ass, so I slip a hand under her stomach and coax her onto her knees. With her wrists still tied, she's mine to do with as I please, and I reenter her—hard. She slumps forward from the force, but I don't give her time to recover.

Anchoring her waist, I slam into her before pulling out slowly, which has Justine moaning in pleasure and pain because she wants to come. But when she does, I want her so lost to ecstasy that she won't realize I'm stealing from her.

The sight is a glorious one, but it doesn't matter how perfect Justine feels. It's only thoughts of Darcie that will make me come.

"Are you scared?" I ask, gripping Justine's hips so tightly it'll leave bruises.

Her head bobbles as I fuck her with such force. She thrashes back and forth, back and forth, on my cock as I force her body up the bed.

Winding her hair around my fist, I yank her neck back and turn her cheek so she can see me completely dominating her.

"Good. Never forget I was the one who took from you because you welcomed me into your home."

She moans, clenching her muscles around me, not realizing my words have taken on a totally different meaning.

She will, though...

Letting Justine go, I grip the back of her neck with one hand, and the other, I fix to her waist and fuck her until she explodes with a muted cry. She convulses around my hard cock, and although she feels fucking incredible, I can't come.

But as thoughts of Darcie cross my mind, of her standing in that bunny onesie, of her standing her ground with fire in those fucking green eyes, I pump harder and faster. I am engulfed with thoughts of her and my need. My craving suddenly kicks me in the guts, and I come with a guttural, animalistic growl.

I fold in half, almost covering Justine's back with the force of my orgasm.

Fuck...

I've not come like that—ever.

Once I catch my breath, I pull out of Justine, who slumps onto her stomach breathlessly.

She begins speaking, but she's still gagged, and I ensure she stays that way until I get what I really came here for.

"Shh..." I order, placing a finger over my lips.

I grab my pants and boots and walk into the bathroom to clean up. Once I'm dressed, I leave Justine tied and gagged to her bed as I rob her house and do so with a smile.

It seems prom night is truly an evening to remember...

CHAPTER NINE
Darcie

It's funny how trust is usually automatic until someone breaks it.

Or breaks you.

Just being in the vicinity of people and the familiarity of their faces and movements in your daily life creates trust. Every day, I go to school, and not for a second would I assume that any one of those humans would do anything untoward.

Yeah, they are all dicks mostly, but who thinks the company you keep could be the company of a malicious criminal? Perhaps I'm naïve. Maybe everyone has the ability to snap and do something crazy for no other reason than entertainment.

The truth is, we are either the hunter or the rabbit.

Do we get to choose which role we play?

I don't think so.

It's a game of whose team is stronger or sicker in the head. One of those two.

I was on the wrong team tonight.

Football will never mean the same thing to me again. Big sweaty boys, panting and battling it out for points on a scoreboard. They strive for greatness and get off on discipline. They berate each other on the field and in locker rooms, and it only fuels their fire to win at all costs.

What makes them snap?

Is it a pedophilic coach? Parents who pressure them to try harder or they won't get that scholarship? Or are they just pure Neanderthals put on the field to release excess testosterone?

"What are you doing out here, little one?" Foss steps out of nowhere in the dark parking lot, overlooking the football field.

"Nothing. Was looking for someone," I reply dryly.

The nerve of that asshole ditching me at prom. Who does that? Men are pigs. Rev is the leader of the pigs. Once again, misplaced trust. *Go me!*

"Come drink with us," says Foss, grabbing my hand. It's sweaty and calloused from weight training and ball handling.

I pull my hand back quickly, and his fingers catch mine to find another grip.

I can see Buckets and whatever his fucking name is standing under the goalposts, fooling around. They're lit by the moon and joking around, taking practice punches on each other.

I think about it for what seems like a minute, and since I've been left high and dry, I figure why the hell not. I'm not going back inside to wander aimlessly around the punch bowl like a loser.

I think about Rev, and while I want to hate him, I really miss him. I shake my head as the same thoughts roll around in my mind.

Why did he leave me?

Maybe he's coming back since his car is still here. He's probably off banging some chick. I feel jealousy build up inside me, and I look at the boys partying on the field and think, *See how you like this, then, Rev.*

I follow Foss, and I'm guessing he's wasted since his hair

looks as drunk as he is. He's pulling me over to his friends even though it's quite obvious that I'm following and don't need encouragement. The grass is wet, but I'm wearing my boots. I give myself a little pat on the back for that choice. I pick my dress up with one hand.

"Ehhhh!" says the big one, Buckets, as I approach them. He hands me a bottle with golden liquid inside it.

"What's wrong? Need a glass, princess?" He laughs, amused. A big dumb bear chuckling like he just made the best joke of his life.

I roll my eyes and grab the bottle.

Cheers to being ditched.

Cheers to my dead parents.

Cheers to my stupid aunt's face that gawked at me as I left and the punishment I'll receive when I return.

Cheers to Rev for getting inside my head and then ditching me for some chick in the back of her daddy's car, no doubt.

"Let's play a game," says Blake, who seems to have recovered from his sleepover in the bathroom stalls at The Planet. His eyes are inky black and he looks like a vampiric Ken doll.

I don't think I've ever seen eyes like this, but it's like he has the soul of a shark. It's a little unnerving, but his smile is darkly inviting.

"It's like spin the bottle." He takes the bottom of my dress in his hands and lifts it a little too high, completely taking me by surprise.

I'm holding the bottle of alcohol I've been drinking and almost fall over.

"Let's spin you around and see if you can walk straight."

Foss is laughing in the background. I don't think he ever stops.

Suddenly, I'm spun around by the hem of my dress. My boots collect together and cause me to fall to my knees. Blake and Buckets hike my dress up higher and start cheering because they can see my underwear.

I struggle to battle against it and push back against my dress to force it down, but I'm failing. I can feel the icy air whip up my thighs, and my teeth begin to chatter.

"It's not funny!" I yell and throw the glass bottle at Blake, hitting him in the head. The boys go quiet suddenly, mouths hanging open as they look at Blake to watch his response.

"Ohhhhhh!" Foss says like I've just made a huge mistake.

This is the moment my heartbeat begins to thump in my head.

Blake stares down at me like his head is made of steel and he didn't feel it. He grabs the bottle off the ground, and the neck of it is covered in mud.

"Oh, you wanna play rough, hey? What's your name, Dhalia?" Blake is talking through his teeth. "Why don't you have another drink and calm that little temper down?"

"I don't need to calm down! Why don't you just fuck off! I'm leaving," I say, scrambling to get to my feet and trying to dust the wet mud off my hands.

Before I have a chance to shift, Blake grabs my face, stunning me into silence and pushes the muddy bottle into my face. It smashes against my teeth and forces my mouth open.

"Thatta girl, drink it all!" he coos, and I feel my throat choking and closing over against the dirty glass.

I need to run.

Suddenly, I'm the rabbit caught in a trap, and I can see my way out, but I can't free myself—yet.

Once I do, they won't catch me because I can run faster than those muscled meatheads with quads too large to be aerodynamic. I've spent my life running from fires I've started when I've spent too long watching them burn shit down before leaving at the last minute to escape the felony.

I clasp the bottle and push back against his force, but I can't budge it from my throat.

I can't breathe as the whiskey fills my throat and runs down the sides of my mouth as I try to reject it. I'm choking and gagging, which I know only creates desire in men like this, but I can't stop.

I'm drunk, which isn't helpful either, in the sense that I need to move and my muscles feel like jelly, but at least my sense of pain is hindered enough for me to take this fucked-up "game."

My body heats up like I'm on fire on this cold, wet night, and I can feel sweat emanating from my hands, chest, and face—fear chemicals that only add to the seduction for predators to feast harder. They live off it and desire it.

My eyes begin darting around, then stop to focus on someone sitting in the shadows of the bleachers. A lit cigarette is sparking with each inhale, and I try to scream out for help.

Blake pulls the bottle out from my throat and crouches down in front of me.

"I like the way you took that bottle. Pity these teeth are in the way." He reaches into my mouth and begins pulling at my front teeth.

I smack his hands and try to turn my face away, but he slaps me back, laughing and poking at my teeth again while I spit at him.

I'm screaming, I think, but it's like noise into a pillow with barely any sound. I feel like my vocal cords are damaged, and I'm squeaking like a mouse.

The field is so vast and wide that no one would hear me anyway, even if I could scream. The effort to try is futile.

I need to be smarter than that.

I feel a fist pull my hair at the back of my head, and it's Buckets. He's leaning over me from behind, and his head is upside down, looking into my face. He spits into my mouth while Blake holds it open.

"She needs some lube, man! The booze is drying her out!"

Foss is standing idly, looking around. I can see him watching the guy in the bleachers, and he uncertainly raises his drink as if to say cheers. "All right, come on. Let her go now. It's not funny," Foss says as if he's nervous.

"Shut the fuck up, you virgin pussy! Get your goddamn dick out," Blake snarls back at him.

He has his hand around my throat. I can hardly make a sound, and I feel as though my body is shifting. Leaving this shell of a green dress to stand by and watch from a distance.

Am I going to die?

I want to die.

But I also want to fight.

"I SAID take your fucking dick out, Foss. I'm not going to ask you again." Blake stands up and punches Foss square in the face.

His surfer curls tumble back, and I see blood dripping out the corners of his mouth. This fires Foss up, and he stares at his challenger with pure ferocity as he rips his belt from his pants.

"You want this, bitch?" Foss says, still staring down Blake.

I try to shake my head, but Buckets grabs my shoulders and shoves me down onto my back.

The lights are blinding me, and I can hardly see. My eyes roll back into my head, and I'm taken to another place. Out of this body, out of my mind.

I feel knees on my shoulders, pinning me down. My legs are kicking, and Blake has his foot pressed against my ankle, twisting it into the dirt. I twist and turn to look over my shoulder to see he's smoking a cigarette casually and looking out across the field.

"Do it," he says to Foss, who is standing there with his big ugly prick out.

"Mind those teeth. Don't bite," Blake continues laughing clouds of smoke into the cold night air.

I feel it come at me fast, the heat and long injection of his dick pushing past my lips and down into my throat.

I want to stop breathing.

Stop existing.

I think of Rev when he turned up at my door, wishing I could press rewind. Go back inside, and slam the door in his face.

I can see curls bouncing over me. Foss has his knees on my shoulders, and he's fucking my mouth like it doesn't have a human attached. I can feel someone ripping my underwear down my legs. Big hands, grabbing at my cold, slippery skin.

I'm exposed.

I know I am, but I can't see.

My body is no longer sacred and no longer mine. I feel large fingers enter me, and I can't stop them.

"She's so fucking tight, man!" hollers Buckets. He spits on me, and I feel the cold, wet grime hit where his fingers move.

"Go easy, boys. Save some for me," says Blake, who just watches calmly from above.

At this point, I'm begging God to let me die. I feel like I'm in and out of consciousness, but it's not the alcohol. It's trauma. My brain is trying to check out, but it's not working. I need to leave my body and shed my skin like a snake slipping out of its shell.

Rushing back into reality, I bite down on the meaty dick invading my mouth, and Foss screams like a baby, quickly pulling out.

I gasp for air like I've just come up out of a deep ocean of water. I begin to throw up, and I'm trying to kick Buckets in the face. I'm sure I collect his jaw with my foot at one point, and the pain from my twisted ankle surges up my leg.

"Move, fool!" orders Blake, and he shoves Buckets away from me. The big dopey mountain of a guy falls to the side, laughing like he's giving his friend a turn at pinball.

Blake gets on the ground, reaches for me, and slams me over onto my face, throwing my dress over my head. It provides a small comfort as now I feel somewhat disembodied from the situation. I'm under my dress, telling myself it's okay.

I'll be okay.

My fingers dig into the dirt, and I try to scramble forward. Hands grab at my hips and yank me back hard.

"You've been a bad girl," says Blake through his teeth, his enjoyment clear.

He grabs my ass and slaps it really hard, which makes my whole body rattle, but I don't feel it. I knew it should sting, but I'm numb. I feel myself being entered.

Suddenly, my ability to feel pain is back as I'm torn for the first time. Wide open and bleeding. My life has ended here in the most brutal and embarrassing way. I want to scream for my mom, and my voice shudders against the dirt beneath the dress, hiding my face from this horrific show.

I can hear the little girl inside me saying, "Mom."

"Mom."

I break inside my head, all of my thoughts now twisting and turning into the evolution of who I'm going to become.

A warrior.

A beast.

He thrusts hard, forcing my mouth into the dirt. I can taste it on my tongue, mixed with the whiskey.

I need to vomit. Over and over again. Vomit out the old me who is now dead.

Heat moves its way down my thighs, trails of blood-colored tears from my body. So this is what it's like to lose my virginity.

He goes harder, and I buck to try to get out of it, which only encourages him to thrust deeper. The hem of my skirt is ripped away from my face. A gust of cold air hits my eyes, and I see Buckets kneeling beside me, laughing with spit all over his mouth and teeth.

He's a rabid dog.

He holds my head down and pushes his fingers deep into my mouth. My eyes are tightly shut, and I'm vomiting over his hand. Blake lets out a deep growl like a Lycan and pulls out of me. I'm heaving and screaming like a wild animal and searching for the man I saw in the bleachers, but all I see is black.

I'm being dragged over to where he was as if they could read my mind—take me over there. I need help.

Mud smears down my dress and collects in my boots. It's not over. It's never going to be over.

"Let's make this bitch scream! I know she loves

it," says Foss, laughing. They throw me down against the bleachers.

I'm not in my body anymore. I'm plotting my revenge with each act they inflict upon me.

I feel a belt wrapping tightly around my head and into my mouth.

"Bite it, princess," Blake whispers into my ear. He's the one calling the shots.

"She's too pretty," says Buckets, drooling, and soon changes that when he punches me with one of those fists bigger than my head square in the face.

My head flies back and cracks open against the edge of the wood behind me. I see stars, and not the ones watching me from above. I cough, and blood squirts out between my teeth and over the leather belt that tastes like sweat in my mouth.

Foss is drunk out of his mind. I get a sense that he's not really okay with this, but he's going along for the ride—weak piece of shit. I start to kick with all of my power as I feel the alcohol begin to wear off.

I don't think I can really fathom what happens next, but at this point, I make a promise to myself that each one of these fuckers will die.

And die slowly...

"Lick that slut pussy, Foss. You know you can't leave a chick wanting more!" mocks Blake. I wonder why he hates me so much.

But the feeling is mutual.

I fucking hate that motherfucker with every fiber in my body, and I'm imagining pulling all of his teeth out and making him eat them.

Foss shoves my knees back and starts biting into me. He's not licking, he's literally eating my skin like a lion tearing at its prey, and as I start a guttural scream, Buckets starts laughing and grabs my head and bashes it against the bleacher.

"Don't come yet!" he says, laughing, as my head cracks like a watermelon.

He wipes the drool from his mouth with the back of his hand and gets super close to my face. I can feel his hot breath against my skin,

"Don't come yet, I said!" he repeats and pokes me in the eye. "Close your eyes. Enjoy it!" He pokes my other eye, laughing.

Blake has Foss by the back of his head, and he's pushing his face hard between my legs.

"You like that, don't you, little brat?" Blake snarls between his teeth.

He grabs an empty bottle and shoves Foss off me.

"Fuck off!" he yells to his two goons.

They back away, and Blake picks me up and drags me off to a dark corner. He rams my head under a bleacher, facedown, and spits in his hand.

"Nearly done, darling," he says, yanking the back of the belt buckle behind my head to reposition me.

I don't have enough screams in me, and it feels like it's coming from someone else.

I'm not me anymore.

I don't know where I went, but I feel like I'm standing behind Blake, like an apparition just watching him destroy a girl on her first time at prom.

I feel a rip, and it's my body.

He's entered me from behind, and I'm crying as he violates my back passage. Fingers, dick, something else—I don't know what it is, but if I thought I was in pain before, I really had no idea how bad it could get.

"There's a girl," he praises happily. "Whoa, nelly, take it easy."

And I feel him break me in two.

I want to die. But he won't kill me.

He pulls me back and forth over whatever he's inserted into me like he's riding a horse.

"I'm training you, my darling," he says as he pushes in hard and keeps it there, waiting for me to relinquish tension.

My throat screams hard against the belt in my mouth, and I feel like I've gone crazy.

"Let it go, Darcie," he says against my ear. "Just let go, baby girl. You got this."

I can hear the other boys laughing in the distance like they are very far away now, and I've fallen down the darkest canyon.

Blake thrusts again, and my body lurches back and forth over the bleacher, my head collecting against what feels like a hard concrete wall. I want him to bash it harder so I can break my body on it for good.

There's no coming back from this. I'll never be the same again. The light of day will only burn me with realities I'll never be able to face.

But still, there's a small flicker of fire in me just dancing lightly over a version of me that knows nothing ever will or can break me. They just made the biggest mistake of their putrid lives.

CHAPTER

TEN

Rev

I have the stamps and pistol. But it's not enough.

I don't know what it is about stealing that just gets me off. It's in the dark and depraved where I thrive. I was born to do this, and no matter how much I have, I always want more. Which is why I decide to swipe the antique Persian dagger which sits prettily in Theodore the Third's office.

With a name like that, he's lucky I'm not taking a lot more.

Peering at the clock on his desk, I see I've been gone for a lot longer than I thought. Darcie is going to be fucking pissed. But I know she can look after herself.

Just five more minutes...

Just as I'm replacing the glass over the dagger case, I hear the front door open.

"Darling? I'm home early. Vinnie has food poisoning. I told him not to eat that clam chowder. Darling?"

Peering into the heavens and cursing silently, I know it's time to bounce as Justine's husband wasn't supposed to be home for another hour. I shouldn't have been greedy. I should have left earlier. If I had, I wouldn't be stuck in this office with no escape, and Darcie wouldn't be waiting for me to return.

Fuck.

But that's the thing about hindsight—it's fucking useless.

All I thought about was June, and how the more I steal, the sooner we can blow this town. Away from the ghosts that haunt us both every single day.

Creeping toward the window, I see that the drop into the garden below will probably hurt, thanks to the barberry bushes. But it'll just add to the numerous cuts and scars I already have.

Ensuring I have everything I came here for, I quietly open the window but quickly retreat when I see a car pull up the drive. The headlights allow me to see Theodore hightailing it to whoever just pulled up. Fair to say, they weren't invited.

A woman exits the car, clearly agitated. I can't hear what she's saying, but I can feel the sting of the slap she just delivered to Theodore's cheek.

Whoever this woman is, however, she's a godsend as it allows me to leave without needing to pick prickles out of my ass.

I quietly open the door and decide to exit the way I came—through the back door. However, I realize Justine is still gagged and tied to the bed.

I should leave her because her excuse as to why she's tied to her bed would be quite comical. But after seeing that her husband is caught up with another woman, I feel guilty for judging her. Her husband is clearly an adulterous asshole too.

Jogging to her bedroom, I see her eyes widen when she sees me. She muffles around the tie in her mouth, giving me visual clues to untie her, which I do. Before she has a chance to speak, I take the gag out of her mouth and slam my lips over hers.

"Thanks. I had a nice time. By the way, your husband is outside with some woman. It doesn't look good...for him." I wince. "Or you."

Her eyes narrow as she's clearly wounded by my detachment and also my revelation, but it is what it is—and what this was, was me using her as much as she was using me.

I don't wait for a reply and quickly make my way through the house.

Thankfully, Theodore is still outside. I wonder if his other cheek has been slapped yet.

Grabbing an apple from the fruit bowl, I take a big bite and keep it in my mouth as my hands are full carrying my stolen goods. That won't do, so I hunt through the cupboards and find a shopping bag to dump everything into.

Just as I'm about to open the door, I hear voices approaching the kitchen, and they don't sound too happy.

Quickly retracing my steps, I head back upstairs and decide to steer clear of Justine's bedroom and stick to the original plan of jumping out the window. Just as I open it, my cell vibrates in my pocket. I would usually ignore it—considering this is the first time I'm seconds away from being caught—but I'm worried it's Darcie on the other end, calling to see where I am.

But when I see the caller is June, my heart instantly drops, and all thoughts of being caught red-handed are forgotten.

"Is everything all right?" I ask, holding my breath.

She doesn't reply, and I don't think her pause is for dramatic purposes. "I'm so sorry."

Now I'm the one with a mouth full of nothing.

"I've been a horrible mother."

Yes, she has been. She's been fucking horrible. But I

don't hold any grudges. I understand she's broken and damaged. I accept that. I'm okay with that because I'm doing all of this to repair whatever pieces of her that I can.

Climbing out of the window, I sit on the ledge and peer into the sky for a moment, listening to my mom confess her sins and wondering why now.

"I will be better. I promise. No more. I'll get help. Please forgive me."

Most would feel a sense of relief hearing those words. But they're ones I've heard before. I know her pattern because I'll be throwing her ass into the shower tomorrow to sober her up again.

But I entertain her nonetheless.

"It's okay."

"No, it's not," she stubbornly argues. "Your father—"

"Let's not ruin a nice conversation by mentioning him," I interrupt, realizing now is the time to bounce.

Swinging my legs, I don't brace for jack shit, and instead, I just jump, knowing full well what I'm in for. The freedom of falling is indiscernible. For a moment, I feel like I can fly.

I land on my feet, but my pants are snared in the barberry bushes.

"You have every right to hate him."

Kicking my way out of the garden, I ignore the prickles sticking out of every part of me and keep to the shadows as I press the phone to my ear.

"I don't hate him," I state firmly. "For me to hate him would mean I care, and I don't. Now isn't the time to have a deep and meaningful—"

"You're exactly like him. So stubborn."

"Mom, enough," I say, not interested in talking about

this asshole. "I'm getting you out of here. Where you can start a new life, away from this...shit."

The contents in the plastic bag I hold is just another stepping stone in confirming this.

Although I feel like a total ass for ditching Darcie, I know she'd understand. We do what we have to, to survive.

"I want to tell you about him. But...I'm not ready."

And this is something I've also heard before.

"Well, I'm not interested," I rebuke because I'm sick of the pedestal she has him on.

"You need to know. You need to know who he is. Who your—"

"I know who he is," I reply. "He is someone who doesn't deserve a second of my time."

"Aug—"

"Mom, enough!" I repeat, suddenly irritated she has "seen the light," only to talk about this motherfucker—he's the reason she is the way she is. "I don't have time for this."

"Don't have time for your mother?"

"For fuck's sake," I mumble under my breath as I ensure the coast is clear. It is. "You don't get to do that. You don't get to unload all your bullshit just because you want to have a chat. I'm not a little kid anymore. We are doing this my way.

"I need to drop Darcie off, then I'll be home, and we can talk all you like."

The moment I hit the sidewalk, I exhale in relief because that was fucking close. I don't like close calls, which means I need to work harder to get out of here sooner.

"Who's Darcie?"

"Just a girl..."

"There's no such thing."

And for once, June and I agree on something.

I never gave leaving this town a second thought, but now, I actually think I'll miss it, and that's because of the girl who's set my world on fire—in every sense of the word.

"I—"

That sentence never eventuates, however, because a blood-curdling scream, followed by the piercing shrill of a car alarm, chills me to the bone...

CHAPTER ELEVEN
Darcie

Now

And then they were done.

I had nothing more to offer.

Suddenly, I'm alone. The belt's gone from my head. My mouth lays in a sticky pool of saliva against the bench seat. I lift my head, and my neck crunches. I begin to vomit. Hot bile from my stomach with the stench of whiskey.

I purge every last one of them from my insides out. I have no one to hold my hair back. My head is spinning, but I stand.

My hands are shaking, and every nail is broken with dirt filled beneath them. I wipe my mouth with my forearm.

A beast was born within me tonight.

I stomp out onto the wet grass and cross the field toward the dimly lit parking lot. I can see Rev's car still parked there, watching me approach as if mocking me. I wonder if he's in the back seat with someone from prom.

Marching forward, I swipe the frost from the driver's window to peer in and then bang on the glass. No one is in the car. Where the fuck is he?

I begin to wonder if the evil trio had kidnapped him after leaving me. I knock on the trunk of the car. No one's inside. Unless he's gagged.

"Darcie?" a soft voice behind me asks.

It's Carson.

Always creeping up on me and the last motherfucker I want to see right now. His face is covered in concern, and I wonder if it's fake. Where was he tonight? Why wasn't he there?

"Leave me the fuck alone," I croak.

"What happened to you? Are you okay?" he asks, stepping closer.

"Don't," I say, holding my arms out. "Do I look okay to you? What the fuck!" I'm standing there, quite obviously bruised and torn from head to toe, and he's asking me if I'm okay.

I'm angry, but all my bravado is an act because on the inside, I want to die.

He grabs my shaky hands, and my knees buckle, and then my tears begin to flow. I try everything within my power not to let him see me do this, but it's like trying to prevent a river from flowing.

"Come here," he says and gently wraps his big arms around my body and strokes my ratty hair like it's silk.

"Shh, shh, it's okay," he soothes softly.

My face buries within his chest. I'm heaving tears into him that I didn't know I had left. My mouth is dry and hangs open against the fabric of his shirt. I'm weak, and every muscle in my body begins to shake and fail. My voice is hoarse, and I don't sound like myself at all. Full of rasps and asthmatic wheezes, I just cry harder as the sounds begin to fail.

Pulling back, I search his face. "Where are they?" I ask with my fists clenched in his shirt.

"They?" he says, gently grabbing my fists to unlock them.

"Those fucking bastards! YOUR friends!" I spit angrily and rip myself away from him and hold myself tight. "Where the fuck are they?"

"Honestly, I don't know. They disappeared over an hour ago. I've been inside all night." He raises his hands in surrender.

"You need to find them and destroy every one of them! Foss, Buckets, and Blake!" I cry, staring him dead in the eyes. My lips are tight, and I have a frown to end all days.

He takes a moment. And then two before he speaks.

"What did they do?" he snarls and clenches his fists. "Why do you look like this? Did they hurt you? I'll fucking kill all of them with my bare hands, Darcie." He searches my face for answers.

Nothing he can do or say will make an iota of difference now. I just need them dead.

"Come to my car. I'll get you home. You shouldn't be out here like this." He puts an arm around my shoulders to guide me forward.

"Home? I can't go home like this!" I start to yell, and Carson searches our surroundings for any attention we might be getting.

I dig in my heels as the last thing I want to do is go anywhere with him. He's just one of them. Football jocks who think they own the world and can have any girl they want.

"I'll take you anywhere you want to go, Darcie. Just come to my car so we can get out of here," he says, and I do feel like he actually cares. Maybe he's not like them at all. He said he was different at the bonfire.

I have no transport, no phone, and no money. I have no idea where my purse went. And I'm certainly not walking back into the school gym like this to start a rumor mill about what just happened.

So with no choice, I allow Carson to lead me toward his car. He opens the door for me and helps me inside.

His car smells like cheap aftershave and my feet forage around the floor, looking for a spot to place them amongst the empty beer bottles. Glancing behind me, I see blankets strewn across the back seat like he's slept there a few times.

"Do you want a blanket?" he asks, reaching for one.

But I shake my head.

I don't want anything...heavy on top of me.

"All right, let's get out of here," he says, and he starts the engine and places a reassuring hand on my leg. I'm shaking under his touch, and I don't like it. I shift my body away from him until I'm almost smashed up against the passenger door.

"It's going to be okay," he assures me and drives slowly out of the parking lot. But it'll never be okay ever again.

The farther away we drive, the worse I feel. Panic rises in my stomach, and nowhere feels safe anymore. Not out there, not in this car, not in my body. I don't even feel like this is real. The urge I have to murder those disgusting jocks robs me of air. I can still feel their hands...their fingers...their tongues... I clench my eyes so tightly I feel like my head is going to explode.

Suddenly, I need to get out. I need to get out of the car right now.

The reality of what just happened rushes back in with a harsh slap of ferocity and threatens to choke me to death, and I can't breathe.

"I'm going to be sick!" I say and reach for the door handle.

"What?" Carson slows down and faces me from the driver's seat. "Oh shit. Let me pull over."

He reaches out and puts a hand on my arm, which causes me to lurch and rip open the car door. We are still moving, but not fast enough for me not to get the fuck out. I jump out of the car and tumble down an embankment.

Death at this point would be a mercy.

My name echoes in the darkness, but everything all morphs into their laughter...their smell...the intense pain and invasion of my body.

I thump into something, and I realize a large tree has broken my fall. I simply lie on my back on the ground, twigs and rocks digging into me, but I feel nothing—I am numb. I stare into the starless sky and wonder what stares back at me. This has to be a bad dream.

Are my guardian angels ready to finally intervene? I think about God and start laughing. Holy fuck, God really fucked up this time.

"Darcie!"

I can hear Carson's distressed voice and the gentle rustling of grass as he frantically tries to find me. But I make no attempt to move or speak.

"Oh fuck, you've got to go to the hospital."

Good to know I look as shitty as I feel.

My bird's-eye view of the universe is suddenly blocked by Carson's head as he stands over me and attempts to help me stand. But all I see is Blake's face over me, and I can smell that same alcoholic stench that I feel saturated in. I can't stand to be touched, so I elbow him in the face when he tries to grab my arm.

He pulls back, swearing something I can't hear over my own panicked yells. Yells that don't seem to be coming from my body, but I can hear them. No matter how hard I try to stop them, they only get louder and more frantic.

"Let me help you! Please!" It comes out muffled as he's holding a hand over his bleeding nose. The bright red in the moonlight matches the color stained over my thighs.

And just like that, the numbness turns to maniacal rage and adrenaline.

I need to get out of here, and I need to get out of here now.

I run.

Faster than I've ever run.

Up the embankment, down the street, and into the night.

Carson doesn't chase me, and the old Darcie would feel a slither of guilt for being so awful to him when all he was trying to do was help. But that Darcie doesn't exist anymore.

Until I'm in the safety of darkness, with only dim flickering streetlights dotting their way toward my destination to nowhere, do I breathe again.

I just need to be anywhere away from here, and for that to happen, I need wheels.

I'm in some neighborhood. Nothing looks familiar, but I am now looking at the world through different eyes.

Picking up a rock in a garden bed, a strangled laugh leaves me when I see the words: *Angels walk amongst us*, written on it. My angel clearly was on a sabbatical tonight, then.

I walk to the silver Honda parked by the curb and smash the rock through the driver's window. A loud shrilling has me covering my ears, and I realize hot, sticky liquid oozes down my arm—more blood. At this rate, I'll bleed to death, but that wouldn't be so bad.

Opening the door, I check the glove compartment, middle console, and the visor for the keys but don't find anything. Looks like I'm going to have to hotwire it. But I can't get my hands to stop shaking, and my vision, it's blurry and burns.

I claw at my throat because I can't breathe again. This is really it this time.

"Darcie!"

I am sick to death of hearing my fucking name. I'm going to change it. Maybe to Chloe or Veronica? Veronicas have all the fun.

"Who's Veronica?"

Arms wrap around me and drag me out of the car, and even though I know his scent, even though his presence calms me, I still want to claw out his fucking eyeballs.

"You left me!" I cry, violently flailing to escape his arms.

Rev lets me go.

I spin to face him and do the other thing I can—I slap his cheek. Hard. But he doesn't move. He simply stares at me, his golden eyes wide, his mouth slightly ajar.

"Wh-What happened? Blood?" It seems he can't construct coherent sentences, either.

I want this dress off me.

Gripping the collar, I tug at it violently, and the moment I hear the first rip, I know what I must do.

"They need to pay. All of them," I snarl, the bubble of hysteria about to pop as I claw at the dress with hysterical fingers. "So in everything, do unto others what you would have them do to you..."

Hardly the time to be reciting the Bible, but an eye for a fucking eye...and I plan on taking those bastards' eyes and then some.

Spittle dribbles down my chin, and I'm certain I'm a

rabid animal, ready to bite any fucker who dares to cross me ever again.

"We need to get you out of here."

Rev shrugs out of his suit jacket and wraps it around me as my dress lays in a bloody, ruined heap by my feet, and I am standing in nothing but my soiled underwear.

Porch lights flicker on in a sequence, reminding me of regimented soldiers preparing for battle, which seems fitting seeing as I am about to go to war.

Rev takes my hand, but I don't want him touching me. He left me, and I will never forget it.

"I'm sor—"

Before I can hear those words again, I slap his other cheek just as hard as the first. "Don't you dare say you're sorry. It's too late for that."

He nods once, accepting his punishment, his long bangs falling over his eyes.

I follow as he runs down the road toward a house where a man and woman are arguing in front of an idling car. They don't even seem to realize we're here, and I realize this isn't a coincidence. Rev was here. He left me to those vultures so he could get his dick wet.

And when he throws a shopping bag into the back of the fancy sports car, I realize not only did he leave me to get his dick wet, he left me to rob the woman he fucked.

"Un-fucking-believable. You mother—" My sentence is muffled under his palm as he places me into the car. Before he has a chance to remove his hand, I bite his fingers. I want to bite them clean off.

He's stone-faced as he runs to the driver's side and gets in. He looks over his shoulder and reverses out of the driveway and takes off into the night, quicker than I can say...this is the beginning of the end.

I don't know where we are going. All I know is that wherever we're headed, I plan on paving the path with blood, violence, and revenge.

CHAPTER TWELVE

Rev

I've driven fast before, but if we survive the night, I'll be very fucking surprised. I just can't stop because the farther and faster I drive, the farther away we get from whatever the hell happened to Darcie.

She lays curled in a ball in the seat, dead asleep. The only thing that hints that she's still alive is her chest sporadically shifting when she inhales a pained breath.

What the fuck happened to her?

I can't even guess because every scenario wants me to rip out someone's spleen—mine included. If I hadn't left her, none of this would have happened. I was only supposed to be gone for a little while. But seems that "little while" was a long fucking time for Darcie to end up bloody, beaten, and her eyes robbed of the light which perpetually shined.

I slam my palm against the steering wheel over and over again.

This is my fucking fault, and I will do everything I can to make it up to her.

A strangled moan suddenly leaves her, before she shoots upward, a guttural scream tearing from her lungs. She frantically peers around, on the defense, and I know here, now, that someone fucking hurt her, and hurt her fucking badly.

I wanted to believe that maybe her injuries were self-inflicted. That maybe she got herself into trouble by setting something on fire.

But no, that scenario is one that would make Walt Disney proud.

This is stuff that lines the mind of the vile and depraved, and Darcie is living proof that evil fucking exists.

"Stop looking at me," she angrily says, folding her arms across her chest.

She flinches, and I know she's in pain. She was running on adrenaline, but now that that's worn off, she is going to be reliving everything that happened. And when she does, I don't want to be driving one hundred miles an hour.

I take a sharp left and detour down a bumpy road. We both jerk to every pothole I drive over, but Darcie doesn't complain. She simply stares out the windshield, crossed-legged with a blank look on her face. However, when her lips twitch, I know her mind is running a race she's already won.

A derelict motel soon comes into view.

Truck drivers and five-dollar hookers only use this place as sleeping in a cardboard box by the highway would be preferable to staying here. But desperate times call for desperate measures.

I pull up around the back, needing to keep the stolen car out of sight—not that anyone would come out here. But I still need to be careful.

The motel sign has long stopped flashing, but every so often, the T on the sign buzzes to life, shrouding the parking lot with a flicker of red.

Darcie jolts when the T suddenly flickers. "Fuck you, T. You lost your chance to shine long ago. Always trying to steal the limelight, aren't you?"

If I don't get her inside, that T will signify what we will be in—trouble.

"Let's go." I open the door and step outside, knowing

better than to offer to help her. The last time I did that, I got both cheeks slapped.

The gravel crunches under her bare feet as she follows, but she doesn't complain. Compared to the rest of her injuries, I suppose this is a walk in the park.

The stars have gone into hiding, and we walk in almost complete darkness to the front door. The bell sounds like it's about to be sick as I open the door, and that seems fitting, seeing as this décor is enough to make anyone want to puke. And the smell...it smells like stale beer and cat piss.

"Wow," Darcie gushes from behind me. "Don't go all out on my account."

This place looks like a hunting lodge on steroids. Not sure who decorated it, but I'm pretty sure it wasn't an animal activist because the furnishings consist of a lot of camouflage and stuffed animal heads. The tall lamp in the corner of the room looks like it was bought from the Ed Gein estate.

And on cue, speaking of serial killers...

A man waddles out from behind a frayed red curtain, wearing a tuxedo. A snort escapes Darcie. I need to get her into a room, and now.

"Good evenin'," the man, whose name tag reads Earl, says. "Are you here to fix the shower in room eight?"

I have no idea if this is code for something other than I am a fucking crazy bastard. But I entertain him nonetheless.

"I tell you what, I'll fix your shower if you give us a room and forget you ever saw us?"

Earl peers over my shoulder. On instinct, I sidestep, so he can't see Darcie. But that doesn't mean he can't hear her.

"Nice suit, *Earl*. Where's the party at? I had a pretty dress. But it's now ruined..."

Earl's tuxedo looks like it's never been washed, and his

white shirt has a smear of ketchup down the right lapel. The jacket itself has layers of dust on it, as well as fuzzballs. And his bow tie is askew.

This would be fucking comical if not for the fact that I know Darcie is seconds away from losing her shit.

Reaching into my pocket for my wallet, I slap a hundred-dollar bill onto the counter, a plume of dust floating into the air. Earl reaches for it with his bony, nicotine-stained fingers.

I watch as he retrieves a silver key from the wall behind him with a fluffy white rabbit foot keychain. "Room five."

He places it on the counter, his beady eyes peering between me and the key.

"Thanks." I quickly reach for it and grab Darcie's hand to hightail it out of here.

But stop dead in my tracks when Earl says, "Hey. You know what they say?"

My back is turned, and if this motherfucker wants to play ball, then it's game on because I am not in the mood for fucking guessing games.

But Darcie is. "No, what do they say, Earl?"

I squeeze her hand, subtly shaking my head as we don't want to antagonize him, for fear he'll call the cops.

Suddenly, a morphed version of "Don't Worry Be Happy" fills the office, and I slowly turn over my shoulder to see Earl has pressed the button on the Big Mouth Billy Bass as it opens its mouth to sing to us.

I have no idea how to respond when Earl hums along to the singing fish.

"Don't worry, be happy now," he says with a wink while I give him a clenched-teeth smile because, what in the ever-living fuck is going on?

I drag Darcie from the office, who hums along too. I

know she's in shock, and this is her way of coping with whatever the fuck happened. Trauma affects people in different ways—my mom is a perfect example of this.

I can't get into the room fast enough and slam and lock the door behind us. Darcie casually peers around while I use my finger to part the stained lace curtain to check that Earl isn't following. We are in the clear—for now.

Sliding the heavy burgundy curtain closed, I turn to look at Darcie, who is still humming under her breath. I don't know how to broach this, but I need to know what happened. I need to know how to fix it.

To fix her.

"What happened?"

She toes at the ugly vomit-colored carpet, her eyes downcast, humming that fucking song.

"Darcie, talk to me. I'm pretty sure you've gone into shock."

"How do you know, Mr. Smarty Pants?" And she blows a raspberry.

"Don't fucking do that," I say, shaking my head. "Talk to me. I need to know what happened."

Finally, she stops humming and lifts her chin to look at me...and slays me where I stand when I witness the detachment in her eyes.

"You want to know what happened *now*?" she questions. "I could have used that concern about an hour ago when—" But a wheeze gets caught in her chest, and she struggles for air.

I rush over to her and gently wrap an arm around her shoulders. "Just breathe."

She shrugs me off. "Don't tell me what the body is designed to do! I don't need direction on a basic human function, fuck you very much."

I step back and raise my hands in surrender. "I don't want to fight. I just want to help."

"Help?" she scoffs, angrily. Good, I want her angry. "There is only one way you can help me."

"How?"

We stand facing one another in the ultimate standoff because I know the next few seconds will change the course of our lives forever.

"They need to pay for what they did. They need to pay," she repeats, placing her hands over her ears as she violently shakes her head. "Make it stop."

"I'll try, baby. Just tell me how." The term of endearment just slipped out, but it felt natural.

I gently place my hands over hers and slowly remove them from her ears as I bend low to look into her eyes. I've had enough experience with June to know how to deal with someone in this distressed state.

Although Darcie is far stronger than my mom, she is still suffering, and if she doesn't face her demons, they will fucking eat her alive.

"Who are they?"

The walls suddenly close in on me when Darcie wets her lips before confessing in a small voice, "Buckets. Blake. And Foss."

She swallows deeply, as it appears even saying their names makes her want to be sick.

"What—what did they do?"

Only after she is done detailing what no human being should ever endure does she allow a single tear to fall. I, however, am fucking numb.

I stare through her, unable to process her ugly words as truth.

"Say something," she whispers, her lower lip trembling.

But I don't know what to say.

I don't know what to think.

Her face hardens, and she lifts her chin high, letting the jacket I had put around her to drop to the floor.

She stands there in her tattered underwear, staring at me, daring me to look at her body, but I won't. She grabs my hand and places it against the skin around her waist and hips.

A car pulls into the parking lot, and the headlights shine through the cracks in the curtains, briefly illuminating the side of her face. I almost don't recognize her.

"Darcie, don't..." I begin.

"Shut up," she says and reaches for my face as if she's blind and touches every line of it—my forehead, which suddenly relaxes from tension, down my nose, until her fingertips reach my lips.

I'm not going to move. I don't know what the fuck this is, but the last thing I want to do is tell her to stop it.

Darcie

He's so beautiful, and I am destroyed inside. I don't know if I'll ever feel anything again.

His lips are softer than I expected. I touch them, and I feel like I'm going to kiss him. Maybe use him. I'm in control now. We are playing chicken, and neither of us will break eye contact.

He's breathing shallow breaths, but I feel like I'm

running and haven't stopped. I brush the hair back from his face so he can see me properly.

I remove the remains of my underwear, carefully lifting my bra straps over the cuts on my shoulders. The musty, cold air sends shivers across my skin, causing goose bumps all over my body, but inside, I'm burning. Blood is crusted down my thighs, and I see him glance down.

"I won," I say, knowing the staring contest was mine to be had.

His face is still, and he doesn't react, though I see the pain in his eyes. Like he's taken all of mine, I'm devoid of feeling.

I'm naked, yet I feel like I'm wearing armor. No care about my body being exposed. The world has made me invincible now.

My eyes dare him to touch me, but he is unmoving. I reach forward to feel what might betray him against his pants zipper, but there is nothing.

I'm horrified.

"I care about you, Darcie," he says, and it sounds like an apology.

"Do you? Because it doesn't feel like it," I reply, disgusted that my naked body has had no effect on him. "Prove it, Rev!" I'm talking louder. I don't know whose voice I'm hearing, but I guess it's my own.

"I'm trying," he states, reaching down for the jacket to cover my body.

I rip it away from him angrily and throw it hard to the floor. "Fuck me," I demand, challenging his eyes.

All I see is pity. I slap him for the third time that day.

He grits his teeth and says a muffled *fuck* through them while trying to remain calm.

"Stop." He puts his hands up, creating a barrier.

"Stop what? Fuck me now, or I'm leaving," I bluntly say.

"You don't know what you're saying," he says, and his eyes are like two healing lakes of liquid gold that I just want to smash out of his face.

I grab him and slide my broken mouth over his, demanding he kiss me back by forcing my tongue into his mouth. He resists and tries to talk to me instead. He tries to make me see reason.

"Oh, for fuck's sake!" I scream at him. "Am I too trashy for you now? Did the boys make me too dirty for you? Mr. Holier-Than-Thou can't get his cock dirty, can he?"

I'm ready for a fight, but at the same time, my shoulders are shaking, and my body betrays me with tears. I fall down to the carpet and curl into a ball.

Make this day end.

Make this day just a dream.

I want to die.

Set me free.

I go into my mind, and I can't move.

I feel his jacket drift soft air over the top of me, landing across my body, and his big arms scoop me and the jacket up. "Shh, it's okay. It's okay," he hushes me. "I've got you."

Rev carries me into the tiny bathroom and knocks on the shower taps that cause it to cough and splutter brown water into a midget-sized bathtub. He pulls the mold-covered shower curtain back so it doesn't touch me.

The water runs clear, as my mind does, and I suddenly feel naked as he removes the jacket from my body and takes me under the water. I feel like I'm being baptized as he remains fully dressed.

He places my feet down gently and faces me away from him. I tip my head down to see blood and dirt circling the drain. Water hits my scalp, and I wince as if my skull has been cracked open and someone just poured acid onto it. He gathers my hair into his large hands carefully behind me and sweeps it all back off my shoulders.

"It's washing away, Darcie." His voice is soft and nurturing, and I suddenly feel guilty for what I did to him. What I said. As if hearing my thoughts, he says, "It's okay."

He reaches around and offers me a sliver of used soap that is cracked and hard. I remove my hands from clutching my chest and shakily take it.

He steps out of the shower and draws the curtain across to give me privacy. "I'm right here."

My body is racked with pain, and every movement feels like I'm breaking bones. I wash. Everything. Over and over until my skin is raw.

The water runs cold, and I slide down to the bath floor, letting it hit my back.

With a screech, I hear the taps being turned off and the pipes in the walls banging hard like the pounding in my head. I look up to see Rev standing with a yellow towel open for me, and his eyes averted.

I'm hugging my knees, and behind him, I see a hole in the wall. "Norman is watching," I say with a half laugh.

"It's Earl, isn't it?" Confused, he turns to peer through the hole.

"No, Norman Bates," I reply flatly.

"Did you know that in the legendary shower scene, Perkins wasn't even in the scene—it was his double?"

"I have no idea why you know all of this shit." And I roll my eyes.

Standing slowly, I conceal myself and take the towel from him. I stare at him for a minute until he gets the hint and leaves, closing the door behind him so I can dry off.

Rev?" I say quietly through the closed door.

"Yes?" he replies immediately, as if he's never left the other side.

I put my hand on the door as if to reach him. "Will you do something for me?"

"Anything," he replies softly.

I rest my cheek against the door.

"Help me."

"Help you?" he questions and begins to open the door, which I nudge closed again.

I see death in my mind. Their screaming hearts and bleeding faces. I set Foss on fire and blind Blake. Buckets gets a hand job, and not the kind he wants.

"Help me...help me make them pay for what they did. I want them...all of them."

There is silence behind the door.

"I want all of them...dead."

Rev

I know she isn't talking in the metaphorical sense.

I don't reply, but she doesn't need me to because she knows my answer.

As I slump onto the end of the bed to take off my boots, all I can hear on repeat is Big fucking Mouth Billy Bass singing.

Don't worry...be happy now...

It appears the only thing that'll make Darcie happy is

killing those motherfuckers who deserve a punishment worse than death.

I angrily rip off my tie and then commence removing my soaked clothes. I toss them into the corner of the room and decide after what Darcie's been through, seeing a half-naked man is the last thing she needs. So I slip under the scratchy covers.

I won't be getting a wink of sleep tonight, but I'll make sure Darcie does. She's exhausted—mind, body, and soul.

The bathroom door opens, and Darcie walks out, wearing a white robe. She toys with the end of the belt.

"I found this under the sink," she explains. "It smells like someone died in it, but oh well."

Nodding, I focus on the TV even though the reception is flickering. Some black-and-white movie is playing, but it's only on to provide some light in the room. I imagine Darcie won't want to be in the dark for a while.

I am on my back with my fingers interlaced behind my head. The blanket rests under my arms, so not a lot of chest is showing, but I wonder if Darcie would feel more comfortable if I gave her more space.

I subtly shift across the mattress to lie on the edge. One wrong move and I'll be taking a swan dive onto the carpet. But I don't want to crowd Darcie.

She, however, doesn't seem to appreciate the sentiment.

"Don't do that," she says, pulling back the covers and slipping underneath. "Don't be weird. Please. I couldn't stand it."

I understand what she means.

After what she's been through, she doesn't want anyone looking at her with pity because Darcie isn't a victim. And the fact that she asked me to kill those three fuckers proves it.

Most would be crying about the injustices done to them, but not Darcie. My little firecracker is done crying. There is one thing I want to ask her, but I don't know if it's the right time.

When I sigh, she reads my mind, however. "Spit it out."

She keeps to her side of the bed, and I keep to mine.

"It was just those three?"

"What, that isn't enough for you?" she snaps, turning her cheek to look at me. Bruises are starting to form, and I know tomorrow they will be a lot worse.

"No, I didn't mean that," I correct. "I just meant...where was Carson?"

When she told me what those fuckers had done, I was convinced Carson was somehow involved. But she never mentioned his name. I know those boys don't do anything without Carson's approval.

She tongues over her grazed lip before replying, "He was the one who drove me out of there. The one who saved me in a way. He was nice."

"Oh bull-fucking-shit," I snap, incredulous and angered she would see him in that way. "Carson says jump, and those fuckers say how high."

"Well, you're wrong because he was there when you weren't! He was the one who showed me kindness when I was passed around like a fucking football! He was the one who chased after me when I threw myself out of his car, wanting nothing more than for this entire nightmare to end forever!

"So think what you want, but what I *know* is that he was there when you weren't."

The TV reflects the shine of her eyes, but she quickly brushes away her tears with trembling fingers.

I know she didn't mean to snap, but it's the truth.

Carson *was* there for her when I should have been, and I will forever make amends for that mistake.

"Did you mean what you said?"

She doesn't look at me. Instead, she stares blankly at the TV. "Yes."

I don't need to elaborate on what I mean. She knows. It's the only question that seems to make sense.

I've done some shitty things in the past, but this, this is something else.

"I don't expect anything from you," she says frankly. "But don't try to stop me. This is happening with or without you."

This may not make sense to most, but seeing Darcie this way, talking about murder, just has me falling deeper and deeper under her spell. I've never met anyone like her, and I don't think I ever will again.

"I understand—"

But I cut her off. "I'm all in."

She turns to face me slowly. She wears the perfect poker face, but I know my admission has stunned her into silence. So there is only one thing to do.

With the smallest of movements, I shift toward her. She does the same thing to me, and the space between us suddenly feels worlds apart. But when she is close enough, I reach for her, and with a tender touch, I pull her into my arms and everything else simply just...exists around us.

At this moment, this is all that matters.

She wraps herself in my arms and cuddles close, lowering her walls just this one time because come tomorrow, I know her barricades will be impenetrable.

She inhales deeply, nuzzling into my chest, and I like it. I don't like cuddling because it's never been like that with the women I've been with. But with Darcie, it feels...nice.

"You smell like coconuts," she sleepily says. "I like it."

I stroke her damp hair and realize I would do anything for her. I mean, I just agreed to murder our classmates, and I don't feel a fucking lick of shame for it.

I think of June and what that would mean for her. All I've done my entire life is look after her, and I don't think she'll know how to survive without me.

"What are you thinking about?"

"My mom," I confess, which is hardly the appropriate thing to say when you're cuddling with a girl. But Darcie gets it. "She is probably passed out on the bedroom floor in a drug-induced coma by now."

"Oh...did you—"

But for once in my life, I don't put my mom first. "Tomorrow, we need new wheels. The cops will be all over the one I stole. We also need some clothes. I think it's best we lay low for a couple of days."

Her head bobs once as she nods. "Agreed. I'm sorry I yelled at you."

"Don't even worry about it."

Our breathing fills the silence, but I want to clarify one thing. "What you said before...nothing will ever change the way I see you."

The semi I have is proof of that. I know she feels dirty, but I'll never see her as a victim. Rather, I see her as the victor. She survived, but the ones who broke her won't.

Darcie affects me in every possible way, which is why I can't let this go, why I can't let *her* go.

CHAPTER THIRTEEN

Rev

I did as I said I would and fixed the shower for Earl.

He offered to give me a tuxedo, but it was a hard pass. I did take him up on the offer to use his phone so I could call Nonna since my battery was dead. She told me what I already knew—my mom was passed out after crying into her bottle of vodka.

I told her I wouldn't be home for a couple of days, and I asked if she could look out for June while I was gone. Of course, she agreed.

With that sorted, I'm surprised the bag of stolen shit I swiped last night is still in the car. It seems trivial, but we're going to need collateral for the shit Darcie wants to do, and this is a good fucking starting point.

I open the bedroom door to see her sitting on the end of the bed, biting her nails. She's dressed in my jacket, which hangs off her small frame.

Her face is a fucking mess. So are her legs which poke out from under my jacket.

But I don't make a fuss.

"Let's bounce."

Remembering the Advil I swiped from behind Earl's desk, I toss her the bottle. She catches it and throws back three pills. I know the sensible thing would be for her to go to the hospital, but I know that ain't happening.

A snort suddenly escapes her, which she catches with her hand.

"What?" I ask, arching a brow. At this point, anything could be funny.

"I broke curfew...oops."

"Even more reason to lay low until we find out what the fuck is happening back home."

I need to have eyes on Carson as there is no way his little lapdogs won't be rehashing what they did to Darcie. Then we will see just how much of a hero he really is because the pull his asshole dad has in town would mean those three clowns would be ruined forever.

But I know that won't happen.

When push comes to shove—assholes stick together.

I don't tell Darcie my thoughts, though.

I offer her my hand, which she accepts.

"So where to now?"

"It's time to get the hell outta Dodge."

Darcie

I need clothes and a goddamn machine gun.

We're on the road, searching for a convenience store. I walk in, wearing his jacket like a dress, and ignore the pervy sixteen-year-old boy behind the counter.

There are security cameras dotted around, so I keep my head down. I dunno what the penalty is for stealing a car. I see some workman's overalls and a hoodie with the convenience store logo on the front.

Great, why not just tell everyone where I've been?

I grab them anyway because the alternative is an apron saying Happy Father's Day on it with nothing to cover my backside. I grab some men's boxer shorts from this sexist piece of shit store as well. Luckily, my bra is still intact, and I washed it last night in the sink.

A TV is playing behind the counter as I go up to pay with Rev's money, and I see a woman bawling her eyes out to a man, holding a microphone in her face. She's talking about a young man who broke into her house and stole her heirlooms and diamonds. A man in the background is trying to comfort her, but she's shrugging his hands off her like he's a disease. Well, that marriage is over.

"That'll be eighty dollars," says the clerk. And then it happens.

There's our car—well, technically, the car we stole on the TV—it's a photograph, and the loser husband is saying it was stolen as well. In seconds, there's an old-school photo of Rev on the screen.

"Excuse me, ma'am, that'll be eighty dollars," the boy croaks at me.

"Holy fuck," I whisper, ignoring him because, what the actual fuck?

"It's on sale with a discount of thirty percent, plus you get a free bumper sticker!" he pleads, desperate for the sale or for me to leave—I can't tell which.

I stare at him. "Fine, give it to me. Hey, do you have hair clippers?"

"No, ma'am, we do not."

There goes my idea of shaving my head to disguise myself as GI Jane.

We're fucked.

Thoughts of my aunt come into my head, and I bet she's called the police too.

Just then, I hear a jingle, and the store door opens to reveal two cops walking in and over to the donut stand. I glance outside to see Rev in the car, tapping the steering wheel while the engine runs. We've gotta get the fuck out of here. I bet he doesn't even know he's all over the news. That dumb bitch probably had the best sex of her life and is now claiming he broke in and robbed her.

I chuck some money at the clerk, take the damn bumper sticker, and walk slowly like I don't have a care in the world out to the car. Rev stares at me through the windshield like I've lost my mind.

"Go," I say calmly, watching the cops stand at the counter to pay for their coffee and donuts.

"Umm...yeah, all right. You okay?"

I smile sweetly. "You're on the news, so what the fuck do you think? Get the hell out of here slowly."

Rev turns to see the cop car behind him and then looks at me.

"Go!" I cry and stomp my foot over to his side of the car and hit the accelerator, which, in hindsight, was stupid because Rev was in reverse and hightails it straight into the cop car.

"What the fuck, Darcie!" His mouth hangs open, and he slams the car into drive and exits the parking lot a little faster than expected as my head flies back into the headrest.

I can hear sirens, and Rev is speeding and turning down random country roads and trying to weave us into farmland when we need to get back to the motel off the highway.

"Now we're fucked!" he says, and I notice his face turn a pretty shade of pink.

I feel like laughing, but I hold it in and watch a few scarecrows whisk by, and some cows nonchalantly chew as we pass.

The sirens become faint, and I know we've lost them. But now, we can't stay here. Now we have begun something we can't turn back from.

"We need a new car," Rev says, suddenly calm and collected.

He checks his phone, then rips the back off it and throws it out the window into a field.

"Well, that was a little melodramatic. You could have just destroyed the SIM and kept the phone. But you do you."

I get a stiff upper lip in response.

We'd been driving for a while, getting farther and farther away from the motel. I'm glad I didn't have any belongings in there. Our license plates are smashed from the police car incident, and I'm feeling safe.

"That one," says Rev, pointing toward a small wooden house sitting quietly on acres of land with a long dirt road driveway leading up to it.

The gates are open, and a sign says, *"Home is where the heart is."* A large barn is next to it, and a four-wheel drive is parked carelessly in front. The doors are open. Taking a careful turn, we make our way down to the house.

"Do you have a plan here?" I ask, pulling on my men's overalls and hoodie in the passenger seat.

"You go to the door and say you're lost and looking for directions while I go scope out the truck. The gates are open, so we should be able to get away quickly, and whoever is in there won't be able to run fast enough to catch up with us. I'll disable this car while I'm out there."

"Seems like a solid plan," I reply as we quietly exit the car and put the plan into play.

When I walk to the house, I see that the door is ajar, but I knock on it anyway. I can hear music playing, old '50s rock.

This place is creepy as hell. I push the door wide open from my standpoint on the porch.

"Hello?" I singsong, but there's no response. I turn to see where Rev is, but he's already rounded the corner.

"Is anyone here?" I continue. This feels like a movie where the chick stupidly walks inside and then gets hammered in the face with a chainsaw.

So I walk in. Down a long hallway with cracks in the walls and creaky floorboards.

"Hello?" I sound like a broken record.

I find myself in a dining/kitchen area, and the dishes are piled high in the sink with buzzing flies over them. Some are caught having seizures in the Venetian blinds that are bent and crooked. It looks like someone tried to let some light in but failed and bashed the side of them to death. It smells like cat piss, but I don't see any cats.

The music is coming from a room farther in. I'm guessing whoever is in there couldn't hear me because it's so loud.

Not my vibe at all, and I'm guessing the person living here won't be either.

I push my way past cluttered kitchen chairs toward the back room where the music is coming from. It's a closed, dark-red door and I can hear whimpering from inside. God, I hope no one is having sex to this music.

I hold my nose as the stench overpowers me and knock on the door. A sudden shriek emits from inside the room—a female screams bloody murder, and the hairs on my neck go apeshit. My fight-or-flight senses switch to fight, and I open the door—fast.

"Get me the fuck out of here!" shouts a young girl about my age from a urine-stained bed with no covers on it and barely a sheet tucked in beneath her.

She's kicking and bucking. Her arms are tied above her head, and her face is swollen and red. She looks like she's been beaten.

"You gotta help me! Untie me before he gets back! Untie me! Untie me!" she begs, sobbing her heart out against her naked chest.

She's completely exposed, and I'm so hyped up by what I see that I clench my fists automatically.

"Stop fucking screaming," I say to her through gritted teeth. She starts screaming louder and louder in my ears as I try to rip off the plastic straps locked around her wrists.

"For fuck's sake! Hold still!" I yell at her. "And shut UP!"

"Fuck you!" she snarls and spits in my face.

Clearly, she is traumatized, so I forgive the behavior.

I get one arm free, and she reaches over to rip at the other side.

"Well, well, we have a little party on our hands," says the gruff voice of a big fat bastard in a plaid shirt and stinky old jeans standing in the doorway. He's laughing and adjusting his belt buckle.

"You invited a little friend over, darling?" he mocks his

pet on the bed, and his beady eyes are hungry and buried deep within his ample cheeks.

The girl starts screaming...again.

"Oh, fuck me," I curse and grab the heavy lampshade from the nightstand.

I slam the end of it full pelt into the asshole's face, and surprisingly, he rolls back like a babushka doll and hits the deck.

Unfortunately, he's not out, though, and grabs my ankle with his big meat hooks and pulls me down to the floor. He really picked the wrong girl to mess with, and while the girl is still on the bed, struggling with her wrist tie, I start bashing his face.

Something in me suddenly snaps...

"Fucking rapist asshole! How do you like that?" It sounds like I'm punching raw meat with porcelain. Over and over again.

"Did you fuck her in the ass? Did you?" I demand and smash him again before he can attempt a response.

The girl starts wailing again behind me.

"Men like you don't deserve to breathe," I say, and my body regenerates like a battery plugged into a charger. "Rapist c—"

"Stop it! Stop it!" shouts the girl. "You're killing him!"

That's the point...

I proceed to grab a shard of the lamp shade now broken and jam it into his face. I turn to her while he's staked to the floor through his eye.

"You really should have more self-worth than to defend this asshole," I say matter-of-factly.

I start wrapping the electrical cable around his neck and yank hard on it like Princess Leia did to Jabba the Hutt.

"You're a fucking psycho!" she screams and frees herself

from the last tie and hightails it buck naked out the window.

Moments later, Rev appears, looking down at me straddling Mr. Mutilated, and gives me a, "Tsk tsk," as he folds his arms and leans against the doorframe.

Damn, he looks hot.

My eyes mischievously lock on his like he's just caught me eating birthday cake before the big day. His hair falls carelessly over one eye, which he shakes out of the way and runs his big hand back through it. He gives me that big Joker smile I'm becoming addicted to.

"Don't let me interrupt," he mocks with a wave of his hand, telling me to finish what I started.

I bring my leg around, jam my foot under Billy Bob's chin, and yank back harder on the cord—this motherfucker just won't die.

The song changes, and I start singing, "Bbaabbyyyy."

The guy looks at me with one eye like he knows it's the end.

Rev sighs. "Okay, he's had enough. We gotta bounce."

I give up trying to attempt murder in the first degree because clearly, I'm not well practiced.

The asshole is moaning, and I think he's gone into shock. Maybe I should've just cut his dick off. I could have gifted the chick with a memento to take home in a party bag.

Looking at him, I see that he already had a face only a mother could love, and now, I don't even think his mother would.

"Get cleaned up," Rev says, nodding toward the bathroom. "I'll deal with our friend here."

Rev smiles sweetly, hands in his pockets, looking down

at him. I can see him analyzing the guy and figuring out how heavy he would be.

I grab some clothes I need from the floor that the girl must have been wearing—she had some style I'm really liking. Baggy army pants, long coat with a hood, and old combat boots held together with silver gaffer tape, which have been decorated in black pen drawings with stars and broken hearts.

I think we would have gotten along had the setting for our first introduction been different.

I walk into the bathroom and look into the dirty mirror at all the blood spatter on my face. I don't hate what I see.

I find a tube of lipstick in the pocket of my new jacket and try it on without cleaning my face.

Ruby red.

Something I'd never wear, but when in Rome...

I kiss my hand to get the excess off and open the mirrored cabinet in front of me. Not bad.

I slide open one of the drawers, and what do you know—pretty little hair samples all lined up in a neat row. Tied so meticulously with childlike silk ribbons.

There's a blonde, several brunettes of all shades, and a fiery red.

He's a collector.

Fucking sick bastard, I did the world a favor.

Rev suddenly appears. "It's time to go."

CHAPTER FOURTEEN

Rev

The truck is quiet as it seems both Darcie and I need some silence after what just happened back at the farmhouse.

I don't know whether to be turned on or traumatized by what I saw—maybe a little of both.

I knew she'd snap sooner or later. And when she did, it wouldn't be pretty. But her nearly killing that asshole was something else...

My dick twitches at the thought.

There is just something so fucking...hot about a woman taking control and owning the ass of a chump three times her size. And with her fuck-off clothes and fuck-off attitude, I don't stand a chance.

"What are you looking at?" she says, snapping me from my thoughts. I didn't even know I was looking at her.

She's leaning back in her seat, her knee bent as she rests her boot on the edge of the chair. She has no idea how beautiful she looks. She also has no idea that her rage is just the tip of the iceberg. There is so much more to come.

"Are you hungry?"

Not only did we steal this truck but we also robbed that asshole of everything we need—food, water, clothes, gas, and money. We don't need to hit a store because our truck is filled with supplies.

Darcie unbuckles her seat belt and reaches into the

back, rifling through the bags of food. I hear the crinkle of a packet and know she's gone for the bag of Lay's. She slumps back into her seat, not bothering to fasten her seat belt, and rips open the bag.

She takes one out, looks at it, but then tosses it back into the bag, changing her mind. Her emotions are running riot, which is why I don't know what to do.

Like I said, this is just the beginning. And I don't know what to do about it.

Should I help her like I said I would? Or should I be the one who sees reason in an unfair world?

"Do you think that chick is going to call the cops?"

All I caught was her naked ass falling out of the window, but from the state of the room, I know that whatever happened in there can't be good.

"Probably," I reply, keeping my eyes on the road. "She *was* held hostage in the house out of *Texas Chainsaw Massacre*."

"I don't get it," Darcie says, and I arch a brow.

"Don't get what?"

"How could she not have wanted to kill that bastard after what he did?"

I understand her anger. The need to hurt anything like she was hurt. She needs to take back what was stolen to try to heal.

"I suppose she was more concerned about getting out alive than revenge."

Biting her thumbnail, Darcie is quiet, appearing deep in thought. "All I could think about was making that fucker bleed."

"Darcie—" But she doesn't let me finish.

Instead, she reaches for the steering wheel and violently

turns it so we are now driving on the opposite side of the road.

I try to fight her off, but she bites down on my wrist. "Live a little, Rev."

When I attempt to stomp onto the brake pedal, she is like a damn spider monkey, crawling all over me so I can't move or see a damn thing.

She straddles my waist, her front facing me and blocking my view. I am literally driving blind into oncoming traffic, or we are seconds away from careening down a steep embankment.

But if this is what she wants...

"Okay then, little rabbit," I calmly say, lifting my hands off the steering wheel, eyes locked on hers. "You choose whether we live or die."

She is pressed tightly against me and the fact that we could be moments away from death strangely gets me hot. My cock instantly hardens, and Darcie's eyes soon widen when she feels the response she evokes in me.

I can see it in her eyes—fear, panic, and excitement. The unknown excites her, just how almost killing that redneck at the farmhouse did. It's only in the eyes of danger does she feel alive, and after wanting to die, the taste is one she will soon become addicted to.

It is one she will not be able to live without.

Just how it gets me off stealing from the rich—the rush is indescribable. And for Darcie, toeing the line between life and death is her poison.

When we hear a horn blaring in the distance, I lick my top lip, daring her to make the choice.

Live or die. She chooses.

"You know you want to take the wheel," she challenges, her green eyes so vibrant.

In response, I interlace my hands behind my head and lean back into the seat.

"Rev," she warns, a slight panic in her voice.

"Darcie."

The horn gets louder.

This is us playing chicken—blind. Not only with the oncoming vehicle but also between ourselves. Who will cave first?

"Take the wheel."

I stomp my foot onto the accelerator instead.

"This is your game," I say, never breaking eye contact. "You make the rules."

The horn is now a constant stream of noise, alerting us that we have seconds to make a decision.

"So choose."

Her cheeks are flushed, her beautiful mouth parted as she can't seem to take in air fast enough. The sight has my cock throbbing in absolute need for this woman.

"Fuck you!" she cries, quickly turning and taking the wheel. She swerves so hard we run off the road but miss the oncoming logger truck by mere millimeters.

I slam on the brakes with her propelling forward, so close our lips are a hair's breadth away. Her chest is rising and falling quickly. Her accelerated breaths fan the hair from my face. Her gaze drops to my lips, and I know she wants me to kiss her, but I don't.

"So you *do* want to live. Remember that."

I had to show her that that is something no one can ever take from her—her fight, her fight to live. Even though she feels like she wants to die at times, her fight for survival will prevail in the end.

They may have broken her body, but what makes Darcie, Darcie, no one can *ever* break that.

Something comes over her, and I see the reflection in her eyes. "I would give up my life...for them."

I suddenly realize she's talking about her parents. "They died in a car accident?"

She nods, chewing on her bottom lip. "I was in the car with them, arguing over something so fucking stupid. I survived. They didn't. The end."

This is her way of telling me she doesn't want to talk about it, and I respect that. But knowing she was in the car with them when they died just has me respecting and admiring her all the more. It also explains a lot. It explains why she is beyond courageous...and that is when I make a decision that is sure to change everything.

"Only in the eyes of death do you realize how much you really want to fucking live," I say, brushing a lock of hair behind her ear. "Which is why..."

"Which is why what?" she coaxes, leaning into my touch.

The action just makes me harder.

"Which is why you're going to sit your ass in that chair —" Before she can curse me out, I place my finger over her lips. "And we're going to take a nice little drive so you can see just how badly you want to live...only to watch others die."

Her eyes widen.

"Yes, little rabbit...I'm going to take you on an adventure, and oh yes, blood will be spilled."

I remove my finger, only to press my lips against hers.

It's not a kiss as such. More a promise of things to come because I plan on taking her to Buckets's farm.

I too have made a choice—I've never played by the rules, and I don't plan on starting now.

All I can hear on repeat is Jim Morrison singing that this is the end.

Darcie sits forward in her seat, peering out the windshield at Buckets's family farm. The choice is hers. We either do this, or we walk away.

When she unsnaps her belt, I know there was never a choice to be made—it was always going to come to this.

"What's the plan?" she asks, her voice animated but also filled with nerves.

"Follow my lead," I reply, reaching into the back seat for the suit I swiped from the house of horrors. One never knows when they'll need to dress snappy.

I leave on the ripped jeans but take off my T-shirt and slip on the white shirt. I roll up the sleeves. I then fasten the black tie. Darcie is watching me closely, and I like it. I like how she looks at me—like I'm her next meal.

The attraction between us only grows.

She also found some women's clothing stored away at the house and grabbed a few things. A white dress is what she decides to wear. I give her some privacy, but not before grabbing the first edition of *The Catcher in the Rye*.

Once she is dressed, she steps out, and I take a moment to admire her—she looks like the fucking devil in her Sunday best. I swallow past the lump in my throat.

We walk toward the tattered farmhouse, and off to the side is a big red barn. I don't have any weapons on me, but I have a feeling Darcie won't want to make this quick. I don't doubt for a moment she can follow through with her murderous impulses, but when push comes to shove, can we really take the life of another?

When we walk up the porch steps, it seems we will soon find out.

I knock once on the weathered door, and when it opens, I smile at the little old lady who is wearing a silver crucifix. "Good day, ma'am. My name is Holden Jameson, and this here is Veronica, my wife. Do you have a moment to talk about our Lord and Savior, Jesus Christ?"

Darcie does her best to keep a straight face beside me as I hug the book to my chest, faking it's the Bible.

This must be Buckets's grandmother.

I've not paid any attention to the rumors because I honestly couldn't give a fuck, but apparently, Buckets's mom left him with his dad and grandmother and ran off with the farmhand when he was five.

I don't know much else other than Buckets is a dumb shit who failed first grade—twice.

The lady smiles as the prospect of speaking about God seems to please her. She opens the door and welcomes us inside. The place has seen better days. It's layered with dust, and the outdated floral furniture has faded over time from the sun.

Someone is watching a football game, and when we approach the kitchen, we see it's an older man. Buckets's dad.

He is eating a casserole at the table, and when he sees us, he pauses with a mouthful.

"These lovely children want to talk about the Lord. Shall we say a prayer?"

Buckets's father shakes his head and places his fork on the rim of his plate. "Mom, what did I say about letting strangers into the house? Sorry, kids, she hasn't been the same since—"

But he doesn't finish the sentence.

Since her grandson turned into a rapist motherfucker? I silently fill in the blanks.

His mother ignores him, however, and begins to dish up some casserole for us. It would be rude to decline, so Darcie and I sit at the table. Buckets's father appears to humor his mom, and I wonder how his son turned out to be such a rotten son of a bitch when his dad and grandmother seem like nice people.

He goes back to watching the TV while Granny smiles, hinting that she wishes for us to eat the meal she prepared for us. But not before we join hands and say a prayer, of course.

The food is good, and this *is* as ridiculous as it sounds as we *are* sharing a meal, "the last supper," with the family of the bastard we are about to hurt—very, very badly.

When I hear the staircase creak and descending footsteps, Darcie pushes her untouched plate away from her because it's time to play ball.

Buckets rounds the corner and stops dead in his tracks, blinking once to make sure he's actually seeing what he is— Darcie and I, sitting at his dinner table and eating his fucking beef casserole.

Darcie waves with her fingers while I smile. I'm not sure if he recognizes us, to be honest.

"Samuel, these two lovely youngsters wanted to talk about the Lord."

Buckets doesn't make a move because the penny drops, and he knows, grandma or not, I will do what I have to, to ensure Darcie gets what she came here for.

"You could learn a thing or two from them. Or you

could always come to church with me instead of playing your video games."

Buckets isn't listening to her, though. He knows he has three seconds to get his grandmother and dad out of here before they witness him being gutted like the pig he is.

"Mr. Donaldson called earlier and asked if you could drop off the bags of grain by tonight."

Buckets's father drops his fork, it clanging loudly against his plate. "And you decide to tell me this now?"

"Sorry, I forgot."

"I should give you a good hidin', boy. You know Mr. Donaldson is our biggest client." Annoyed, Buckets's dad pushes back his chair, scraping it along the linoleum.

We watch as Buckets's grandmother raids the kitchen for a Tupperware container to put his leftover casserole in. This would be quite comical if not for the fact that I am scouring the kitchen for objects to use as weapons. That grater on the counter looks rather fetching.

Buckets's dad grabs the truck keys from the hook near the back door. He doesn't say goodbye and slams the door behind him, rattling the porcelain display plates that hang on the wall.

Darcie leans back in her wooden seat, resting on two legs. She rocks back and forth, back and forth, the chair creaking each time she moves. The air is filled with a heaviness—it gets me fucking hard.

"What do you want?" Buckets asks, talking big as he folds his arms across his chest.

His hands are massive, and when I remember what those hands did to Darcie, it takes all my willpower not to break every bone in them.

Darcie is composed. Too composed. This means fucking war.

"What I want?" she questions, laughing. "What I want is not to remember the feel of you inside me. What I want is not to remember those big hands forcing their way into me. That's what I really want. But I will never forget...which is why I'll settle for the next best thing."

"And what's that?"

Darcie stops rocking and deadpans him. "Your hands."

"Samuel?" his grandmother bleats with a look of horror on her poor little face.

My eyes never leave Buckets because in about five seconds, I'm going to launch across this table and rip out his fucking spleen.

"I suggest you leave, darling," I say to Granny. I don't look at her, but she knows I'm talking to her.

She doesn't skedaddle and instead starts wailing.

I roll my eyes and, with a sigh, take her hand and gently escort her into the pantry and close the door, securing it with a fork across the handle so she can't get out and witness the reckoning.

I'm not sure who attacks who first, but Darcie jumps onto the table before leaping onto Buckets, causing him to lose balance, and tackles him to the ground. He fights her off easily as he has about a hundred pounds on her. She goes sliding along the kitchen floor like a hockey puck and comes to a stop when she crashes into the oven door, smashing her head on the glass.

When I see blood, *her* blood, I leap across the kitchen and grab Buckets by the back of the neck as he launches for Darcie.

She shakes her head, appearing to need a moment to catch her breath.

"She fucking asked for it, man!" he yells, trying to fight me off.

In response, I smash his head into the microwave door—once, twice, three times. I only stop because the door buckles under the force.

He attempts to buck me off, but I am running on pure rage and use his face to clean the dirty dishes off the counter as I run his head through them.

Glasses, plates, and pots tumble to the floor, adding to the bedlam, but it's not enough.

With my fingers still wrapped around his nape, I drop the plug into the sink and turn the cold water on. He is desperately fighting, but he isn't going anywhere. I can hear Granny bashing on the cupboard door and squeaking for help.

"Why are you fighting for her? She loved it! Her tight little pussy was begging for our cocks! So was her a—"

He doesn't get a chance to speak those vile words ever again because I dunk his head into the sink, forcing him to gulp down the water. He slams his big hands against the sink, his bare feet slipping and sliding in the spilled water and blood seeping from the cuts on his feet, thanks to the broken glass.

I lift his head out and watch as he gasps for air like a fish out of water. "Tell her you're sorry!" I scream, turning his cheek to look at Darcie, who seems to be coming to.

He spits at her in response.

"Fine, have it your way then."

I submerge his face once more, gripping his hair so hard that clumps of it come free in my hand. I cannot stop. Knowing what he did to Darcie has me wanting to kill this motherfucker with my bare hands.

Suddenly, Granny comes out of hiding with a broomstick. Wiry old thing she is. I see the fight in her, but really, now is not the time. Darcie runs over and grabs the broomstick from her hands and sweeps her out the back door.

Buckets gargles, bubbles floating to the surface as he tries to take in air, but the only thing this fucker will be taking is a broken glass in his ass if he keeps talking smack about Darcie.

"Rev." It's only Darcie's voice that makes me see reason.

Turning to look at her, I watch her as she turns off the TV, only to search the old radio for a song. When "Heart of Glass" by Blondie comes on, she smiles and starts to dance around the kitchen, lost to Debbie Harry's voice.

The song is happy and upbeat, a complete opposite to how Buckets is feeling with his face in a sink full of water.

As she hums to the music, she dances over to me, leaving me speechless because the look in her eyes tells me she's about to shake my world up beyond repair. She leans in close, singing the chorus as she removes the plug from the sink.

The water swirls down the drain, each chug allowing more air to reach Buckets's lungs. And when I hear him inhale deeply, I smash his face against the side of the sink, angered he's still alive.

She places her hand over mine, and her touch is like a ten-thousand-volt shock throughout my body. It's sensory overload, and she feels it too.

I let Buckets go, only for Darcie to take hold of him and lift his head as she bends her face low, making them eye level.

"They call you Buckets because of your big hands, right?" she asks, her eyes alight with devious excitement. "Those big hands could have been used for good, but instead, you poked those fucking things where they don't belong!"

"You liked it," he snarls, baring his teeth. Is this what he tells himself so he can sleep at night?

"No, no, no," she whispers, pressing her nose to his. "I really didn't."

It looks like she's about to kiss him, and when she turns on the garbage disposal, I realize this is something he isn't going to like.

Before he can blink, she jams his hand down the disposal unit, holding him down with all her might. He tries to free himself with his other hand, so I slam it over the edge of the sink, breaking his wrist. His bones crunch in time with the music.

Soon, Buckets goes into shock, his hand getting sucked farther and farther into the garbage disposal. His face is pale, and he hangs like a limp piece of meat while I stand back, so fucking turned on at seeing my girl take revenge, covering herself in his blood.

She then reaches for a corn cob holder in the shape of a little yellow corn with its sharp little prongs poking out and jams it at full force into Buckets's left eye. There is something personal in that action. She is taking something back he stole from her.

He screams bloody murder as if that hurt more than the garbage disposal making a meal out of his hand.

She wipes the blood splatter across her cheek, marking her face like the true warrior she is, and I can't help myself. I grab the back of her head and slam my mouth over hers. At first, she freezes, but when I nudge her lips open with my tongue, she opens to me and kisses me back.

I tangle my fingers through her hair as she stands on her toes to reach my mouth.

We kiss like it's our last days on earth, and when Darcie feels me harden, she runs her hand over the front of my pants and grips me through them. She pulls back to look me dead in the eyes, cheeks flushed, mouth swollen, and says, "Let's fuck, right now."

Buckets is feet away, and I know this is her final "fuck you" to him.

She turns around, lifting the hem of her dress to expose her ass as she braces herself on the kitchen counter. This is all shades of wrong, which is why I pull down my jeans and rub my cock along her underwear, then quickly pull them aside to tease her, then flick them back into place.

She whines as I'm about to retreat but turns over her shoulder and grips my hand. "Don't you dare stop." She grabs my hips and pulls me against her ass.

I am hers.

She fucking owns me—mind, body, soul.

She coaxes me to move, and when the head of my cock inches into her, we both groan at the connection. Buckets is groaning too as his blood flicks around the room and across her sweet face. Her cheek is pressed into the bench as she stares at him with strands of bloody hair over her eyes.

She is fucking fire.

I thrust into her hard. Her hips smash into the counter, and she pushes back into me.

"Fuck yes!" she cries, wanting every inch of me.

Gripping her hips, I sink into her, and her body grips my cock, almost strangling it. I want to come. But there is no way I'm coming until she does.

Buckets is crying—poor bastard, he'll never be able to wank with that hand again or grip any hips like this.

It feels so good that I don't even care about this macabre scene. The sick part of me that I cherish fucking loves it. I punch him in the face with excitement and knock the corn cob holder clear out of his eye socket, taking the eyeball with it.

Darcie begins to bounce on my dick, meeting me thrust for thrust as I drive into her hard. I hold her hips, and she holds on to the counter, so we meet one another with equal force, and it's fucking beautiful.

I pull out, only to slam back in.

She groans and reaches for the hot tap, slamming it on over Buckets's already mangled arm, and he screams loudly as I fuck her relentlessly. He's the soundtrack to this sex show.

Even though I'm being rough, I know this is what she wants. She turns her cheek to watch Buckets as I sink into her over and over again, replacing every bad memory with this beautiful one. I'm healing her while his glassy eyes watch as we fuck.

The kitchen steams up from the hot water rising up over his face, his consciousness slowly ebbing away as his hand turns into ground beef.

Bending over Darcie, I kiss the side of her neck as I bury myself deep inside, pushing in as far as I can and holding it there while she begins to spasm. She moans, which fucks my mind, then turns her cheek so we can kiss. With one hand anchored around her waist holding her tight, I grip her chin with the other and angle her face so I can fuck her with my tongue and cock at the same time.

She moans around my tongue, sucking it in deeply as she clenches around my dick. She feels so fucking incredible, and every other woman pales compared to her, to this. And I know that's because what I feel for Darcie, I've never felt for anyone before.

It scares and excites me.

I run my thumb down her chin and cup her cheek. I

want her to know this means something to me. As fucked up as this is, seeing this dumb jock about to pass out from massive blood loss, I want her to know that this changes everything, and the next time we do this—and there will be many next times—I'm going to take my time.

But now...it's time for her to come.

Pulling out, I spin her around, stunning her, and before she can ask what I'm doing, I drop to my knees and worship her like the queen she is. I bury my face between her legs and eat her out how a man should take care of his woman.

Her body convulses, which is what I want because I want her to associate me with all aspects of sex—not just fucking. I want her to replace that night with this one. I want her to replace the memories of them with me because I am hers for as long as she wants me.

She threads her fingers through my hair and presses my face in hard, riding me how I want her to. She places one leg over my shoulder and opens herself up to me, grinding against my mouth violently. I grip her inner thighs and fuck her with my tongue, pushing my thumb against her clit while her legs begin to shudder. I shove two fingers into her, and a strangled gasp leaves her before she drags my mouth to her clit.

My greedy little baby.

I use my mouth and fingers in unison, and before long, her body arches back against the bench as her legs lock my head in tight, and she shakes. Darcie comes hard, and her screams echo through the kitchen walls loud enough for the neighbors to hear acres away.

I reach up and cover her mouth with one hand and finger fuck her hard right through her orgasm to give her more. She comes over and over again on my fingers. Everything she deserves and needs.

Her mouth opens and closes beneath my hand, and she bites hard into my fingers, screaming in euphoria. I release her and stand, gripping the back of her head. Pulling her to me, I slam my mouth over hers so she can taste herself on my lips. She kisses me back ferociously, and even though those motherfuckers took something from her I can never give back, I can give her this. I can give her me—over and over again.

She collapses against my chest, breathing heavily, but when she realizes I didn't come, she grips my cock and starts jerking me off. I don't stand a chance.

With our eyes locked, I come so fucking hard all over her legs and dress, I can't see straight.

I lean forward, resting my forehead against her shoulder, and she caresses the back of my neck.

We are entwined—sticky, bloody, and spent.

Buckets is still alive and partially witnessed the whole thing in some way or another, in and out of consciousness. Poetic justice, really. He tried to break her, but he could never.

Darcie turns off the tap and garbage disposal, and we watch Buckets slide down to the kitchen floor with a thud. His hand is no more. All that remains is a mangled mass of meat and tissue. A nice deep hole in his head from the missing eye too.

His blood begins to stain the white floor as he lies on his back, staring at the water stains on the ceiling.

We don't discuss whether we should call an ambulance or not. Let the Lord decide. He *was* the one who brought us here.

CHAPTER
FIFTEEN
Darcie

The night is thumping—in my head, in my legs, and in the air. I wonder if this is what serial killers feel like after their first murder. Like a mix of oxytocin and adrenaline far greater than any drug could provide.

The wind is soft and much warmer than the cold nights we've been having. Rev keeps reaching his big hand around the back of my neck to caress the bare skin there.

I hate theme parks, but it's like I'm seeing one for the first time, and my eyes are alight with all the neon colors and smells of candy apples, popcorn, and cotton candy. I'm suddenly craving that rush of sugar to the system after you put that pink fluff on your tongue, and it immediately dissipates.

Teenagers are squealing on rides turning every which way with distorted faces like a bunch of horror masks laughing.

I grab Rev's hand and pull him over to the guy selling cotton candy.

"I want it," I say, licking my lips.

"You always get what you want, don't you?" he asks against the back of my ear as he wraps his arms around my waist from behind.

"Always," I reply, grabbing the cotton candy and throwing some coins at the guy.

Rev immediately takes a bite out of my perfect pink tree, and I slap his hand playfully. Is this what love feels like? Or is it lust? His mouth is cheeky and sticky, so I grab his face and lick it right off his lips.

"That's mine." Staring into his eyes, I dare him to try again.

"What is? Me or the cotton candy?"

"All of it." I laugh and pinch a ball of it to stick in my mouth, and then another before I'm finished.

Our boots scuff along the dirt ground covered in junk food wrappers and game ticket stubs. There's a head of a soft toy elephant on the ground, and I kick it.

"Oh, poor Dumbo," jokes Rev.

"Fuck Dumbo," I say. "He couldn't keep his head on straight."

In the distance, I see a group of boys trying their hand at the strength game, smashing a hammer down and watching a marker fly up to ding a bell. They're clearly drunk and really annoying the attendant.

Rev leads me over to them. "Hey, I bet you that jacket that my girl Veronica here can smash the bell right off its hinges."

He has his hands in his pockets again. He's so cool that it's ridiculous. He's unflinching and stoic with the undertone of a devilish broken angel. I'm staring at him. Full trust that whatever he's doing, it's okay.

"And what do we get if she doesn't?" a clearly wasted blond guy challenges.

"The keys to my car. It's the truck over there by the hot dog stand," he says, pointing.

"Fuck yeah!" They all cheer and push each other around.

I'm hearing a song beating in the background, some old '80s track.

"Final Countdown"?

The hammer is in my hand, and as much as I want to perform well for Rev, I've got no chance.

I smash it down as hard as I can, and the marker slides halfway up before falling back down. I look at Rev. He's still staring at them like he's analyzing their reactions and calculating things.

"Hand 'em over, pony boy," slurs drunk guy number one.

"Best of three," says Rev, folding his arms, pretending to feel worried. I know he isn't.

For fuck's sake, I feel like I'm the clown now, on show for everyone watching.

Bang!

Metal on metal and no prize as the bell is untouched. I hate this game. Now I'm getting annoyed and scowl at Rev. He gives me a sweet smile.

"One more time, Veronica," mocks drunk guy number two.

Oh, he can count to three. Well done.

"Veronica?"

Fuck off.

I throw the hammer back and swing it like a roundhouse, inches from the drunk idiot's face.

"Hey, princess!" he shouts, tumbling back into his friends.

Rev rolls his eyes and looks at me. He's suddenly alpha, and he wants me to do what I'm told. It's hot, I won't lie. I don't even put any effort into the last swing, and the marker barely rises.

"Keys, motherfucker!"

Rev throws our keys to him in seconds, and my mouth hangs open in shock. The blond guy holds them in the air as they all try to grab for them like a pack of wolves on a hunt. They all start rushing off, eager to claim their prize.

"What are you doing?" I ask, suddenly feeling like my celebration night has been destroyed.

"We need fingerprints. They can't start the car. I disabled it," he coolly explains. "Let's go to the fun house."

He points at the laughing mouth doorway in the distance while I remember to close my mouth because this man continues to surprise me.

Rev

olding Darcie's hand is a fucking adrenaline rush.

I know that makes me sound like a simp, but she's such a hard-ass, except when she's with me. When she lets her guard down, I see the smart, witty woman I'm falling hard for.

After what just happened, I thought coming here and doing something "normal" might help Darcie. I mean, she did just brutalize Buckets, where we fucked in his blood.

Sounds macabre to some, but to me, it's fucking hot. It's carnal, filled with bloodlust, and I'm becoming addicted to the taste.

I'm not sure if he bled out or not. One can only hope.

Darcie skips toward the fun house, her hair catching the breeze. She looks so carefree, which is ironic, considering what we just did. I give the attendant our tickets, who doesn't bother to peer up from watching the porn on his phone.

A lame exaggerated clown laugh booms above us as we climb the stairs. It sounds like Krusty the Clown on crack. Darcie never lets go of my hand as we enter via the diabolical mouth. It's a splash of neon blues and pinks, making it hard to see.

We make a right where the hallway is suddenly spinning. We have to cross a rickety bridge, and the red-and-white-checkered walls rotate, throwing everything off center.

"This is fucking lame," I say while Darcie laughs, dragging me toward the bridge.

We cross it while Darcie puts out her arms, faking balance. At least she's having fun.

She jumps off the end, and when I follow, a man dressed as a tree comes out of nowhere. I punch him square in the face, and ironically, he drops like a tree. It's a knee-jerk reaction.

"Timber!" Darcie shouts, skipping toward the next adventure.

I step over the guy I just knocked out, and when I see a room full of mirrors, I curse this horrible idea. But with nowhere to go, I follow Darcie, who is cackling at her reflection in one of the silly mirrors that morphs her into a giant.

"I'm the prettiest girl in all of Tulgey," she says, pointing at the green painted sign slapped on the wall.

Apparently, we are in the enchanted forest of Tulgey.

Double lame.

Grabbing Darcie from behind and wrapping my arms

around her waist, I kiss the side of her neck as we look into the mirror. Now we both look ridiculous.

"I could have told you that," I confess, loving the way she leans back into me.

Her breaths suddenly quicken, and I wonder if she's thinking about what we did in the kitchen. I am. I can't stop.

"Catch me," she says, suddenly twisting out of my arms and running away.

The room of mirrors is now a fucking maze.

"Darcie!" I call out as the lights become a strobe effect. "Stop fucking around."

Of course, she ignores me, her laughter joining in with the mechanical one over the speakers.

I make my way through the room, cursing when I bump into a mirrored wall. Turning around, I stop and assess my surroundings because there is always a solution to every problem.

However, who I see standing behind me has become one big fucking problem.

"I never took you for the 'fun' type," Foss says, folding his arms and talking big. "Or is stealing from my family fun for you?"

Yeah, not my proudest moment. I did steal from Foss's family. I also fucked his mom. Mrs. Kingston, aka Foss's mom. He must have seen his mom's crocodile tears on the news when my mug was plastered on the TV.

Things just got interesting...

I laugh in response. "I like to do all sorts of fun shit...like fucking your mom."

"You motherfucker!"

"Yes, yes, I am. *Your* mother fucker."

Foss comes charging for me, but the weak asshole has no muscle on him, and I sidestep him. His head crashes into the mirror, and the glass slowly cracks, piece by piece in the middle.

I laugh hysterically.

This fun house is a fucking hoot, after all.

I'm about to kick Foss in the teeth, but two guys suddenly grab my arms. They are jacked on something because when I look up at them, I see bulging neck veins and an uncontrollable temper, which is undoubtedly coupled with a tiny dick.

"Think you're funny?" one of them says as he headbutts me.

I stagger back into the mirror, winded.

Gripping my side, I grin. "I am fucking hilarious."

Taking a closer look at him, I see that he looks a lot like Foss. I take a stab and guess this is his big brother.

"Ask your mom...she can vouch for how funny I am when I was eating her pussy."

"Motherfucker!" Big Foss charges at me, smashing his meaty fist into my lip, splitting it open.

"I really wish you'd stop using that term." I cough up blood and spit it at his feet. "It only looks bad on you. You know what else is really bad? Fucking your mom."

I really should stop because I can't win this fight. But the moment the three boys start whaling on me, I feel free. Each punch and kick winds this coil inside me because they better kill me. If not, I will be coming for their fucking heads.

Big Foss kicks me under the chin when I land on my knees after being punched in the stomach. I fall backward, an imprint of my body in the mirrored wall as it smashes around me—kind of like a chalk outline, marking where my dead body will soon lie.

All I can think about is Darcie. I hope she has the good sense to stay away.

They beat me until I hear a deathly rattle coming from my punctured lungs.

That fucking macabre laugh jolts out of nowhere, grating me raw. That, combined with the three assholes' laughter, has me wishing they'd knock me the fuck out already.

"Say you're sorry!" Foss says, acting tough in front of his brother as he kicks me in the ribs.

"The only thing I'm sorry for," I wheeze, rolling onto my side, "is that I didn't fuck your mom in your bed."

I burst into laughter because, why the hell not?

"Talk about my mom again. I dare you," Big Foss challenges.

I, of course, accept the challenge.

"These fingers..." I hold up my pointer and middle fingers. "They made your mom co—"

I don't get to finish my sentence because Big Foss bends down and snaps my middle finger backward, it cracking with a loud snap.

Big Foss looks at me like I'm supposed to react, and I do, just not in the way he thinks I would.

I laugh in his face, flipping him off with my broken finger.

He punches me in the nose, which is the perfect opportunity for me to slouch forward and steal Foss's phone from his back pocket as he's high-fiving his brother.

They continue beating me until all I can taste is blood. Big Foss grips me by the collar of my shirt and presses us nose to nose.

"You're going to give back what you stole from my family."

"Chill out, man," I slur, my head lolling back like a rag doll. "I'll give you back your paintings."

"Paintings?" he spits. "You stole stamps and my grandfather's pistol."

"Oops, my bad."

He headbutts me, angered I am not submitting and merely laughing hysterically when I'm the one being beaten to a pulp.

When it's clear I'm not going to budge, Big Foss kicks me one last time before calling out to his boys like the good little dogs that they are. They chase after him while I'm left in a pool of my blood, coughing and laughing because I won.

I close my eyes and try to feel some part of my body, but everything is numb and hurting at the same time. I just need five minutes, and I'll be good to go.

"Rev! Oh my God. I-I'm sorry," Darcie stutters, her frantic footsteps running toward me. "I was hiding. I didn't know. I thought—"

"Shh, little rabbit." I cough, trying to reach for her, but I think my wrist is broken. "As long as you're having fun."

"I'm not having fucking fun!" she cries. "You're hurt. In what universe would that ever mean I was having fun?"

"Stop it," I wheeze, flinching as I pry open my eyes. "You're gonna make me blush."

"Who did this to you?"

The room won't stop spinning, but I scoot up and lean against the mirrored wall. I look at my reflection across from me and cringe.

"Jesus, that's gonna leave a mark."

"Stop messing around!" she yells, gripping my bicep. When her fingers are covered in blood, she recoils. "Oh fuck! Sorry! Let me help. Can you stand?"

"I just need two minutes to feel my...body."

She bites her nails as she crouches near me, nothing but concern reflected in her eyes. It touches me. I've never had anyone give a shit about me before.

She's shaking, and I suddenly realize that the feeling is mutual. She's always had herself to rely on, like me. Two broken misfits have somehow learned to become a little less broken by finding one another.

"I'm going to be okay," I assure her, and with bloody fingers, I leave two marks across her cheek. "It's just a scratch."

"Don't leave me," she whispers, her lower lip trembling.

"Never, baby." I grip the back of her neck and draw our foreheads together. "Promise."

That seems to appease her, and she gets down to business.

She tears the bottom of her T-shirt, which reveals an expanse of perfect pale skin on her stomach. Even though I am bleeding profusely and can't see out of my left eye, she is the fucking hottest thing I have ever seen or half seen.

"What color eyes do I have?" she cryptically asks.

"Not really the time to be discussing eye color, baby."

"Answer me," she says, getting her boss game on, holding my gaze.

I squint, trying my best to look at her eyes, but I should have known this was a ploy to distract me because as I slouch forward, she reaches down, and with a hard crack, she snaps my finger back into place.

She smiles while I bite down on my tongue.

That smile soon fades when her attention drifts to the shard of glass sticking out of my bicep.

Before I have a chance to fight her off, she yanks the piece of glass out of my arm. She winces, wrapping the torn

T-shirt around the gaping hole in my bicep while I focus on the way she bites her bottom lip in concentration.

Who needs painkillers when Darcie is my own personal drug?

I inhale her into me, and suddenly, I can breathe again. I also sense we are not alone.

"You?" Foss gasps, looking at Darcie, unsure if it's really her.

She smirks, and the devil spreads her wings. "You."

This fun house is about to get a whole lot more fun.

At first, I can see Foss doesn't recognize Darcie, but when he does, it's too late. I assume he came back, looking for his phone.

She lunges for the shard of glass she pulled from my arm and stabs it into Foss's pec. Stunned, he staggers backward and smashes into the mirrored wall, and it cracks around him. The sight is a fucking glorious one.

His fingers fumble as he tries to remove the glass embedded in his chest, but Darcie kicks him, pushing the shard of glass deeper into his pec. His mouth opens and closes like a fish out of water, but no sound comes out.

"Not laughing now, are you?" Darcie screams into Foss's face. "Like you were laughing the night when you thought it was funny to fuck my mouth because you're a gutless clown."

Something comes over Darcie, something which can only be described as a veil of darkness, and it's fucking beautiful. She switches in the blink of an eye, and I know that's because she has gone to a place that allows her to feed her demons that linger beneath the surface, waiting to be fed.

I sit, watching from the floor, because this is Darcie's show.

Foss knows it's now or never and dives for Darcie, but she twists, which has him charging straight into the mirrors, headfirst. Blood stains the glass, a bloody outline of where his head was rammed through the mirrored wall.

Darcie grabs the back of his collar, yanking his head back so she can snarl into his face, "What are you doing out here, little one?"

I know this dialogue is one that was used the night that changed her forever.

Foss twists and turns, but Darcie is not letting him go. "Do you remember what you did to me? Do you remember how you bit me? Do you remember when you fucked my mouth?"

Before Foss has a chance to answer, Darcie knees him in the balls. "Rev, hold him down."

I jump up, not sure what she's got planned, but I'm here for the ride.

Foss looks up at me, begging I show mercy. I merely laugh in response, flipping him off with my broken finger. "Sorry, broken finger."

I throw him to the floor, and before I pin him down, Darcie says, "Hold him down with your knees on his shoulders."

I don't ask questions and do what she says.

Darcie stands in front of Foss, peering at him so he views her upside down. "You want this, bitch?"

She doesn't care what he wants when she grabs a handful of broken glass and pries open his mouth in a pistol grip. He gasps for air, but it's the last time he'll be breathing with any sense of ease because Darcie stuffs his mouth full of glass.

All I can do is stare in utter fascination as Darcie places her hand over Foss's lips, forcing him to keep the glass in his mouth. Foss is gasping for air, his face turning beet red as he struggles to breathe.

He swallows, moaning in pain as the glass is clearly cutting his esophagus.

Darcie removes her hand, watching as Foss tries to spit out the glass. It cuts at his mouth, blood dribbling down his chin.

Darcie grins. "You really need to learn to shut your mouth."

She takes one look at Foss, knowing he won't die, or maybe he might, but regardless, she is clearly satisfied with her handiwork nonetheless.

And it's here when Darcie grabs my hand and skips away from the chaos she created.

We exit from the fun house, discreetly slipping past the crowd who are too distracted stuffing their face with popcorn and guzzling down cheap beer.

I think I'm fine until I'm spinning faster than the Tilt-A-Whirl.

"Rev!" Darcie cries, looping her arm around my waist to stop me from falling on my ass.

I lean into her, trying my best to keep most of my weight off her because she's small, and I'm worried I'll crush her.

When she sees an unattended ambulance up ahead, I know what she's planning to do. When we approach it, she gently helps me lean up against the side of it and then leaps inside, stealing the first aid kit from the floor.

We stagger away, me trying my best not to fall. We sneak through a makeshift hole in the wire fence at the back of the carnival, which leads to a grassy field. Darcie walks as far away as possible, wanting to avoid any witnesses.

When we pass through a clearing in the tall trees, things quieten, and the screams of the carnival fade into the darkness. We venture deeper into the now dense woods, which is actually pretty fucking nice. There is a small lake ahead.

Darcie never lets go of me, and although I feel like a crybaby, it's nice to have her give a shit about me because she is the first person to do so. That reminds me of the stolen phone in my pocket. I really need to check in with June.

"Can you sit?" Darcie asks, looking at me with nothing but concern. A totally different look from when she was shoving glass down Foss's throat.

She helps me to the ground, and I can't help but flinch because fucking ouch!

My white T-shirt is soaked in blood, so without thought, I reach for the back of the collar and take it off, then pitch it to the side. I immediately feel better, and the breeze against my bruised skin helps a little.

Darcie is frantically rummaging through the first aid kit, tossing items she doesn't want over her shoulder. I watch on, unable to stop my smile because she is one stubborn lady.

When she finds what she's looking for, she turns back to look at me, but a winded breath gets caught in her throat. I have no idea what's wrong until her eyes eat me alive.

I am throbbing for an entirely different reason now.

Normally, this would be the time she looks away. But she doesn't.

She brings two fingers to my lips, running them across my bloody mouth. She doesn't care that her fingers are covered in blood.

"Your lips are so hot," she says, surprising me with her candor. "I like when they kiss me."

"They like when they kiss you too."

She smiles, appearing happy we're on the same wavelength.

She pops two painkillers into my mouth but doesn't remove her finger. Instead, she circles her finger on my tongue. It's a knee-jerk reaction, and I curl my tongue around her finger.

A whimper leaves her. "No wonder you can fuck anything that walks."

"Hardly," I reply, swallowing the painkillers when she removes her finger.

"So you don't fuck every woman you steal from? That's not the reason you're able to steal from them? *They* want to fuck *you* and look past why you're fucking them when you can have anyone you want."

She soon seals her lips, regretful for revealing too much.

I thumb over her bottom lip. "You say the sweetest things to me."

She rolls her eyes and begins cleaning my wounds as best she can because honestly, I should be going to the hospital. But that's not an option, so Nurse Darcie will do just fine.

She brushes back my long bangs, cleaning the deep gash on my forehead. "Those fuckers," she mumbles under her breath.

"Pretty sure Foss learned his lesson."

She goes quiet, and I know she's thinking about what she did. "Do you think I'm a bad person?"

"I'm really not in a position to judge. But no, I don't think you're a bad person. Brave? A little crazy? And a lot hot as fuck? Then yes, I think you're that."

A blush spreads over her cheeks. "I think you're a lot hot as fuck as well, even though you look like shit at the moment."

"So romantic," I quip with a grin. "Even though we've butchered the English language."

"True dat," she adds.

I love this playful side she has. I love that I've watched her do some fucking macabre things, but she can still be cute as fuck as well.

Maybe we're just as fucked up as one another.

She cleans the many gashes and cuts I have, both of us deep in thought.

"I have to call my mom," I reveal because sharing personal stuff is what people are supposed to do, I think. I've never wanted to share anything with anyone before, but with Darcie, I want to tell her every secret I have. "I stole Foss's phone. That's why he came back."

Darcie nods. "Do you think he's dea—"

I shake my head before she has a chance to finish her sentence. "Doubt it, but he definitely won't be chewing gum for a while."

When she cleans over the cuts on my chest, her chest begins to rise and fall a little quicker. I try my hardest to keep still, but the way she touches me has everything demanding more.

"What's wrong with your mom?"

"Honestly, I don't know. But I will do anything I can to save her."

I instantly regret my words because of what Darcie shared about her parents. They couldn't be saved. At least my mom is alive. Well, kind of.

"Fuck, sorry, I didn't—"

"It's okay," she interrupts. "And I really mean it this time. I know this is going to sound fucking morbid, but hurting those who hurt me helps me heal. Most would say going to therapy is healthy, but talking about my feelings isn't going to help."

"If you ever wanted to talk or whatever," I casually say. "I have ears, and you know, they are happy to listen."

I sound like a fucking lame simp.

Darcie bites her lip to stop her chuckle. "Thank you, but only one thing will make me feel better."

I know what that is, but not now. I'll tell her I know where Blake will be later because now, I want to surprise her.

"Close your eyes."

She arches a brow but thankfully does what she's told—for once.

Ignoring every inch of my protesting body, I limp toward the lake's edge because something amazing is about to happen. The sky lights up with thousands of lights, and it's fucking beautiful.

Cupping my hands gently, I smile and hobble back over to Darcie.

Dropping to my knees before her, I say, "Open your eyes."

When she does, she meets mine, then looks at my cupped palms. I open them, and her reaction is worth almost toppling over in pain.

"Oh my God," she cries, steepling her fingertips over her mouth. "I thought they only came out during the summer."

"Not all of them."

We both watch as the firefly I caught lights up the space between us. It hovers between us, not appearing to be in any hurry to join its many friends.

"It's beautiful," Darcie says, her eyes glued to the firefly, and I know she sees the beauty in something so simple as well.

No matter what we've done, no matter what we do, we're just a couple of misfits trying our best to survive.

I hook my thumb over my shoulder, and as the moon comes out of hiding, so do the thousands of fireflies, lighting up the night sky.

"Rev," she gushes, coming to a stand and running toward the lake's edge, her arms spread out wide like she too wishes she could light up the darkness. But little does she know, she lights up mine every single day.

Our little friend flies away, knowing his job here is done.

I join Darcie, standing by her side as we silently peer into the sky littered with fireflies. She reaches down and loops her fingers through mine. The fireflies soon pale compared to the fire burning between us.

As usual, the world fades into the background until it's just Darcie and me.

"Thank you for bringing me here," she says in an almost whisper. "It's my first date."

"Sorry I bled through half of it."

She smiles, and the sight takes my breath away.

"Why do they light up like that?"

"Because of a chemical reaction caused by the organic compound, luciferin, in their abdomens," I reply without thought.

"Luciferin," she repeats softly. "Sounds kind of diabolical, which is ironic, considering it relates to something so beautiful."

I can't help but compare her analogy to herself—Darcie is kind of diabolical, but she is the most beautiful girl in the world.

I've always hated the word love. It gets thrown around so easily, losing its meaning. But luciferin, now that is a unique word. And this right now, this feels something like luciferin.

I shock myself with the thought because I never thought I'd ever feel it, but with Darcie, I do. And that scares me because she has now become my collateral.

Clearing my throat, I dig into my pocket, deciding to call Nonna to check on my mom. I don't release Darcie's hand, however.

"Hello?" It's good to hear her pissed-off voice.

"What's up?" I say coolly as I know she'd be beside herself with worry. "How's Mom?"

"Rev! Where have you been?"

"Sorry, I got into some trouble."

"Yes, I saw whatcha did on the TV. So did your mom."

Her tone makes my stomach drop.

"Where is she?"

Darcie turns her cheek, realizing something is wrong.

"Nonna, answer me." I don't mean to be rude, but her silence only confirms my worst fears.

"She saw what you did, and I don't know...she took too many pills."

"For fuck's sake! Where. Is. She?" I don't have time for guessing games.

"She's at Oakland Villa, Rev. She OD'd."

I don't give her time to say anything else because I hang up, dragging Darcie away from her paradise.

"What's wrong?" she asks, trying to keep up with *me* now. But my injuries are obsolete compared to the one on my heart. "Rev!"

She digs in her heels, forcing me to stop and explain.

I release her hand and, with a roar, punch the trunk of a tree. "Fuck!"

"Stop it. You're hurting yourself—more than you

already are." She knows not to touch me. "Is your mom okay?"

"No, Darcie, she is not fucking okay." I instantly regret speaking to her that way. I need to calm down.

I take three deep breaths and meet Darcie's eyes.

"She's at the fucking psych ward she was at when she tried to kill herself. And just like I did when I was ten years old...I'm going to break in and get her the fuck outta there."

CHAPTER SIXTEEN

Rev

I've asked Darcie to keep watch because I don't know what shit I'm about to run into.

The last time I did this, I promised myself it would never happen again because my mom would never be trapped in this place again. It was the reason I decided to better our lives any way I could.

But as I jump over the high brick wall, it seems life has a fucking sick sense of humor because here I am—again.

I keep to the shadows, sticking true to my name because no one sees a Rev. I sneak to the back door where I know lazy orderlies spend most of their nights, smoking or dropping the drugs they stole out of the medicine cabinets.

I poke my head around the corner and see a plume of smoke fill the starless sky. A man in white scrubs smokes a joint while scrolling through his phone. I weigh my options —I can take him out, or I can play it smart and find common ground.

I decide to go with the latter.

Putting my hood on, I keep my chin low to hide my injuries and casually walk toward the man.

"Hey! You can't be back here."

"Shh, chill out, man," I reply calmly because if I act like something is amiss and I'm not supposed to be here, my cover is blown.

"I'm calling security." He reaches for his walkie-talkie.

"No, you're not...Michael," I counter with a chuckle, peering at his plastic name tag. "Pretty sure they wouldn't be too happy knowing you're getting high on the job."

His bravado soon dies, just how I knew it would. "What do you want?"

I stop a few steps away because if this plan fails, I will have to resort to option number one.

"My girl is inside. I'm here to tuck her in." I don't offer any other explanation.

The man snorts a disbelieving laugh. "Are you fucking joking?"

Removing my hood slowly and lifting my chin, I take great pleasure in witnessing this asshole gasp and take a small step back when he sees my beaten face. "Does it look like I'm fucking joking?"

"I ca-can't let you in there."

"Who says?"

"I'll get into trouble," he lamely replies while I roll my eyes.

"Only if you get caught."

He looks from left to right, clearly wrestling with his morals. So I decide to make it real easy for him.

Digging into my pocket, I pull out a couple of hundred bucks and a small bag of weed I stole from the glove compartment of the truck we stole. I knew it would come in handy.

"I won't tell if you don't." I offer him the cash and weed while he eyes it hungrily.

People are so predictable; it is actually fucking sickening.

He reaches for the bribe and quickly shoves it into his pocket.

"We good?"

He nods, taking a last drag of his joint before putting it out. "Follow me."

The moment I step foot into this place, memories assault me, and it takes me a second to adjust.

The medicated smell mixed with desperation still lingers in the air, and I want to be sick. The stark white walls are amplified, thanks to the fluorescents, and I suddenly have the urge to slip on some shades to block out everything this place represents.

My boots squeak across the polished linoleum, and I hope I leave a trail of mud behind to tarnish the perfect floor. This place should be a haven for those who need help, but in reality, it's just a shiny prison.

I can't stop thinking about the many times I broke into this place when I was a kid. No wonder I'm so fucked up because as macabre as this place is, it still feels familiar, like home.

"What's her name?" Michael asks quietly as we walk down the corridor of endless doors.

The only glimpse of the outside world the people locked behind these doors have is a small glass panel. But most are handcuffed to their bare beds for their "safety," so the only real view they have is that of the ceiling they stare up at, counting every second which feels like years.

"June Blackwood."

Michael's keys stop jingly against his hip as he comes to a brief stop and turns over his shoulder. "*She's* your girl?"

I deadpan him. "Yes."

He doesn't pry any further and continues walking, stopping when we reach a door. I know what's behind here.

He unlocks it and leads me down the corridor paved with maniacal ramblings and laughter that chill me to the core. I hate that she's in here again; the ward for the "special ones." The place where the hopeless are sent. The place for people society will forget about because they are considered too far gone to help.

I peer into each door as we pass by, my stomach twisting in knots with every step I take. Most of them are bound to their beds with brown leather straps. The ones who aren't are rocking in the middle of the floor, crying for their mothers to come save them.

I want to save them all, but how can I when I can't even save the one person I promised to protect?

"She's in here." Michael stands by the last door on the left, appearing to give me one last chance to back out.

If only it were that easy.

When he sees I'm not going anywhere, he unlocks the door. But unlike the other doors I had no issues looking into, I can't look into this one because the person inside isn't a random face. I know her secrets, and it just makes me love her all the more.

With a deep breath, I walk into the room to see my mother strapped to her bed by her wrists and ankles. She has a white bandage around her left wrist because it seems OD'ing wasn't enough. She had to slit her wrist as well.

The door closes behind me, sealing my fate as I stand silent, needing a moment to process what I'm seeing.

She doesn't deserve this. She never did. But it seems some people are just destined for a certain path, no matter how badly they want to change.

June lifts her head from the mattress, her eyes widening when she sees me. I'm surprised they haven't sedated her.

"Rev?" She blinks once, appearing incredulous that I'm really here.

"Hi, June."

A sob escapes her. "You can't be here. You'll be in so much trouble if they catch you.'"

"When has that ever stopped me?" I walk toward her bed, trying my best not to let her see my agony at seeing her tied this way.

Dropping to my knees, I commence unfastening the buckles at her wrists, but she shakes her head. "No, leave me here. It's better this way."

"Being tied up like an animal is far from being better than any possible scenario. It'll be just like last time."

"What happened to your face?" Her concern unsettles me as I can't remember the last time I heard it.

"Don't worry about it. Let's just get you out of here."

"I said no!" she cries, which stuns me because this is new. "Not this time. I won't allow you to get into any more trouble. I'm the one who should be protecting you, but I haven't done that in a very long time. Let me start now. Let your father—"

But I don't allow her to finish. "Enough! Now is not the time to talk about that loser."

"But he's not. Your father is a very powerful man. He"— she pauses, her lower lip trembling—"he owns this town."

My blood runs cold, and time stands still.

"What did you say? He lives *here*?"

She nods slowly.

"And you only thought to mention this now? Your stories varied from him being the postman to a random naval officer you met one night in a bar!"

"I know, and I'm sorry, but I wasn't ready."

Suddenly, untying her is the least of my concerns.

Jumping up, I begin to pace the room like a caged tiger. "You weren't ready?" I scoff, running a hand through my snarled hair. "You are in this fucking place because of him!

You should have gotten your shit together and forced yourself to face your demons, not drown them in the bottom of a whiskey bottle!"

My body trembles in rage and something else I've never felt before. It's a combination of every fucking emotion known to mankind multiplied by ten thousand.

How could she do this? How could she be this selfish?

She made me believe he walked out on us my entire life, but to know he's been here this whole time...I don't know how to feel. Everything I've done is because of her, to better our lives and to forget what he did.

"I couldn't tell you because I was afraid."

"Afraid of what?" I bellow, interlacing my hands behind my neck and peering up at the ceiling, wishing I could escape.

"Afraid of this," she whispers, confirming I look as crazy as I feel. "Afraid of what you'll do when you find out who he is...and who is your—"

But she pauses, which confirms there is so much more to come.

When I think I can speak, I meet her tear-filled eyes. "Does Nonna know who he is?"

She nods slowly.

Every person I trusted has lied to me.

"Motherfucker," I curse under my breath before rage overtakes me and I strike out with violence—it's the only way I know.

With a roar, I punch the wall over and over again, ignoring my battered body protesting with every strike because the pain feels good—it makes me feel alive.

"Rev!" June screams, begging I stop.

But I can't. I'm afraid of what'll happen when I do.

Only in the darkness and the depraved do the voices subside and I can breathe.

Blood stains the floor from my busted knuckles, and the contrast of it against the polished linoleum reminds me of the twenty-thousand-dollar painting I stole from Ms. Pitcher's house months ago. It raked in a small fortune as I sold it to a guy who knows a guy.

I did that, I've done all of this for June to get us the fuck out of here to better our lives, but it was a waste. All I wanted to do was protect her, when in reality, my mother is a fucking liar. If only she told me who my father was sooner, I could have confronted him and asked why...why did he leave her?

Why did he leave me?

If he has lived here this entire time, then he would know who I am. He would have watched me grow up, yet he chose to remain silent. He chose to watch me from afar because he didn't want to be my father.

He never wanted to be. If he had, he would have told me who he was years ago.

The thought destroys me in ways I never imagined as it was easier accepting him to be a nobody, just some passerby my mom had a one-night fling with. But to know he's been here this entire time, it fucking stings.

He could have told me anytime he wanted, but he didn't because he never wanted me to know.

My body surrenders, and I slump to both knees, cradling my head in my bloodied hands. In this circumstance, the normal response would be for most to cry. But I can't. I physically can't shed a tear because my body refuses to shed one ounce of sadness for a man who never cared.

And I'm not a fucking baby.

I think of Darcie and how none of this would have

happened if I had never left her alone the night of prom. I made that choice with June in mind. I chose her over Darcie's safety, and I'll never forgive myself for it.

But lesson learned because I'll never make that mistake ever again.

My life suddenly seems so pointless. I've done all this for a liar, for someone who could have chosen to better our lives. But she chose the coward's way out, and instead of facing her demons, she fucking ran away.

On this cold floor, I am reborn, and as I lift my chin to look at June, she knows it too. She knows this is it this time. I am done saving her because the truth is, she never wanted to be saved.

I lift my broken body, on the inside as well as on the outside, but I use the pain as my motivation not to look back.

I take one final look at my mother and memorize her face because I don't know when I'll see it again.

I will find out who my father is and the secrets he protects on my own because that's all I've been my entire life; until I met Darcie. We are two broken pieces who somehow fit together, and I'll try for the rest of my life to help put her back together again.

I don't bother with goodbyes.

Turning my back, I cut ties with the old Rev and make way for the new me.

"I'm so sorry. Please forgive me," June says, her voice quivering. "I love you...Augustine."

And with that, I leave behind the woman who is nothing but a stranger to me.

I don't bother finding Michael on my way out. The hollowed cries of the patients follow me into the darkness, and when I step outside, I lift my face to the heavens as it pours around me.

The downpour is heavy, and most would be seeking solace indoors. But for me, my solace is in the rain where I wish for it to wash away the sins which weigh me down with every breath I take. I stand in the shadows, the rain pounding in time with the frantic staccato of my heart.

Everything is different now. I had direction. My life was mapped out for me because of June, but now, that has changed.

All that matters is Darcie and putting her back together again. And there is only one way how.

Breaking into a sprint, I feel nothing exists but the world we created, and I find her where I left her—she is the only person who hasn't let me down.

Her eyes widen when she sees me running toward her, and before she has a chance to speak, I slam my mouth over hers and breathe new life into us both. She could have waited inside the car, but she didn't. She waited in the rain, as desperate to see me as I was to see her.

We are obsessed, consumed by the other, and nothing has felt more complete.

Lifting her, I slam her ass onto the hood, our lips never missing a beat as I own her mouth like she owns my heart and soul. She threads her fingers through my wet hair, pulling hard and before long, we are both pawing at the other, desperate to consume the other whole.

I'm still unsure of what's okay with her, so I let her lead as her deft fingers unfasten my jeans. She slips her hand into them and when she feels my cock is hard, her gasp fills my lungs. She commences stroking me, but when she shoves my jeans down with the other hand, I know what she wants.

What we both want.

Her body pressed to mine fills every void—physically and emotionally. I'm falling deeper and deeper down the rabbit hole, and I know I've passed the point of no return.

The rain continues to belt down around us, but moving isn't an option for either of us. In the rain, we are both reborn.

I tear at her clothes until she is bare, and without breaking our kiss, I slide into her, condemning us both to this blissful hell. She bows her back as she lays on the hood, her arms spread out wide to hold on as I begin to fuck her hard.

Gripping her hips, I slide her toward me and fuck her with passion and love, because I do. I love this strong, brave woman, and I would kill—literally—for her.

She cups my cheek, peering into my eyes, a silent touch to show me she understands. That she too can feel the war raging behind my eyes. It's us versus the world, and anyone who stands in our way is about to pay with blood and tears.

I gently wrap my fingers around her throat, coaxing her to arch her neck, because the imagery of the rain and the glow of the headlights in this abandoned field is fucking beautiful.

She wraps a leg around my waist, opening herself up to me, and my heart swells at the fact that she trusts me after everything she's been through. I fuck her hard, her body moving up and down with the momentum. I want to devour every inch of her, but right now, I need to come.

Reaching down, I thumb over Darcie's clit and watch as her mouth opens and closes in pleasure before her guttural cry fills the night air. The moment she comes, I drag her closer toward me and fuck her with vigor so our bodies become one.

When the last tremor rocks her, I pull out, coming on her stomach with a sated groan.

I bow forward, pressing my lips into the crook of her neck. Her rapid pulse beats against my mouth, and on instinct, I bite down and suckle her rain-soaked flesh into my mouth.

"What happened?" she breathlessly asks as I arrange myself back into my pants.

But there are no words.

Instead, I do the only thing I can do—I drop to my knees, surrendering everything I am to her.

The rain distorts her form, but it's like something out of a comic book. I focus on her eyes and beg she doesn't do what every goddamned motherfucker has done to me my entire life.

And when she slides off the hood, only to drop to her knees too, I know that she won't.

She presses her hand over my frantic heart, reading me without needing to say a word. "I'll never leave. I promise."

And just like that, my world turns on its axis and finds its true north.

"The other guy who did this to you. Blake?" I ask, even though I know the answer.

She turns her cheek, but I cup her chin and gently encourage her to look at me. I want her to see that I am with her—every step of the way.

Eventually, she nods.

I can read her vacant expression, and I know that what this fucker did to her was unimaginable, so I run my thumb along her lips, catching the raindrops clinging to her pink mouth.

"I know where he is."

Her eyes widen, but she bravely pulls back her shoulders. It's time.

"Show me."

CHAPTER SEVENTEEN
Darcie

We walk down a cold, wet alleyway toward the club.

A small narrow door with a sign says *TRES-PASS* on it. Trespass being the name of the underground club that Blake frequents. He often carries matches with Trespass logos on the packet. A heavy golden door knocker of a lion with its mouth open hangs on the door, staring at us.

"Three knocks, followed by a three-second pause, then one further knock, and the door will open," Rev casually says to me. He lights a cigarette with his back to the wall.

I'm still wondering how he knows this shit, but that's a conversation for another day. I'm wearing a tight black dress that strangles my rib cage and laces up the back. I'm also wearing a gold embroidered velvet mask over my eyes, the dress code for tonight.

Rev has a leather mask over his eyes, and his black hair is slicked back. He wears a crisp white shirt, the starchy collar sits around his freshly shaven neck, and his large shoulders are shrouded in a black trench coat. His attire covers his injuries, but I know the ones that aren't seen are the ones that hurt the most.

The door opens, and a woman with long, red flowing hair and wearing a 15th-century bustier stands sulking in the entrance and chewing her nails. She has tattoos all over her fingers and greets us without words. She pats both of us down; not that I could fit any weapons in my outfit. She pays special attention to Rev. I feel like they've met before.

He stares at her like they're having a telepathic conversation. Her eyes avert, and she steps back, clearing the doorway for us to enter.

My mind races, and that's because I'm jealous. But I need to focus. Where the fuck is Blake?

The club smells like incense and sex. Black velvet covers the walls, and I see birdcages with exotic birds hanging around the room. It pisses me off, and I want to set them free. Standing in front of one cage, I see a large macaw staring back at me with one eye. His cage is lit up like a stage, and he shimmers red, blue, and yellow. A hand reaches in front of me and opens the cage door.

"They're free to go," says a voice behind me. It's Rev.

I turn to him, probably still looking in horror, and he closes my mouth with the back of his hand beneath my chin.

"They just choose not to," he reveals, smiling.

I stare back at the macaw, who watches me calmly. The door is wide open, and he begins to preen and pick at his feathers.

"I guess we learn to adapt," I reply, thinking how I can relate. "Sometimes, we're safer in a cage."

Rev nods, his golden eyes appearing even more hypnotic under that mask as he scans our surroundings. His eyes are alight in the darkness; he likes this place.

The club isn't big, but it's filled with patrons, and I know this place is invite-only. It's elite, and I wonder if there is some kind of secret handshake to get invited. Of course Rev is here, blending in like he belongs. I like the way he adapts to any situation like a chameleon and comes and goes unnoticed, always getting whatever it is he needs.

There isn't anything I don't like about him. I wonder if he feels the same way about me. I've never had anyone care about me the way he does. It's brutal in every way, and I'm addicted. I don't believe in insta-love, but I feel like I've known Rev through centuries of past lives. Always meeting and falling over and over again.

A tragic love story sealed with a bloody kiss.

Our connection is warped and unconventional, but it's our story, and I'll be damned if I allow those monkey footballer bastards to take everything from me.

And now...it's *my* turn to take.

I look beyond the cage and see an alcove tucked away behind a red velvet curtain upstairs. I know Blake is in there. I can feel him like a sickness lurking behind my ribs waiting to end me. My heart begins to race, pumping blood around my mental insanity. I can almost taste the pain he will endure, and it's my elixir.

Rev peers into the direction I am focused on. He reads my thoughts. "Go."

He runs a finger down over the back of my shoulder, and I know he won't be far from me. It feels like the music playing is throbbing to egg me on. I'm excited and angry; it's a feeling I'm getting used to. A delicious cocktail of emotion I'm beginning to crave.

I discreetly circle around patrons who are being whipped, led around by chains, strung up and caressed. The beauty of submission is that they hold all the power despite appearances. I'm not judging. I know why they want to be trained and adored. There are no rules here. Anything goes. We can all be our depraved selves, living out fantasies that serve our primal needs.

Climbing the stairs, I part the red curtain, and my eyes take a moment to adjust. When they do, I see a small, narrow corridor that looks like a medieval foyer. More ornate doors are blocking my view, and I am careful to keep hidden within the shadows, listening until I hear...him.

Putting both hands on the doors, I push and don't bother being discreet about it. I see Blake with a woman. There's no one else in the room.

It's amazing how someone can be so devastatingly sexy yet walk around as the most disgraceful human on the planet. Blake is a pretty face with damage behind his eyes. His dark hair and dark eyes mirror his dark heart, but those fucking lips are like the most heavenly raspberry jubes I want to run my tongue across...right before I slice out his tongue and swallow it whole.

His jawline square, lightly dashed with a five-o'clock shadow against his skin. He's not wearing a mask, but his "pet" is. Her hair is tied back painfully in a rope-like plait.

It would appear that he's a Dominant with an ugly little "brat" submissive trying to press his buttons to receive her punishment. But he's bored. I know what he likes.

He likes me.

Someone who really fights, who really cries, who really knows how to take the pain—for no real reason other than for his pleasure. Someone who will sacrifice their own soul to feed his.

The submissives are boring him, and he's starting to feel like he's serving them. It makes him sick. I can see it in his eyes when his gaze drifts over to me. The room is dark, but a blue light is hitting all my skin's highlights.

He doesn't even appear surprised to see me here because he knew...he knew I would find him.

I remove my mask and drop it on the floor. He's transfixed on me, and I can almost see the pulsing in his neck while his blood begins to pump harder. Like I've lit a match and thrown it on pure gasoline, he is on fire.

Blake stands, and with heavy leather boots, he kicks his sickly brat to the side. She giggles in excitement, thinking her punishment is on its way, but when he bends to her and mouths, "Fuck. Off," she realizes playtime is over.

She pouts at him, and he grabs her by her high ponytail braid, dragging her past me before he throws her out the door and over a metal railing. I hear a few screams from the people in the surrounding lower level of the club, but not for long when they realize who did it, like it's a regular occurrence.

Blake returns seconds later and kicks the doors shut to silence her screams.

"Well, it's taken you long enough to come back to me," he says with a smirk; a smirk I want to carve into with a knife. "Get on your knees, Darcie. It's customary when you enter my room."

"Get on yours," I counter, unafraid.

Blake throws his head back and laughs. He seems delighted. He likes a challenge.

I watch as he unscrews a long vial from his neck chain and brings it to his nose. He sniffs hard, and his eyes roll back into his head.

I stand still, observing him with no expression on my face.

He sits down in a red velvet chair which is akin to a throne, his legs wide and his arms placed on the armrests. The room has old Victorian vibes, ornate trimmings, a large brocaded mirror on the heavily wallpapered wall with a bureau beside him. Upon it sits candles, an ink pot, feather pen, crystal wineglasses, handcuffs, cat-o'-nine-tails, a knife —which I've locked in my memory bank, and some half-used lines of powder.

"It's not how this works, darling," he states, wiping his nose.

"I've seen how it works."

"How could you with your back turned, my petal?" I see flashes of the wooden bleachers I smacked my teeth against as he invaded me over and over again. I run my tongue over my teeth just to remind myself they're all still intact.

His gaze slithers down my body.

"I am not your darling or your petal," I retort. "I could be your worst nightmare."

His hand playfully reaches out to a melting candle, and he teases his fingers on the flame.

I see Rev appear behind him as if he had been there the whole time, but I had never heard him enter. His presence makes me feel alive.

"Get on your knees, Blake." I hate repeating myself.

He mulls over my comment before standing slowly and walking over to me. Big leather boots creasing with each catlike step.

Rev retreats back into the shadows, just watching quietly because this is my show.

I lift my chin as this six-foot-four man towers over me. I can smell his sweaty arousal, and it's familiar. He smiles and leisurely lowers himself to his knees, his mouth brushing down the length of my body as he does so. My stomach lurches, and I can barely contain my need to strike out like an angry cat.

I don't know why he's submitting, as it's so out of character for this dominant asshole.

My eyes glance behind him, and Rev nods gently from the darkness to encourage me to do whatever I need to.

"And now?" Blake asks, awaiting instruction. He seems on the verge of laughter, which makes me want to choke him out.

"Lie on your back."

"Do I get a pillow?"

"No," I respond coldly. *Well, maybe a pillow to suffocate your fucking face...*

Blake lies back against the cold floor, his dark jacket flapping open like a crow fallen. The shine from his belt buckle catches in my eyes from the reflection of the dotted lights in the ceiling. The music in the club is a throbbing electric bass, a perfect soundtrack to this meeting. If he screams, no one will hear it.

It's like I've made a wild animal surrender, and while I feel powerful, I know that at any given moment, the animal could bite and destroy me. Or strike out like a snake, and it would be too late for Rev to get to me.

I place my heels on either side of his body, and his eyes come alive as he stares up at my dress.

"There she is," he says, focusing between my legs, licking his mouth.

I slide my dress farther up my thighs to give him a better view since it will be his last. Blake's excitement is obvious, and I feel like stomping on it.

Rev is merely a smile in the darkness like a Cheshire cat observing.

It's time to show him what I have planned. I like Rev watching me. I know he will reward me later for my performance with his beautiful body.

I crouch down and lower myself onto Blake's face. He

laughs as he's smothered by my silken underwear. It's a funny game to him, but a game that doesn't end well.

I grind my hips harder, pleasuring myself on his mouth, and feel him gasp for air, his jugular jerking and hands almost reaching up to move me away, but stop and fall back down to the floor. It's almost like he wants punishment. To feel what it's like to surrender. He's going to fall on his sword.

I feel myself getting wet, but it's not out of desire for this monster; it's excitement over the power. Suddenly, I'm beginning to understand him. The mind of a predator. A filthy animal. Perhaps I am just as filthy?

Rev steps toward me from where he was watching patiently and positions himself where I can see his beautiful face in the half light. The candles flicker light into his eyes and across the side of his angular jawline and anticipatory lips. He rubs his face and studies the situation.

He's wondering where this is going. I can see his aroused curiosity, but he gives me space to do what I like.

I push down harder, eyes locked with Rev as if it's his face I'm pushing into, and then everything ceases... suddenly, every muscle in Blake stops. He's passed out beneath me. From lack of oxygen or drug-induced, I'm unsure.

I shuffle back and straddle his chest. He's out cold. But breathing.

"Nice work," Rev says with that handsome half smile. Erotic asphyxiation clearly gets him off. "If I was going to die, I'd choose that option."

"He's not dead," I reply, disappointed in myself.

"Well, no. But whatever he snorted seems to have taken effect, and I'd say he's coming back soon. So what are we doing?"

I study Blake's face intently; he's very pretty for a demon spawn. "Help me turn him over?"

"Of course, baby," says Rev affectionately, and he holds my face in his hands while stepping on Blake's head and kissing the side of my mouth.

He helps me stand, and without my help, Rev uses his boot to kick Blake over onto his stomach. I hear a small oomph as air escapes his lungs, and he does a face-plant on the floor.

There is so much I want to do. But time is the enemy, and I know the only reason Blake didn't fight me is because he's a sick puppy. He thought he wasn't in danger because he underestimates me. That's how arrogant and cocky he is.

But he will soon see that he should never underestimate a woman hell-bent on revenge.

I scan the room and pick up a glimmer of an antique knife on the ornate desk against the wall. Blake's out cold—he's not going anywhere for the moment. I look at his pretty face in some kind of slumber. Peaceful, with slow breaths.

How could this person who looks so quietly innocent be such a monster?

I wonder what happened to him to create the darkness he now lives in. But he made his bed, and he's going to have to lie in it, soaking in his own blood, care of yours truly.

I clench my teeth, thinking about how he violated me. It wasn't pretty, and I wish I could erase the images he has of me from his mind. Like deleting shots from a photo reel in a phone. But I can't.

All I can do is leave him with a permanent reminder that it's not okay, and it never will be.

I grab the knife and the ink pot and return to him, sitting on his legs. Reaching around, I unbuckle his pants and unzip his fly.

"Please don't tell me we're cutting his cock off." Rev sighs, rubbing his hands through his hair, clearly not liking this concept.

"No, that would be too easy and a little cliché, wouldn't it?" I think about Lorena Bobbitt driving off with her husband's cock and hooking it out the window like an unwanted hot dog.

I'm still amazed those cops found it before a raccoon had a munch.

Pretty sure her husband didn't do anything nearly as bad as Blake did, but I guess some people have a lower tolerance for bullshit. She paved the way for women's empowerment. Now I'm just doing the same, although it's not his cock I'm going to remove. I think I'm way more creative than that.

I pull down his pants, exposing his pearly ass, and run my fingers over it. A final goodbye to this smooth, beautiful skin. He really shouldn't have messed with mine. I have visions of shoving the knife up his ass, but I just don't think I'm that brutal.

I just want to leave him with a friendly reminder.

And so, it begins.

I carve a C in his left cheek. He stirs, and I see his face contort.

Rev kneels to hold the front of his body.

The C isn't deep enough, so I go in again, and Blake's head shoots up suddenly with a scream.

"Knock him out!" I say to Rev, and in turn, he pulls Blake's head up by the hair and punches him hard in the face.

Blake's eyes roll back, and he flops back with his cheek to the floor.

I continue with an R next to the C, this time knowing I

have to push down harder. Blood is leaking, and I know my makeshift tattoo is probably going to look like shit due to the blood that will push out the ink I'll be pouring over it.

At least it should scar, anyway.

I finish the left cheek with the word CRY.

Moving onto the right, I carve the word BABY, which wasn't easy. You try cutting a B into a pliable butt cheek. But I did it enough to be legible. School showers will never be the same for him again.

I wipe the blood across his cheeks, then grab the dark blueish ink pot and cover his ass in it. That's gotta sting, but he's too out cold to react. I want it to work, but I doubt he'll send me a butt selfie when it heals to show me.

So I keep cutting and pouring ink, making a dark black bloody mess.

Rev raises his eyebrows and muffles a laugh while shaking his head.

"You never cease to amaze me," he says, looking at me with eyes that set me on fire.

Why is it that every time I do something like this, we feel like fucking? Is this some kind of fetish I don't know about? Because I've got it bad. I grab his shirt, yanking his face to mine, and kiss him hard.

My bloody inked hands find his hair, and he doesn't seem to mind. He pulls back, searching my eyes closely.

"What's next, bunny?" He watches my mouth and scans my features on the way back up to my eyes.

"Just one more thing," I say and find his mouth again. It's warm and soft as my tongue slips in.

I just want to be inside him while he's inside me. The intensity I feel is one I can never escape from, and I don't want to. I run my hands over his jaw and clasp my precious dark angel.

Returning back to my messy masterpiece, I grab the knife and pull Blake's right hand behind his back. Staring at each finger, I begin eeny, meeny, miny, moe. That game is so rigged, though. I always knew it as a kid too.

With five fingers, you can end up back at the start, so I begin on his index finger. I'm pretty sure that one along with another reached into my back passage a hundred times while I screamed into the night.

He won't be using it again.

So I begin to saw at it. No idea how I'll get through the bone, but I'm not thinking that far ahead.

Rev grabs my wrist to halt me. "Not that one." He's drawing a line, and I don't know why. "Pick another one."

I sigh, realizing how fucked life would be without an index finger. How would he text me his apology without it? How would he flush the toilet?

I really don't fucking care, and I look at Rev in disbelief. Is he softening? What the fuck?

I keep going, trying to cut this meaty thing off, but in one swift movement, Rev rips the knife from my hand and stabs through his ring finger against the floor. He cracks through the bone and smashes Blake in the face another time for good measure.

He casually hands me his finger as I watch the blood gush around the rest of his fingers on the floor beside Blake's head.

I drop the finger quickly like it's hot because, I swear, I felt a pulse in it. I shiver and make little fists with all of mine. Why does this feel worse than watching Buckets lose a whole hand in the sink? Rogue fingers are just creepy as fuck, I guess.

Pulling myself together, I finish my masterpiece by taking that finger and shoving it as far up Blake's anal passage as I can. I hope it gets lost in there. Grabbing the burning candle, Rev sears his amputation, and I can smell burning bacon mixed with something metallic.

I dunno if that even works, so I slide his belt out from his pants and fasten it around his wrist tightly to slow the blood flow. "Honestly, I don't care if he loses his whole hand. He and Buckets can start a boy band, for all I care."

I'm not making sense, but Rev feels me and knows I'm broken inside. He doesn't question me or give me looks of judgment, and for that, I'm grateful.

The word CRYBABY is beginning to swell, but I think it will be there to stay. No one likes a crybaby. Except maybe prison inmates when they rail that little bitch in the laundry room. The vision tickles my senses, and I can't help the evil smile that creeps across my face.

Rev

Well, holy mother of fuck. I'm so hard, I can barely see straight. Something about watching Darcie in her element is utterly cathartic. I suppose that makes us both fucked up because most would be hitting the road after watching what I just did.

But it makes me want her all the more.

She smiles, pleased with her handiwork as she cuts the clothes from Blake's body, dusts off her hands, and stands. "Don't want his little minions to recognize him," she explained why she disrobed him. "Let's go."

And just like that, she's done.

Or so I thought.

I stand, but when Darcie hunts through the drawers of the bureau, I know we are far from done. She holds up a gun, her eyes wide with excitement. She retrieves another and smiles.

"We're going to take a walk. Rev, I need your trench coat."

It seems she's thought all of this through. I toss her my coat.

Peering at Blake's ass, I see there is one single word.

CRYBABY

A snort escapes me because that shit is fucking funny.

Blake is still passed out, so I yank him up by the scruff of the neck and help Darcie dress him in my coat. Darcie slips the guns into the deep pockets, and then we lead him from the room. To onlookers, he is merely drunk, swaying from side to side, so when we descend the stairs, no one heeds any attention to us.

It's just another day in the office for us friends.

Darcie makes her way toward the entrance, but I shake my head. I know a back way.

She follows my lead without asking questions. I know she'll ask how I know about this place. The security doesn't look twice as they open the door for us. The moment we're outside, the cold air slaps life into Blake, who inhales sharply.

Darcie holds on tight, but I know she doesn't stand a chance if he decides to fight. So I let him go, only to head-butt him out cold. I don't bother catching him, and he collapses to the concrete with a thud.

"A shame, really," I say, gripping both of Blake's ankles. He's still wearing his boots. "I really liked this coat."

Darcie arches a brow, but when I commence dragging a passed-out Blake along the ground, she understands after tonight, we're all ruined in some way, shape, or form.

I retrieve the guns from his pocket before tossing his ass into the back of the pickup we stole. We both quickly get in, as we don't want to cause any more of a scene with the cops on our asses. The truck roars to life as I take off into the night, never looking back at the mess we made.

Darcie's attention is fixated through the windshield, and when she gives directions on where to go, it seems she has the backdrop for the final act set in mind. We drive in silence. The only thing filling the truck is some tragic country ballad.

"How did you know about the club?"

Clenching my hands around the steering wheel, I confess, "Some pervert with a fondness for underage boys."

Darcie waits for me to continue.

"He was a rich fucker. Married with five kids. But it was all for show. He owns the club. I wanted a fifty-thousand-dollar painting in his house. So I did what I had to, to get it."

I don't need to fill in the blanks. She gets it. It was at that club I learned a lot about people by watching and learning how to get what I want. And after a while, that life became my norm. It was my norm because I knew it wasn't permanent.

I did what I had to, to survive because I knew it would help my mom.

And what a fucking joke that was.

Darcie doesn't pry, but she knows me just as well as I know her.

"Here," she says, pointing at a junkyard.

And what a backdrop she's chosen.

I park the truck around the back and kill the headlights. Even though this place isn't patrolled by security or have any killer dogs on-site, we can't go waltzing in through the front gate. Opening the console, I pass her the guns.

Darcie follows as I get out and check to see if Blake is still out cold. He is.

I'm not gentle as I grip him by the ankles and hurl his ass out of the truck, ensuring to smash the side of his head on the edge of the tailgate.

Darcie's fingers brush over a similar injury sustained, thanks to this sack of shit, which is why I ensured he felt what she did. The finger up his ass is indicative of what he may have done to her.

My jaw clenches, and just for good measure, I make sure his raw ass is exposed to the dirt as I drag him along the ground littered with broken glass and rocks. When I reach a small hole in the wire fence, I gesture with my hand for Darcie to go first.

Her tiny frame fits through with ease.

I use the toe of my boot to pry Blake up like a raggedy doll and shove him through the hole. The barbed wire scratches him. He's going to be one scarred-up mother-fucker once tonight is through because unlike the others, Darcie doesn't want him dead.

He would be already if she did.

Darcie's shoes kick up dirt as she pulls him out of the way so I can fit through the hole. I love that she doesn't mind getting her hands dirty.

Once in, I peer around the desolate field filled with waste which was loved once upon a time. But now, it lays in twisted, broken heaps. We dispose of things so easily when something better comes along.

Blake is still unconscious, but he'll rouse soon.

Dragging him by the arms, I lug him through the junkyard. I don't clear a path for him. Whatever is in my way, I use Blake as my sweeper. When I drag him over a pile of rusted kitchen silverware, a dessert fork gets imbedded into his thigh.

I don't bother removing it.

If he doesn't die from whatever Darcie has planned, then he's going need a tetanus shot. As well as a shower in fucking bleach because when I see a heap of black garbage bags oozing something brown and nasty, I take a slight detour.

Darcie covers her nose with the back of her hand while I sideswipe the bags with Blake's torso. The unidentified goo covers Blake, and it's good to see it smells as nasty as it looks.

With that done, I see a small alcove between a mountain of squashed cars piled high to the skies. "There," I order, and when Darcie follows my line of sight, she nods.

I prop Blake up against some steel railing, and Darcie passes me some rope she found along the way. He is still out cold, so I hold him up with my shoulder as I tie him to the railing. When one arm is tied, I yank the other, and when I hear something akin to an orange being squashed by a truck, I grin because I'm pretty sure I just dislocated his shoulder.

Once tied, I step back and am pleased to see him displayed like Jesus on the cross—it seems fitting 'cause this motherfucker is about to be crucified.

Darcie places some empty bottles and beer cans around Blake's head. "I always wanted to learn how to shoot," she says, turning out her bottom lip. "Now is as good a time as any."

She offers me a gun, and we get into position, standing

in front of Blake. She looks at me, and I smile. "Want me to show you how it's done?"

She nods.

Placing my gun into the small of my back, I stand behind Darcie and run my fingertips down her arms. Her skin breaks out into tiny goose bumps.

Positioning my hands over hers, I say, "Keep your fingers outside the trigger guard. You're then going to use your other hand to steady the gun."

I show her what I mean by aligning her hands how they should be.

"Make sure all fingers are clear of the hammer," I continue, kissing the shell of her ear.

A gasp leaves her, but she stands her ground.

"Fix your gun on the target." I raise her arm, aiming for the corroded Budweiser can left of Blake's head. "Control your breathing."

Her breathing is anything but as she shuffles backward, pressing her back into my front. This is getting her off.

"And then?" she coaxes, her voice wavering.

"And then, baby...pull the trigger."

I bite over the side of her throat, feeling her lashing pulse under my tongue, which instantly gets me hard.

Darcie whimpers before a loud bang followed by her jarring backward into me fills the air.

"Holy shit!" she cries, as that shot was clearly accidental, but when the beer can backflips into the air before landing on the ground with a hollowed thud, it seems Darcie is a natural.

The commotion wakes Blake, who shakes his head in a daze. Darcie and I don't give him time to recover as we get into position, aim, and shoot.

The shots echo into the night, filling the junkyard with

an orchestra of sound. But the best sound of all is hearing Blake's cries for help—the fucker is human, after all.

Darcie continues firing, and we both know she could hit Blake if she wanted, but she doesn't. It takes all my willpower not to put a bullet in his leg.

And just like that, the firing stops. But Blake's cries don't.

Darcie rolls her eyes. "Fucking pussy."

She marches over to him while I dally behind.

"Why?" she asks, and no matter what revenge we seek, this question is at the core—why?

Blake shakes his head. He's a fucking mess.

Darcie isn't playing, however, and pistol-whips him in the temple. "I said why!"

When I hear a trickle of something hit the ground, I know he's pissed himself.

"He...he told me to do it."

And the night falls still.

"What did you say?"

By Darcie's stunned reaction, this is something she never factored into the equation.

"He told me I had to do it otherwise he'd ruin me. I wouldn't get the football scholarship if that shit got out," Blake confesses, looking at me like I'm his savior. "She told me she was sixteen, man! I didn't know she was underage.

"She said she wanted me too. But he knew...and he filmed it."

None of this makes sense as it's the ramblings of a desperate man. But it appears someone blackmailed Blake, and like a pussy, he caved, which makes what he did even worse.

"I don't care!" Darcie screams, getting into Blake's face.

She yanks on his hair and pulls his head back. "Who told you? Motherfucker, who!"

Blake's lower lip trembles. He is actually afraid of this asshole. "I can't tell you. He'll kill me."

With a few rounds left in my gun, I place it against Blake's sweaty temple. "Wrong answer, fucker. Answer her. *Now*."

This is the moment of truth, but the answer is, what's going to happen when Darcie uncovers the truth?

I can see Blake's pulse punching at the side of his throat, his heart desperate to give in because that will be far more merciful than the fate headed his way.

"Carson."

Darcie gasps, and I can see her mind cataloging over the night to determine if Blake is lying. When the full moon catches the tears in her eyes, the answer is clear.

"Please kill me," he begs, eyes pleading with me.

He knows when Carson finds out who the snitch is, death will seem like a mercy.

I look at Darcie, who seems to have slipped into a world where she doesn't want to exist.

However, when the junkyard fills with blue and red lights, I know it's time to bounce. The cops have been on our asses, but I refuse to be caught inside this shithole.

"Baby, we gotta go."

But Darcie doesn't move.

Gripping her cold cheeks in my palms, I coax her to look at me. "It's just you and me, baby, versus the world. Come back to me."

I can hear static over walkie-talkies. The cops are coming.

"Kill me, man, please," Blake says, yanking at the ropes at his wrists.

But I don't have time. I can't draw attention to where we are.

His voice seems to rouse her, and she turns her cheek with deadly precision. "You're already dead inside."

She returns her focus on me and her pain, fuck me dead, I want to eat it and swallow it whole so she'll never look at me with that vacant look ever again.

"Let's go."

Darcie thankfully nods, and we take off, like fugitives into the night, keeping to the shadows...and Blake still breathes...for now.

CHAPTER EIGHTEEN
Darcie

It's late, almost morning, by the time we check into a run-down motel room where no one would look to find us. I'm covered in blood, piss, and ink. I feel disgusting, and the high is gone.

I don't know what I feel other than low seeping dread in my stomach.

Carson did this to me?

Flashbacks leave me winded when I think of him trying to help me in the parking lot. His sweet, understanding smile and demeanor. I close my eyes, and I can see the dark figure that was smoking in the bleachers. Just watching.

Was that him?

A scent drifts under my nose, like a memory that I can literally smell—the scent of his aftershave mixed with... cigarette smoke.

Did he orchestrate this so he could come out looking like a hero? Prince Charming, dashing in with his white sports car to rescue me from his fuckboy rapists? Then what? I fall madly in love with him because he goes off and pretends to beat them up and protect me?

This is fucking messed up.

He couldn't handle rejection. Not the all-star football jock who gets anyone he wants. I fucking hate him. But hate isn't a strong enough word for what I feel.

In fact, I hate everyone except Rev. I can't trust another single soul ever again.

I'm going to make Carson pay, and it's not just going to be a finger up the ass, either. It's going to be both his arms and whatever else I can find. I imagine him screaming and begging for mercy. I want to put real tears on that stupid poster boy's face. Maybe I'll cut his hair off? Maybe I'll…

"Penny for your thoughts? Or…ten bucks if you want," Rev says, pulling a scrunched-up bill from his pocket.

I smile because, just like that, he can make me forget I hate the world.

The motel room is damp and cold. Rev turns on the wall heater, which grunts and groans with the effort, then blows a wave of dust into the room. Warm dust, it's nice.

"I'm just thinking about Carson. About what he did," I respond, my eyes just staring into space. "I can't believe how fucking stupid I was. I actually thought he was trying to help me."

Rev sighs; it's a sound of frustration and sadness. "Well, that's what assholes like him do, they are chameleons. You're not to blame for any of this—he is, and I have no doubt he'll be blowing his own dick when you cut it off, set it on fire, and shove it down his throat."

That visual gets me hot.

"But we need to be smart, my little firecracker. That was too close in the junkyard. We have to be careful."

"Carson has to pay for what he did."

Rev cups my cheek in his big hand. "And he will, but we've been lucky with the other guys. With Carson, we need to—"

"To what?" I coax, my interest piqued.

"We need to smack him in the mouth and knock him out cold so we can take him far away from here, and you can take your time. This can't be rushed. That fucker needs to feel every shred of pain. He's the final one."

"And then what?" I ask because I haven't thought that far ahead. Revenge has been my motivator, and everything else has been second best.

Rev mulls over my comment but doesn't answer. Instead, he takes my black ink-stained hand, guides me into the bathroom, and yanks a cord that turns on a buzzing light. Big hands wrap around my ribs and he lifts me onto the sink and stares at me. His eyes are like glowing embers; the color of gold and hazel all mixed up together. I picture a baby with those eyes, then shake my head.

Rev slips his hands on either side of my face, and before I can breathe, his mouth is on mine. It's warm and needy against my frozen lips.

I try to talk as he's kissing me, but he mutters, "Nuh-uh."

Without breaking our kiss, he reaches out and hits the taps in the shower. We are both pretty filthy, and I can't wait to get under the water.

Rev rips off his shirt, and he's covered in old battle wounds. I notice scars on his torso for the first time and touch them cautiously. His eyes follow my fingers, and he exhales as if I'm healing him. Puncture wounds and cigarette burn scars trail along his chest.

"Who did this to you?" I ask, my heart aching.

But he doesn't want sympathy.

"I did," he replies, staring into my eyes. "Come on, let's shower."

He's not ashamed of his scars. I think they mean something to him. Badges of honor, maybe? Battles won? A sure sign that he was stronger than whatever tried to beat him, which is no surprise because he is my Superman.

The water is hot, and trying to adjust the temperature is futile because it's either too hot or too cold. Kind of like me, really. I'm feeling a little crazy right now. Rev doesn't seem to be fazed by it.

We kiss under the water, and it's deep and honest. As his tongue searches my mouth, I melt into him. My tough girl guard falling into submission. I grab at his skin and feel his tight arm muscles flex under my touch. Although appearing tall and slim, he's very built under the layers of black clothing he always wears.

His body covers mine, and the tension between us begins to grow. He wants me as much as I want him.

He grabs my legs and hitches me up to wrap them around his waist. He then pushes my back against the tiles. I lock my heels together behind his back and hang on tight. I can feel his dick teasing me, and I wriggle to find it and bear down.

As he enters me, I begin to see flashes I don't want to see. Faces that haunt me. I try to shove them aside, but they are taking over. I begin to heave and cry under the water as Rev's fucking my body. I'm trying so hard to stay right here, but I can't. They've destroyed me. I'm not even alive anymore. That girl who Rev first met died that night, and now, I'm just a sociopathic ghost.

"Look at me, baby." Rev's breath is hot against my neck.

My eyes are shut tight, and I'm almost screaming.

"Look at me!" he repeats, as I'm going into a full panic attack.

I open my eyes, and I'm breathing fast; his eyes are strong and safe.

"I've got you, baby." He kisses away my tears. "You're strong. You're beautiful...and you're mine. Now, fuck me."

I stop crying and lock eyes with him as I begin to rise up

and down, his big hands under my ass guiding me. I know what he's doing—he wants me to be present at the moment and replace those horrible memories with moments like this.

He wants it to be his mouth, his touch, I remember—always.

"Don't stop looking at me," he instructs, and his eyes blink through the hot water with large droplets on his long lashes.

"Don't. Stop. Looking. At. Me," he repeats as he pushes his cock in deep and as far as it will go.

I feel so full—in every sense of the word, which is why I let go.

"I love you, Rev." As the words spill from my lips unintentionally, his eyes roll back into his head.

Coming hard in me, he moans, "Fuck, me too, baby. I fucking lov—"

BANG!

BANG!

BANG!

His sentence remains unfinished as the sounds of something earsplitting booms from outside our room. Rev hits the taps off and grabs towels for us.

"What the fuck is that?" I whisper loudly, quickly drying off.

Rev yanks the cord to kill the lights in the bathroom. He grabs the gun he had earlier placed on the toilet cistern and shoves it into the waist of the towel now tightly wrapped around him.

"Stay here," he orders and crouches down low to creep through the room, keeping to the shadows.

I bite my lip so hard that I taste blood. He peers through the crack in the curtains, and my blood runs cold when he bellows, "Fuck!" before the door to our motel room is kicked in, smashing the plaster wall.

Rev

I don't have time to protect her.

I don't have time to reach for my gun.

I don't have time to do anything but fucking watch my world spiral to shit in a second.

"Get down on the floor!"

"He's got a gun!"

"Motherfucker, show me your hands!"

These orders are being barked at me by two rookie cops who can smell their promotion through the ranks by making this arrest.

I raise my hands slowly, but the young cop with a buzz cut waves his gun at me. "I said, get on the floor!"

"Get on the floor? Show me your hands? Make up your motherfucking mind."

Buzz doesn't like my cheek and, in response, pistol-whips me in the temple.

I tongue my cheek, blood trickling down my forehead and seeping into my eye. I don't wipe it away. I stare this fucker down because if he thinks I'm about to surrender, he is shit out of luck.

His partner, who is about ten years his senior, has his gun trained on Darcie. I look at her, and with a nod, she reads my facial charades.

"Pl-Please don't hurt me," she stutters, interlacing her hands. "I'm s-so scared. Please, let me get dressed. I'm c-cold."

Oh, fuck me, this damsel in distress act is too funny.

The cop whose badge reads Tillerman doesn't hide his appraisal of her standing in nothing but a towel.

"Keep looking at her that way, Officer, and I'll feed you your eyeballs."

It works like a charm.

Both cops focus on me, thinking I'm the more dangerous one, which is fucking sexist. I've seen Darcie in action—she's fucking brutal and, at times, sadistically scary, which is why I love her.

Before these assholes burst through the door, I was on the cusp of having the best orgasm of my life and telling my girl I loved her after she told me she loved me.

Looking at her, I don't know how I got so lucky. She's strong, and beautiful, and will happily shove anything into her enemies' orifices and set them on fire.

Speaking of...

Darcie quickly changes into jeans and Chucks and throws on my hoodie, but I don't fail to see her stow away a packet of matches she stole from Trespass into her back pocket.

My little pyromaniac never leaves home without them.

Buzz snatches the gun from my waist, which results in the towel pooling to the vomit-colored carpet. "And you didn't even buy me dinner first," I quip when my junk is on full display.

Tillerman doesn't appreciate my humor and tosses a pair of jeans and boots at me. "Get dressed."

I do as he says because I need a plan, and I need a plan

quick and smart because getting caught was not part of the deal.

The moment I'm dressed, Tillerman elbows me in the stomach and yanks my arms behind my back, handcuffing me. Bent low and attempting to catch my breath, I subtly shake my head because I can see Darcie wants to fight.

But she can't.

We fight.

We die.

We're wanted fugitives.

We need to bide our time.

Tillerman heaves me upright and reads me my rights.

I yawn in response.

Buzz cuffs Darcie, but I can see the young buck is sweet on her as she goes all doe-eyed. "Please don't do them up tight. I won't resist. I promise."

What a fucking chump.

Buzz keeps a stiff upper lip, but I can see he's done as she asked. She's a fucking crazed mastermind, and I am going to fuck the ever-living shit out of her the moment we get out of this mess, because we are getting out of this.

I don't know how yet, though.

We are led from the room, a few bystanders standing in their doorways to see what the commotion is. The cops leading us toward the patrol car are talking amongst themselves, bragging that they caught the two teen delinquents who have eluded police for days.

They're going to be the hometown heroes. Or so they think.

I lock eyes with Darcie, and I can see that she's wondering how we're going to get out of this. But I made a promise to protect her, and I never break a promise.

We're thrown into the back of the patrol car, arms

cuffed behind our backs. Rookie move because they don't harness us in. They think they're safe as houses because a pair of cuffs detain us. They almost deserve the shit show they're about to get because of their arrogance.

They get into the front, and the only thing which separates us is a metal grate between us. I can't believe they didn't restrain our feet. The car kicks to life, and the blue and red lights set the stage for what's to come.

Darcie looks at me, silently asking what the fuck we're supposed to do. But I've got this. I've been in worse situations. I examine our surroundings, peering at the bolts holding the grate in place. They're done up tight.

There's no way I can kick that in without getting shot.

Next plan.

I gesture with my chin that Darcie is to lean forward so I can see her hands. She shifts subtly, and I grin when I see the cuffs are loose. It's going to take some wriggling, but she can do it. The harder she tries, the damper her flesh becomes, and that will hopefully help slide the cuffs off.

I nod, and she leans back, subtly putting our plan into place.

Now, it's my turn to shine.

"So whatcha gonna do with us?" I ask, leaning forward to get up close and personal with Buzz so I can block Darcie from view.

"Shut up, smart-ass," he barks, whacking his baton on the grate in warning.

It's not a deterrent.

"Or what?"

Buzz bares his teeth, ready to strike, but Tillerman warns him, "Enough, McKenzie. The DA is going to have a field day prosecuting this little shit. He's been waiting for him to fuck up for years, and now that he can be tried as an adult, I have no doubt they'll put him away for a very long time."

I can hear a gasp leave Darcie because the DA is Carson's dad—the fucker who owns this town. It is nice to know, however, that I owned his wife's ass when I fucked her six ways to Sunday just 'cause I could.

Walter Beckett doesn't like me. He never has. I don't know what his problem is, apart from the obvious, of course. But he's made it clear that the moment I fuck up, he'll be there, ready to make my life hell. So, no doubt, these cops know what it means for them to be turning me over to him.

No wonder his son is such a jackass. He learned from the best.

"How is the dashing DA?" I ask, pressing my nose against the grate so I look like Little Miss Piggy. "Still got a hard-on for me then?"

Tillerman chuckles, but it's not a pleasant sound. "He's going to be even better when he throws your sorry ass into jail for life. And what perfect timing, with his tenth-anniversary party happening in two days, what better way to celebrate with his colleagues than announcing the infamous Rev Blackwood is finally where he belongs."

Darcie's movements cease, and that's because she realizes what I do—this fucking moron just gave us our golden ticket to where Carson will be as he will be suited up, playing the good son role as he celebrates his father's achievements.

If we're going to do this, then why not in front of an audience where we can show the good people of this fucked-up town who their precious DA's son really is—a fucking sadistic rapist.

Two days is all I need to plan this and plan it well because there is no room for error.

"I'm going to be sick." Darcie's cries have me turning over my shoulder, and I know she's slipped free from the cuffs.

It's time.

I lean back so Buzz can see her. He's sweet on her, which is why he turns to Tillerman. "Pull over. I don't want her being sick in the car."

We're in the middle of bumfuck nowhere, and it's evident Tillerman doesn't want to stop, but when Darcie begins dry retching, it seems he doesn't fancy cleaning vomit off his leather seats either.

"For fuck's sake!" He yanks the car violently to the shoulder, and I jar forward, hitting my head on the grate. "Oops."

Fucker did it on purpose. But that's okay. His head will be bleeding soon enough.

Both cops get out of the car. Buzz on Darcie's side. Tillerman on mine. They draw their guns, and when Buzz opens Darcie's door, she doesn't hesitate. She launches on top of him, tackling him to the dirt as he's totally caught off guard.

His bad for underestimating her.

Tillerman's eyes drift overhead for a split second, and it's all I need to lean back across the seat for support and ram my feet into his stomach. A shot fires into the night sky.

I roll out of the car and don't give Tillerman a chance to recover as I headbutt him—over and over again. I break his nose. And when he tries to shoot me, I hip and shoulder him to the ground, where I pin him with my body weight.

Dirt plumes into the air as we fight for dominance, scrambling to subdue the other. When he raises the gun, I use what I can, which is my mouth, and bite down on his wrist. I shake at it like a dog would at a bone, and when I taste blood, I know I've won.

The gun drops to the ground with a thud, followed by Tillerman's pained cries echoing into the heavens.

With my hands still cuffed, I use the edge of my shoulder to siphon off his air supply as I press it against his throat. His hands smack at me while he wheezes for breath, but he's going to lose.

Peering down at him, I smirk as I watch him straddle unconsciousness. "Oops."

His face turns a beet red, his eyes bugging from his head, and as I press down harder on his Adam's apple, he finally goes out cold.

I don't have time to celebrate, however, because I can hear Darcie and Buzz fighting. Jumping up, I charge for Buzz and hip and shoulder him to the ground. He puts up a fight, and we scramble desperately, but I manage to pin him down.

"Darcie, get the keys!" I order because I can't do jack shit while still cuffed.

Buzz tries to buck me off, but I use all my weight to keep him down.

Darcie slips and slides as she frantically runs over to Tillerman and yanks the keys from his belt. She has the good sense to also retrieve his fallen gun.

"Good girl," I commend, slamming my head into Buzz's face to subdue him.

I try to offer my hands so Darcie can unlock my cuffs, but Buzz keeps fighting. "Stop moving or so help me God, I will fucking shoot you."

Darcie trains the gun onto Buzz, just how I taught her. I'm so proud.

He reads her seriousness and halts. Darcie is able to

uncuff me, but we don't have time to celebrate. I press my boot over Buzz's throat as I stand over him and deliver the fate he deserves.

"No doubt your little friends are on the way."

Darcie gasps, only just realizing the GPS on the car has been tracking our movements. They've already called it in, so asking Buzz to say he made a mistake and it wasn't us he was arresting won't stick, which means...we gotta run.

"Sucks to be you. You thought we were your meal ticket to a promotion but looks like you'll be wiping shit and piss from the county jail cells for letting us go."

Before he has a chance to speak, I drop to one knee and slam my fist into his face. He's out cold.

I don't have time to celebrate. I grab his gun and then Darcie's hand.

However, it seems the shit show doesn't want to end when I hear the unmistakable sound of a gun being cocked. I don't even think twice before I shove Darcie out of the way, where she falls into the dirt, and then I turn to face Tillerman as he fires from a gun he must have had hidden away.

My bad for not checking earlier.

He's a lousy shot, but if I didn't move Darcie, it would have hit her. That is enough incentive for me to pull back the hammer and shoot Tillerman in the kneecap without hesitation.

He drops the gun, and his howls echo in the darkness. "You're lucky I didn't aim higher, you piece of shit."

Offering my hand to Darcie, I lift her, and we run toward the forest, which will be our sanctuary for a little while.

Our breaths ricochet between us, but we keep going because I know the place will be crawling with cops soon enough. When Darcie tires, I pick her up and run with her pressed to my bare chest, her slack arms looped around my nape. I don't stop and continue running as I know there is an abandoned shack up ahead.

When I see it, I hope it's empty because if not, I'll have to use my gun.

The decayed door is hanging off one hinge, and when I walk up the rickety steps, they whine under the force. I peer inside, and the place is still a haven for the misfits.

The floor is littered with empty beer cans and cigarette butts, and it smells like cat piss. It looks to be empty. I gently lower Darcie to her feet and take a few breaths when I do.

"Fuck, that was close. I—"

I don't get a chance to finish, however, because she steps into my chest and wraps her arms around me. "You almost took a bullet for me," she says in awe.

"Of course, baby," I reply like it's a no-brainer. "I love you."

She's quiet, and when I think I've said too much, she presses her lips to the wounds over my chest, before gently kissing over my heart. "I love you too."

Hearing those words breathes new life into me. "Thanks to Tillerman's overshare, we know where Carson will be."

"What are we going to do?"

Kissing over the top of her head, I inhale her unique fragrance into me—it's a scent I've become addicted to. "We do what I do best—I break into his home, and we find something that will reveal to the world what true monsters the Becketts really are.

"And then?" she whispers.

"And then...we kill them all."

CHAPTER NINETEEN

Darcie

I feel like I'm in the cottage belonging to the three bears. I'm Goldilocks, and I could seriously down some cold porridge right now without even blinking. My stomach is groaning like a whiney bitch. There's an old bed that probably has dust mites and semen embedded in it. I'm exhausted, and I just want to lie down. It's probably stupid as hell to stay out here in the woods with the cops chasing us, but I'm tired to the core.

Rev sits on the floor by the bed and toys with his gun.

"What are we doing?" I ask, but the question is rhetorical.

"Come here," he says, patting his lap.

I collapse onto him and lie between his legs, my head on his chest. I just need to sleep. I can't think straight. I feel like I'm inhabiting someone else's body that's done all these evil things.

Who am I?

Did Rev influence me? I stiffen. Why didn't he stop me? I start to question who *he* is.

Why have the police been after him for so long? Have I been groomed and taken advantage of by a killer?

Am I a killer?

These are the neurotic thoughts racing around my head, and I know that's because I need sleep.

So I silence the voices and embrace them—down the

rabbit hole I go, down deep into old memories. Ones with sunshine in them and laughing. I even see a swing in the park, but I don't know if I was ever there.

The reality around me is cold, dark, and dirty, with colors of blue, green, and black. My mind, however, has gone into the warmest amber light, coaxing me back to a better time. Is this what they mean by follow the light?

Cold tears are on my face, but I refuse to wake up. I want to stay here inside my warm mind.

Digging.

The sound of a shovel entering the earth and the cough as the dirt is thrown. It's happening over and over again and rouses me from my sleep. I'm still lying against Rev's chest, but poke him lightly and look up.

Rev's eyes are open, and he's listening.

"Someone's digging outside?" I whisper, unsure whether I'm dreaming or not.

He simply nods slowly and exhales.

We get up and peer outside. There's an old man digging a huge hole out the back of the shack. Beside him is a full bag sealed tight. He's grunting and chatting to someone, and I can't make out what he's saying as he's barely opening his mouth.

The bag is moving, and I'm suddenly feeling a fire ignite in my belly. A game is beginning once again, and my warm memories that soothed my sleep have quickly evaporated.

Before I know what is happening, Rev is outside, casually smoking a cigarette, standing by the semi-dug-out grave this man is digging. Smoke billows in the crisp air, and the trees surrounding us are muted in the fog. It looks like an old painting, beautiful yet hiding the worst secrets. I can't imagine how many bodies may be decaying in this forest.

I hear mewing. Like small squeaky toys and the thick plastic bag is moving.

"Oh, fuck no!" I say, appearing behind the old guy with my gun pointed at his head.

Rev smirks and searches the sky as he chokes out a laugh. "There she is," he tells the heavens and meanders off to take a piss by a tree.

The bag beside the digger has cats in it. I fucking know it, and they are all alive.

The old guy turns to me and rests his arm on the shovel conversationally. "The damn rodents won't leave me be!" he says and spits on the ground.

"Get your fucking face on the ground right now!" I order, completely horrified by what's going on.

He puts his arms up in utter shock, and the shovel drops into the grave. "Lass, I think you need to put ye weapon away. I'm not hurtin' nobody here. I'm just getting rid o' these vermin."

"Get. Your. Fucking. Face. On. The. Ground. Now!" and I shoot a shot into the air, which has Rev running back, frantically zipping up his fly and trying to rip the gun out of my hands, but I hold fast.

"Are you fucking insane! We are lying low, and you shoot your fucking gun?" he spits, and it's the first time I've seen him annoyed with me. This guy, who probably turned me into a psychopath.

The cats are screaming now. Like they know that rescue is imminent. I tear open the bag to see the most beautiful golden kittens pour out. My face fills with tears, and I shoot another shot into the air.

"This world is a piece of shit!" I scream, and the man is now shaking with his face on the ground and his boots kicking the dirt.

Rev is mad. I can see the vein at his neck throbbing with each infuriated breath he takes. "You're going to risk everything for some fucking cats? You've lost your goddamn mind."

I sniff back my tears while I keep the gun trained on the cat killer and reach down to cradle the kittens in one hand.

Behind us, there is a truck, and it's what we need to get out of here. Rev is two steps ahead of me and rips the keys from the old guy's back pocket. He removes his jacket and boots as well, then storms over to the truck and hoists them into the back tray.

"Get in the truck... NOW," Rev orders, his patience shot.

"I'm not leaving these kittens," I whisper, crouched down trying to collect them all. They're crawling over me trying to seek warmth and my heart is breaking.

"Leave the fucking cats. We have to go NOW!" Rev asserts, kicking the door of the truck with his boots.

I can't leave them. I'm lying in the dirt, crying with ten kittens crawling all over me, and I want to save them all. I want to save me.

Defenseless creatures only wanting love. No mother and no one to protect them. I'm gutted, and I feel sick. Vomit rises, but nothing comes out as I dry retch.

Suddenly, I'm yanked by the arm and pulled upward. Rev has lost his cool with me, and I hate him right now. I hate myself, and I hate him.

He places a rough hand on the back of my neck and steers me, marching toward the truck. The kittens are screaming behind me, small dots of fluff in the dirt crying for me to come back. The pain in my heart is excruciating, and now the one person I loved and trusted is turning into a monster.

"I love you, little brat! I'm doing this for your own good, now get in the fucking truck," he says and shoves my small weeping frame into the passenger seat.

I slump over and scream louder than I've ever screamed. Right along with those kittens.

Rev places a large hand over my mouth and pins my head to the back of the headrest. The old man still has his face buried in the dirt, and I wish I'd killed him to save my furry babies. But Rev stopped me. This is all his fault.

I hate all men on this earth because they cause nothing but pain. Nothing but torture. I'm going to fucking destroy Carson with every fiber in my body and...maybe even Rev too.

Rev

Darcie is howling beside me...and all for some *fucking* kittens.

I don't get it. I've seen her torture with a smile, but now she's losing her shit because she's suddenly a cat person.

What the fuck is going on?

"Darcie, enough," I say, trying to focus on the road covered with potholes. But her cries only grow. "I know it sucks, but you can't save everything. We can barely save our own asses, and you're worried about some strays!"

"Fuck y-you," she sobs, not even able to look at me. "You're nothing but a fucking cruel asshole. They are defenseless. We could have helped them, but you chose to abandon them. I don't even know who you are anymore."

"We save ten kittens, and there will be ten more! What fucking difference does it make?" I slam my palm against the steering wheel, furious we're having this ridiculous conversation.

She continues staring out her window, back turned to me.

"Answer me!" I exclaim, angered that she would risk everything for something so insignificant.

"It makes a difference to them," she says in a whisper. "I know we can't save them all, but not saving the ones we can is inhumane. They may not be perfect. They may scratch and bite. But everyone deserves a second chance.

"No one deserves to be abandoned. No matter what."

And suddenly, I get it because we are no longer talking about kittens. We're talking about her. No wonder this was so personal to her.

Something has shifted in Darcie; just how I knew it would. What she's gone through changes a person, and I knew sooner or later, it would catch up to her. I also knew she wouldn't always look at me as her savior.

I'm not her Prince Charming. I left her when she needed me the most. I left her because in the end, I wasn't thinking about anyone other than myself.

"For fuck's sake!"

Darcie's head crashes into the window as I pull an erratic U-turn and press my foot down on the accelerator. I don't slow down because, what's the worst that can happen?

We die?

We're headed for that route anyway. There is no proverbial light at the end of the tunnel for us. We're wanted fugitives, and the longer we evade arrest, the harsher the penalty we face. But I don't want that for Darcie.

I want her to have a shot at life. I want her to have a real chance at being someone because I know great things await her.

And I will do everything in my power to ensure she gets it.

I slam on the brakes and jump out of the car. The dickhead is still facedown in the dirt, and when he attempts to thank me for coming back for him, I kick him in the teeth, knocking him out cold.

The headlights catch the eyes of the kittens, and I curse under my breath as I grab the bag and dump the little squeaking assholes into it. I don't know how many there were, but I'm not going to do a headcount, and storm over to the truck and yank open Darcie's door.

Without a word, I drop the bag into her lap.

I watch as she peers inside, and when she deadpans me, I wish I'd just kept on driving. "There's only eight. There's supposed to be ten."

Gripping the doorframe, I internally count to three and clench my jaw. "Fine."

Turning around, I go on the hunt for these two fuckers. When I see one hiding under a fallen branch, I grip it by the scruff of the neck and press my nose to his. "Where's your brother, you little shit?"

The kitten squawks in response.

It takes me ten minutes, but I find the last turd, sleeping soundly under a tree. He joins his brother in one of my palms because they're fucking tiny, and I pass them to Darcie. She accepts and places the other two with their siblings in my sweater, which she's used as a blanket.

She's only in a tank, so once in the truck, I slam the door

and crank up the heater. We don't speak when I speed away into the night, knowing keeping a low profile is imperative. I don't know where to go because there is no safe place after the shit we pulled with the cops.

But we have a day to kill.

I decide to risk it because there's only one thing we need to ensure we have some shot at getting out of this alive, and that's money.

There's one thing I learned growing up with a mom who is an addict, and that's hide your valuables because nothing holds any sentimental value when a junkie is jonesing.

I couldn't leave my money at home for obvious reasons, which meant I needed to hide it away with someone I trusted, and there's only one person I trusted, and that's Nonna.

I hope to fuck the cops aren't scouting the place, but it's a risk I need to take. We need money. And we need guns.

Darcie is ignoring me, but that's fine. I'm not in a talking mood. I wonder if the honeymoon period is over. I tell a chick I love her, and this is what happens. No wonder I never said it before.

But I keep my head in the game because there's no room for error.

It's late, and no one but crackheads and hookers are out, looking for their next fix of whatever their poison is. I turn down a street and kill the engine.

Darcie looks through the windshield, but this neighborhood is foreign to her. "Stay here."

I open the door and shut it softly, but when I hear the passenger door mimic the same action, I glare at Darcie over the roof of the truck.

"What part of stay here didn't you understand?"

"All of it," she spits, the bag of kittens in hand. "I'm not some airhead you can bark orders at."

"I wouldn't need to be barking orders if you didn't lose your shit over kittens. We're here because you can't do what you're told."

"Fuck you, Rev."

Seems she still hates me.

Knowing this is an argument not worth having, I walk past her and down the alleyway which runs behind the houses I know so well. Darcie's muted footsteps reveal she's following.

I know this neighborhood like the back of my hand because this is my playground. But I don't have time to play. Jumping onto the lid of a silver trash can, I jump over Mrs. Santina's fence and pat her rottweiler, Boris, on the head as I pass his kennel.

He doesn't even raise his head. He's seen it all before.

I continue jumping fences into backyards and kudos to Darcie, she keeps up. About six streets down, I crouch low and peer through the steel links of Mr. Morrison's fence to across the street to where Nonna's house is.

This was the long way to get here, but it's the safest because no one would be looking in that direction for me. But in this street, I have to be careful.

When the coast is clear, I dip my chin and blend into the shadows as I cross the street and walk into Nonna's backyard. Lifting the gnome with the red hat, I dig in the dirt with my fingers and find her spare key.

If I can avoid seeing her, I'll be happy because when my mom decided to step up to the plate and finally be a parent, she divulged Nonna knew who my father was this entire time. I'm fucking angry with the world.

Carefully climbing her back steps, I unlock the door,

and the moment I enter the kitchen, I'm instantly hit with the smell of lasagna. I've had many meals in this small kitchen, but now, I can only think about the lies these walls house.

I need to bounce before I lose my shit.

I avoid the loose floorboards I've memorized by heart and carefully open the door under the stairs. This is where Nonna keeps her Christmas decorations as well as old clothes she doesn't want to throw away.

This is also where I've hidden fifty thousand dollars—give or take. I also have stashed away jewelry and weapons, all for a rainy day.

Dropping to a squat, I run my fingers over the wooden floorboards and when I feel the familiar groove in one, I pry it open. I do the same to two others.

Reaching inside, I begin pulling out zip lock bags filled with cash. Like Darcie and her kittens, I know how many there are, but I don't plan on taking them all. Regardless of what Nonna did, I would never leave her dry as I know she will be the only one to look after June when I'm gone.

I snatch a floral pillowcase from the shelf to the left and begin stuffing it with the bags of cash. I search further into the floor, and when I feel the duffel bag, I yank it out. It's covered in cobwebs and a dark red stain which is blood.

Once I have everything, I replace the flooring and stand.

Turning, I see Darcie watching me from the doorway, eyes wide. I know she's wondering who the fuck she got into bed with. I'm not a good guy, and she now sees that.

I fucked older women to get what I wanted.

I lied to good, honest people to get what I wanted.

And I don't feel a shred of guilt for it.

It's a dog-eat-dog world and if Darcie wants to judge me, then she should see it all.

"Were you going to say goodbye?" Nonna's voice sounds behind Darcie, who spins, stunned.

"You're robbing an innocent, old lady?" she asks, horrified.

"Trust me, she is anything but innocent. *Ciao*, Nonna."

Darcie steps aside, looking back and forth between us, confused. But there is no confusion between Nonna and me —she knows I feel beyond betrayed for her lies.

"Your mother told me everything. I'm sorry—"

I shoulder the duffel and shove past her. "Save your apologies. That time has come and gone."

"It was for your own good. If you knew—"

"Yes, that's right. *If* I knew, but I didn't know because no one thought it was important to tell me the truth!"

"That's not true. Your father, he's not a good man."

"Looks like it wasn't just my looks I inherited from him then," I snap, hearing June's drunken sobs of how much I looked like *him* on repeat in my head.

I thought this was all bullshit, of course, because I thought I was just a product of a one-night stand my mom never got over.

But I was fucking wrong.

"I'll get this laundered and mailed back to you." I hold up the pillowcase and grab Darcie's forearm. "Let's go."

I'm surprised she doesn't fight me, but she must sense how close I am to losing my shit.

I haul her ass through the house, ignoring the pang of sentiment as I pass each room—this used to be my happy place. Now, it's just another disappointment.

"Where will you go?"

"Dunno," I reply, my heavy footsteps in concert with my heavy heart. "I'll send you a postcard."

Nonna has never taken my shit, and now is no exception as she races in front of me like an Italian ninja. "I did what I thought was right. I did it to protect you."

"You know what, I'm sick of hearing that shit. That excuse didn't stick with June, and it sure as shit doesn't stick with you. Goodbye, Nonna."

"Augustine," she sobs, interlacing her wrinkled hands.

Darcie freezes as it's the first time she's heard my name.

"Please don't leave like this. Stay. We will work something out. It's dangerous for you to be out there."

"Don't you get it?" I implore, my voice breaking as I look into her wise eyes. "It's dangerous for me everywhere! But most of all, it's dangerous for me in here." I point at my temple. "And in here." I point at my heart.

"No matter where I run to, I can never outrun myself."

Her lower lip trembles. "You don't want to know who he is?"

The moment of truth...the truth which has come eighteen years too late.

"No. He can rot in hell, for all I care. I'll see him there soon enough."

A tear falls down her cheek, breaking my resolve. But this is for the best. "*Ti amo,*" she whispers, but it's too late. If she really did love me, she would have told me the truth.

I don't bother with a reply and walk to the back door, heart in my throat because I'm a fucking bastard.

Darcie yanks her arm from my grip, but at this stage, I'm starting to think I'm better off alone. I would do anything to protect her, just how Nonna said about me, but I soon see that sometimes, some people don't need protection.

I leave through the back door without Darcie because if she chooses to stay, that's her choice.

I make my way back to the truck, jumping over fences

and cursing into the heavens. There's got to be more to life than this, right?

But the universe isn't talking to me tonight.

I light up a cigarette and lean against the hood, smoking it slowly. I should go, but I know Darcie is coming. She may not want to, but our bond runs too deep to turn away.

The moment I butt out the smoke with my boot, she appears breathless with a hole torn in her jeans. Boris doesn't like her, it seems.

I push off the hood, and we get into the truck. It starts with a roar, and we take off into the night.

The radio fills the silence until Darcie, with her face turned toward her window, whispers, "Nonna said she'll find good homes for the kittens."

Those motherfucking kittens.

CHAPTER TWENTY

Rev

I've left Darcie sleeping because honestly, I need to do this alone.

I left her a note and a gun on the bedside table, hinting my return, not that I think she'd care either way. The dynamics have shifted between us, and I think that's because she's finally seen the real me.

Darcie isn't a killer—her hand was forced by gruesome things done to her, and instead of being a fucking crybaby about it, she took matters into her own hands. That's what doers do—they do. But she wasn't born this way.

It's the classic case of nature versus nurture.

Me, however. The fact that I'm skulking through the Becketts' backyard like a thief in the night has me questioning just who *I* am.

I know the blueprint of this place because I fucked Carson's mom. She was careless and underestimated me and my need to destroy everything I touch. This anger eating away inside me fuels every step I take, and all I can think about is making everyone pay.

Darcie is safe, and that's all I care about.

She didn't question how I knew the mansion on the lake would be vacant when I broke in. She also didn't flinch when I punched in the alarm code because she knew, she knew what I did, or rather, *whom* I did to get intel on the place.

I stole Ms. Klein's antique ring from her finger when she was sleeping. After I fucked her, of course. When Darcie pulled back the Egyptian cotton sheets and rested her head against the pristine white pillows, I couldn't help but feel a sliver of disgust when I remembered fucking Ms. Klein against the headboard.

Darcie was lying in my filth—in more ways than one.

The Kleins are holidaying in Spain, just how they always do at this time of year. I know this because that's what every smart predator does—they watch and learn the movements of their prey. And that's how I know how to break into the Beckett fort without detection.

The DA's home is the biggest on the block—I wonder if the size is making up for something he's lacking in his pants.

The white house exudes wealth and importance to those who drive by. But it's all for show because his wife wouldn't be seeking out the consorts of a high school student if she were a pillar of happiness.

But that's the thing about these rich folk; the more they have, the more they want and before long, everything loses its shine, and they are constantly chasing a new high, something to bring excitement into their structured lives.

Money doesn't buy happiness. It does, however, help you survive, which is what I plan on doing as I slip on my hood and punch the code into the panel on the garage door.

Everything runs on codes in the Beckett household, and I know them all, thanks to finding them written down in Theresa Beckett's notebook. I committed them to memory as I knew they'd come in handy one day.

The beep and green light on the panel let me know it's showtime as the garage door rolls open. I enter casually and curl my lip when I see the DA's numerous sports cars parked in the enormous garage. I've never seen Walter drive any of these, so it's all for show—just another thing to showcase his wealth and importance to his country club friends.

I fucking hate this guy.

He goes around town, thinking he's better than anyone else, but behind that dazzling smile, I know lies a cunning bastard. Everyone is fooled by his bullshit, but not me, which is why I'm here. I know he is guarding secrets; skeletons in the closet, so to speak.

Every founding family like this does.

I plan on discovering those secrets and exposing this family for the lying, cheating assholes that they are. Walter has no doubt cleaned up his son's indiscretions in the past because I have a feeling what Carson did to Darcie wasn't the first time.

It was about power because he'd felt powerless his whole life, oppressed under the shadow of his "perfect" father. He has been forced to live the charade as the impeccable son of the DA who can do no wrong, but Carson and his father are far from perfect, and it's time I expose them.

Unable to help myself, I reach into my pocket for the stolen truck keys and key each car as I walk by them, whistling under my breath. If I wasn't trying to be inconspicuous, I would smash each window before setting the cars on fire, but maybe another day.

I open the door, which leads into the long hallway.

Peering from left to right, I see the coast is clear, so I mute my footsteps as I make my way to Walter's office. I can't help but admire the architecture of the place. It's antiquated, mixed with modern, and if this was anyone else's house, I would think it's pretty cool.

The grand marble staircase is carpeted in red. The paintings on the high walls are worth a small fortune.

Walter may be the world's biggest fuckstick, but he has good taste in art.

I continue skulking through the house, my mind racing because how could such beauty breed such hate? Carson is a bully, a psychopath, and a rapist—it doesn't make sense that someone of his standing has turned out so fucked up, right?

Wrong.

It's because of that that he believes he's untouchable.

When I get to the top of the staircase, I tip my chin and look at the stained-glass dome over me. The full moon illuminates the intricate patterns, which can be interpreted as anything, dependent on the beholder. To me, all I can focus on is the red.

Enough with the sightseeing; it's time to uncover the dirty little secrets which will destroy this family before Darcie destroys Carson—in every sense of the word.

It's not enough that we kidnap his ass and make him pay for what he did. I want the entire Beckett family to suffer and be looked at the way I have been looked at my entire life. I want them to know what it feels like to be an outsider.

I hear Carson's arrogant voice behind his bedroom door. Curiosity gets the better of me and I tiptoe toward his room. I hear him sweet talking some poor girl, assuring her he won't show the pictures to his friends.

But I know she's just next in line.

Unable to stomach his lies a second longer, I make my way toward Walter's office and when I turn the handle, sigh in relief when the door opens. I close the door softly behind me as I enter.

The room is filled with awards for Walter's accomplishments. He even framed a newspaper article where he helped put away the town's first serial killer—good times.

I take a seat in his brown leather chair and peer around the room, wondering what Walter sees. All I see is the lair of a pretentious asshole. I reach for a silver frame on his desk. It's of the Beckett family, smiling happily in front of their lake house.

I toss the frame into the trash can under the desk, envy suddenly hitting me because I wonder how I would have turned out if I were in Carson's shoes.

The desk drawers are locked, no surprise, so I jimmy them open with the silver letter opener. When the top one pops open, I hunt through it, not sure what I'm looking for. I'll know what when I find it, however.

Nothing excites me until I open the bottom drawer and a small silver key catches my eye. I look between it and the tall filing cabinet in the corner of the room.

Bingo.

Grabbing the key, I make my way to the filing cabinet, and the key is a perfect fit. The top drawer is filled with more garbage, and anger hits me because I'm missing something. This is Walter's private space, but it appears too clean-cut like the real dirt is hidden where no one would ever look.

Peering around the room, I take my time to examine every single thing. The books are stacked alphabetically; the paintings hung at precise angles. Nothing is out of place, which I know means it's done entirely for show.

I just need to think like a narcissistic asshole.

Tapping my chin, I look at the small painting above the fireplace. It's of a foxhound with a dead duck hanging limply in his jaws. Why can't I stop looking at it?

Turning my cheek to the right, I arch my neck to view the painting from a different angle, and when I see it's not flush with the wall, I realize I've been looking in all the wrong places.

A man like Walter Beckett doesn't stow his secrets away in a predictable place such as a filing cabinet. I march through the office and carefully remove the painting from the wall, revealing a small silver safe.

There's an old-school dial on it where only the owner would know the combination to open it. But Walter is predictable, and when I turn the dial a little to the left, and then the right, before turning it back to the center, I smile because this asshole is about to go down.

The combination is Carson's birthday. Why do I know when that douchebag's birthday is? Because every year, the football team holds a bonfire in his honor, which every loser is dying to get an invite to—suffice to say, I would rather set myself on fire than attend.

The safe clicks open, and without delay, I open the door.

There's some jewelry inside, a revolver, and a small metal box. I grab the box and open it, elated when I see folded paperwork inside. Opening the first page, I read over a letter from the chief judge pardoning Carson from sexual assault charges against a minor.

I read over his crimes and shake my head. If this went to court, Carson would have done some serious time. Not to mention, tarnished the precious Beckett name.

Each piece of paperwork I pull out is like the ones before it, all pardons from important people, making Carson's rap sheet disappear. No wonder he has a godlike complex; this fucker has never had to deal with any repercussions of his actions.

But what he did to Darcie, that's something which he *will* be held accountable for.

I stuff the documents into my pocket as it's the evidence I need to soil the squeaky-clean reputation of the Beckett family.

However, an aged piece of paper seems out of place with the others, so automatically, I unfold it and read over the words which shatter my fucking world beyond repair.

Time stands still…

I read over the words once, twice, three times, hoping that by some miracle, what I'm reading is wrong. But it's not.

I've seen and experienced a lot in my lifetime. But this, this is unlike anything ever before. I just stare at the page, it trembling in my hands. Every emotion slams into me, and I suddenly can't breathe.

There must be some mistake because if what I read is true…then I am going to burn the entire Beckett kingdom to the ground.

Anger fuels my every thought…my every breath, and I know I need to bounce before I do something stupid.

Pocketing everything I need, I put everything else back the way I found it and leave this house as quietly as I entered.

When I jump into my truck, I work on autopilot and drive, but I know I'm seconds away from losing it. The wipers *swish…swish…swish*—a hypnotic rhythm which, with every sound, feels like it's flaying away at my flesh.

Life undresses me, and before long, all that's left will be a meat suit with a deadened beating heart.

How can life be so fucking cruel? How can I be kicked in the guts, over and over again? Is this my karma for all the bad shit I've done? I suppose I deserve it. But no, not this.

This can't be true because if it is…I don't want to exist.

Turning off the headlights, I push the accelerator to the

floor and let fate decide—live or die...die or live...it's all the same because if this is living, then I will happily embrace death because how am I meant to face tomorrow, knowing what I do?

The landscapes blurs around me as I drive faster, and before long, I can't see a thing, my vision distorted, and that's because I do what I haven't been able to do since I was a kid—I cry.

It feels foreign when those fat, heavy tears spill down my cheeks because nothing has affected me this way before. I often wondered if I was dead inside because nothing moved me, but it seems it takes the most fucked-up thing in the world to make me feel...something.

I really am fucked up in the head.

The truck careers into the night—destination? Who the fuck knows?

If I were to die right here, right now, I wonder who would mourn me. What would my headstone say?

Beloved son of June and...

Vomit rises, and I think I'm going to be sick.

But the sickness, the anger, it fuels this darkness inside me which swirls and dances to the voices in my head that are telling me to kill them...kill them all. But as I close my eyes and lift my hands off the steering wheel, I know the only person I want to kill...is myself.

I don't want to exist in a world where my entire existence has been a lie. I don't want to face another day knowing that he hated me as much as I hated him. But the difference is, he knew who I was, but I was never privy to the fact.

Everyone knew who I was...but me.

A scream tears from my throat, and blinding rage overtakes me. The tires pass over gravel as I know I've veered off the road. Now would be the time to take the wheel if I want to live. Dying would be easy…it's the living part that hurts with every single breath I take.

This hard exterior was erected because I was sick of being hurt, that is until I met Darcie. She was able to penetrate my walls and that shows me I'm not dead inside. If I were to end it now, I would never see her ever again and that's the tomorrow I know I don't want to live.

Opening my eyes, I see I'm about five seconds away from slamming into a tree.

The choice is mine. For the first time in my life, I choose what I want my fate to be.

The choice is simple—I choose her.

Always.

Grabbing the wheel, I frantically turn it and tap the brakes, not to lock them up. The truck slows down before I brake, mere meters from a steep embankment.

With my heart in my throat, I open the door and fall from the truck and begin to pace the desolate road like a madman. With my hands interlaced atop my head, I tip my face into the heavens and scream at the stars.

"Why?" I bellow into the empty sky. "Motherfucker, why? How could you!"

I don't know who I'm speaking about right now because every person involved is to blame.

Reaching for a fallen branch on the ground, I commence hitting the truck with all my might. Each indent is a reflection to the thousand lashes against my heart. It doesn't make me feel any better, but when I'm breathless and soaked with perspiration, do I stop.

"Fuck!" I scream over and over again.

But this breakdown is only the start of things to come because I need to get back.

It's kissing dawn when I return to Darcie, knowing that things are about to get messy.

Opening the door, I smell coffee brewing, so I enter the kitchen. When she sees me, she straightens from her position as she's leaning on the bench, reading from a recipe book.

Her eyes narrow. She knows something is wrong.

"Did you get what you needed?" she asks as the note told her I was going to Carson's.

I nod, pouring myself a cup of coffee.

She waits for me to continue, but I can't. For the first time in my life, I'm scared, scared of disappointing her as I begin wrestling with my convictions.

Turning my back, I peer at my reflection in the splash back wall. I look like shit. I've lost count of which bruises and cuts are from when and where—they all mix into one huge mess.

"So we're all set? Carson is going to die?"

On any other day, I would say hell to the fuck yes, but not today and that's because of what sits in my back pocket like manacles around my heart.

"Rev? What the fuck is going on?"

I wish I could answer her, but I can't. I should want to kill them all, but I don't...and what the fuck does that say about me?

"Tomorrow, we kill Carson and anyone who stands in our way, right?"

Here it is—the moment of truth.

Deep down, I think I always wanted to know who he was because he is half of who I am. I thought that maybe if I knew who my father was, I was to better understand who *I* was.

But now that I know, I realize I was better off never

knowing.

"No," I reply, bracing for the consequences.

"What do you mean, no?"

"No, we can't kill Carson. We'll find another way."

Silence...

I should embrace it as I know it won't last for long.

But the voices inside my head will never be silenced because all I hear on repeat are the words which I read in that document. Unveiling my filthy bloodline.

My name is Augustine Blackwood...and Walter Beckett is my biological father.

Carson is my brother, and we are just two sick fucks from opposite sides of the tracks.

A coffee cup shatters into the splash back in front of me, shards sideswiping my cheek as I see Darcie's unfaltering expression staring back at me.

Let the games begin...

Darcie

Rev turns around slowly and stares into my face. His eyes are no longer those beautiful amber jewels but black holes, like I've just tested the patience of the reaper.

"I don't know what your problem is, Rev, but we are fucking killing Carson like a pig on a spit, and we are going to do it now!" I smash my palms on the counter, knowing full well I just triggered a beast when I threw that cup, strategically missing his head.

He swipes crap off the bench with one arm and hikes over it, sending crockery and utensils crashing to the marble floor, and lands flush with my body. His large hands seize me by the neck, and I see his teeth mash together as he looks down and presses his nose hard against mine.

Spit leaves his mouth as he says, "Simmer down, buttercup. Carson is...my fucking brother." It's a guttural sound that emanates from his throat and into my face.

Time stops, and we are taken to an alternate world with this revelation. I wish he was joking, but I can see that he's not. It's just another fucked-up thing the universe has decided to throw our way.

He begins to laugh like he's lost his mind, rolling his eyes back into his head and gripping the sides of my neck tighter and tighter, offering me no room to breathe. But he literally just took my breath away with the words he spoke.

I begin to panic because something comes over Rev, and I can't help but think...we hurt the ones we love.

I slam my knee into his crotch, feeling his grip release and his body buckle down. I cough hard, catching air, and bolt through the house and down the hallway.

His heavy footsteps follow as he bangs the walls with side punches yelling, "Get the fuck back here!"

"You're a fucking psycho. Just like the rest! I knew I couldn't trust you!" I scream back as there is no way I'm stopping.

I enter a side door that leads to an open empty garage. Searching frantically, I grab an axe off the wall, but it's so damn heavy, I drop it and grab a hammer instead. Rev bashes the door open, and it almost bounces off the hinges and returns back at him as his fist punches a hole through it.

I stand forthright with my back to a carpenter's bench, hammer hidden behind my back.

"Calm the fuck down, Darcie," he warns, rubbing his splintered fist and storming toward me.

With one strike, I swing my arm out from behind my back, hammer in hand, and it just misses his beautiful face as it catches air when his reflexes save him from the blow. Rev grabs the hammer off me and hurls it at the roller door, causing a huge clamor.

Without hesitation, he spins me around and presses my face into the wooden workbench, his other hand gripping my waist. I'm breathing hard and can smell the sweet timber in my lungs.

I gasp and scream as he bends over my body and his warmth and weight talks to other parts of me—parts that want him and desire him so badly. He feels it too and presses himself against my ass, showing me just how this situation is affecting him too.

But no fucking way am I surrendering just because he has a pretty face.

I grab a metal torch and smack it into the side of his kneecap.

"Fuck!" He grunts and rips the torch from my hand.

"If he's your filthy brother, then I want nothing to do with you!" I scream, lying with every fiber in my body.

He spins me back to face him and kisses me hard, forcing his tongue into my mouth. But not today.

I grab a handful of nails from the toolbox beside me, ready to make him choke on them. They puncture my hand, and warm blood oozes out and runs down my wrist. I'm shaking as I kiss him back, violently searching my mind for what my next move is.

Fuck or flight?

Fuck or fight?

Rev grabs my wrist and shakes all the nails out of it; they rain down on the concrete floor.

Before I can headbutt him, he has a rope looped around my neck and circles it one more time. The scratchy nylon pricks my skin.

"You've got to be fucking joking!" I laugh at him in disbelief, both hands reaching up to loosen the rope, but failing.

"If you're going to behave like an untrained puppy, I'm going to treat you like one," he calmly replies and yanks me to my knees, holding the rope like a dog lead. "Get inside."

He begins dragging me across the concrete floor like a reluctant pet.

Hell to the fuck no.

When I spot a hunting knife on the lower shelf of the bench, I grab it. "Hey, Rev," I singsong, and when he turns, I leap up and slam the knife into his shoulder.

A wounded yell leaves him and suddenly, I feel a little bad, but I need to move. I run toward the door, but only have so much slack on the rope. I'm yanked backward against his body.

"Don't be trying this shit on me." He rips the knife from his shoulder and holds it against my neck. "Let's discuss this like adults, shall we?" he suggests like I'm an unruly preteen.

He marches me inside and into the bathroom, where he hits the shower on cold. He yanks my head underneath. "Time to cool off," he says as my breath hitches at the icy cold water drowning my head.

"Fuck YOU!" I gurgle under the water.

"Well, if you insist," he jibes back at me, holding the rope firmly.

"Fuck you, Rev. You piece of shit," I scream under the water, trying to get free.

"I'm *your* piece of shit, baby," he says, laughing at my drowned head. "Had enough yet?" He's clearly getting bored.

"No!" I holler as my head hangs upside down.

"No?" He knocks the jet function on the showerhead. It hits me like a cold knife to the back of my head and I struggle to shake myself out of it. "Let's discuss this calmly!" he yells over the loud rushing water.

I hang limp and give up. I'm so done with all of this. I just need to escape and go find Carson. I pull the crying card, which I know Rev won't handle. He turns off the shower, and it relents, leaving me dripping cold.

I drop to my knees on the tiled floor, feeling the rope rest down beside me.

"You'd think they'd have heated flooring in this house," I say as he throws a towel at my head.

I catch it and shiver inside it as I peer up at him and see all the blood covering his torso from the knife wound in his shoulder.

"You're such a nightmare, Darcie," he says, shaking his head at me.

"And you're a fucking Beckett," I reply, just to test him one more time.

"Touché."

When his shoulders sag, I know I've won this war—for now.

CHAPTER TWENTY ONE

Rev

I feel like a piñata at a ten-year-old's birthday.

Every part of me has been beaten, broken, and bruised. You'd think that would be enough for me to hang up my hat and reminiscence on the good ole days. But nope, here I am rocking a fucking hair net as Darcie and I attempt to remain inconspicuous.

This idea is probably one of my worst, but I am fresh out of fucks. Whatever happens, I'll deal because we are so close—I can taste it.

Darcie still hates me, but that's okay. It's probably better that way. After our cage match, we kept to our corners, only speaking when we had to. I told her killing Carson was off the table, and she replied by flipping me the bird.

We have reached an impasse, and this time, neither of us will back down.

She wants Carson dead.

I don't.

Why the fuck Walter has my birth certificate is another insignificant question that won't fuck off. Was he holding it as a reminder of things not to do when teaching his prodigal son the ways of the world? Was I the blueprint for him to learn from?

Whatever the reason, Walter can fuck off as far as I'm concerned. He knew. Carson doesn't. Well, I don't think he does, which is another reason I need to keep them alive.

I can't be torturing and killing the people who hold the answers to the questions I so desperately seek.

I understand why Darcie is pissed, but this time, there is no compromise. She does it my way. Or, let the better man win. And when I peer over at her, eyeballing the fuck out of me, I don't like my odds.

We are here in the Beckett home under the guise that we're just two teens who want to earn an extra buck working this grand affair. The staff uniforms we wear help us blend in. We stole them from the two unfortunate morons who should have listened to their parents and not talk to strangers.

They are tied up in the forest. But I'm not a total bastard and made sure to throw a blanket over their heads to keep them warm. And who said chivalry is dead?

Security is relaxed, and I think that's because they don't think I would be so stupid and maim Walter publicly, but that's exactly what I plan on doing.

The skeleton in his closet is me. What a fucking plot twist.

We're being sent in every direction, helping to prepare for the proceedings which allows me to move around freely. But we still must be careful because of Carson. I've not seen the fucker yet. No doubt he's looking at himself in the mirror, kissing his biceps and making sure every strand of hair is brushed immaculately.

I still can't believe he's my brother. I also can't believe I fucked my stepmom.

Some asshole shoves some red napkins which are shaped like origami ducks into our hands and orders Darcie and I into the ballroom to help with the preparations. She doesn't look at me and storms off.

Well, this is going just swimmingly. At this rate, I think

Carson is safe as I'm pretty sure it's my head Darcie wants and not Carson's.

We work on opposite ends of the room, but I never let my guard down. I keep my eyes on my surroundings and Darcie because there's no room for error. And when I hear a voice I never thought I'd hear so soon again, it just confirms that we have to be on our A game.

"Did you see the rack on her?" Carson says, whistling.

"How could I miss them?" replies motherfucking—I piss my pants—Blake.

This is bad. Very bad.

Darcie turns over her shoulder, meeting my eyes. It seems only in the face of danger does she not want to rip out my spleen.

I nod discreetly, hinting we're to bounce out the doors which lead into the gardens.

She makes a beeline for them, but not before eyeing the ice statue of a cherub playing a harp. No doubt she is contemplating breaking off his chubby little arm and shoving it up Carson's ass. She's already owned Blake's ass when she went all Shakespeare on his backside.

I wonder what alpha boy Carson would think if he saw the words crybaby on his BFF's butt cheeks.

A chuckle escapes me because that shit is fucking funny.

We manage to make it outside undetected. "That was too fucking close," I say under my breath as some little old lady in a peacock feathered hat passes us by.

"Why is Blake here? This is bad. He has no doubt told the police about what we did," Darcie says, peering over my shoulder. "No doubt your beloved *papa* made sure he came out of this looking the victim."

"Enough with the dad jokes," I warn because regardless

of his relation to me, it doesn't mean I like the guy. "We need another plan."

"You think?" she taunts, rolling her eyes.

Oh, fuck her and that smart fucking mouth.

Gripping her by the throat, I walk her backward and slam her back into the brick wall. We're shrouded by a huge oak tree, but getting caught seems less painful than dealing with the wrath of Little Miss Sunshine.

"If you've got a better idea, then I'm all ears." I don't loosen my grip on her throat, and my dick stirs when she swallows deeply under my rough grip.

"We could just, I dunno...kill Carson?" she suggests, eyeing me something wicked. "Instead of this James Bond shit."

"James Bond kicks ass, FYI. And no, we can't."

"I fucking hat—" I don't let her finish and eat her words as I smash my mouth over hers.

She may hate me, but she sure as shit likes the way I kiss. And kiss, we do.

I press my chest to hers, relishing in the trouncing of her heart against mine. I live for this shit. I live for my little firecracker, who will be the death of me.

As I slip my tongue into her mouth, she moans, and just when I think we're friends again, she bites down on it—hard.

My bad for thinking she'd forgiven me. She releases me, and I know better than to go back for more.

"You gave up that right when turned into a traitorous asshole." She playfully slaps my shoulder, while I flinch. "How's the shoulder?"

"Just peachy...considering you jammed a fucking knife into it."

She giggles, and it's akin to the Satan's doorbell, welcoming me into hell.

Playtime is over, however, when I hear Walter Beckett talking to Coach Anderson.

We sink low, using the tree as our barricade as we watch the guest of honor talking in secret with Coach Anderson. I look at him, really look at him for the first time because I see him through different eyes. I can't believe he's my dad—this fucking chump who wears beige chinos and a polo is my father.

What the fuck was June thinking? And better yet, what was Walter thinking about having sex with my mom? He would never be caught dead fucking someone like her—I mean, what would his country club friends think?

I guess that's why he kept me a secret. He knew I existed. The fact that he was in possession of my birth certificate is proof of that.

I have so many questions, which is why I need them alive.

Carson and Blake are too busy gossiping like little bitches to see the coach, but when they do, something changes in them both. I watch closely and examine the way Carson's cocky demeanor diminishes. He grows almost nervous as he fiddles with his blue tie.

I can't hear what is being said, but Carson looks uncomfortable when the coach wraps his arm around his shoulders, drawing him into his side.

"You don't think the coach is taking his leadership a little too seriously, do you?" Darcie asks, as she too can see what I can.

I don't reply because, honestly, I don't know. But it would explain a lot.

Some abuse victims become the abusers to gain back

their power, and we all know what a megalomaniac Carson is.

This gets more fucked up by the second, but when the guests start arriving, I know the party has just begun.

The house is full of anyone of importance. It's perfect.

Darcie isn't aware of my plan, just yet, and that's because I wasn't sure if we'd be able to pull it off. But remember when I said money talks? Well, money talks to a computer geek who has just became my new best friend.

We've ditched the staff uniforms and changed into the outfits we packed in the duffel we hid away in the green house. It is a black-tie event, after all. So we've adhered to the dress code. I have on black suit pants and a crisp white shirt. I'm wearing suspenders and a black bow tie.

Black Chucks complete my outfit.

Very dashing, indeed.

Darcie wears a red silk strapless ball gown. Seem appropriate because I know come nightfall, she's going to burn this kingdom to the ground. The dress is ruffled and long at the back and short at the front, showcasing her shoes which are black combat boots.

It reminds me of prom. That seems like a lifetime ago, but that was the night that kick-started this shit show, so it seems appropriate she goes back in time.

Her hair frames her beautiful face and regardless of the fact that she wants me dead, I still love her with every breath I take.

We look like every other jackass here, but we still need to keep to the shadows because no matter how badly I want to watch the fall of the Beckett empire, there's something more important—and that's giving Darcie the vengeance she deserves.

What I have planned is just a decoy because the real prize is Carson.

The guests are ushered into the ballroom like good little sheep and talk amongst themselves, sipping their French champagne. The sound of a microphone tapping kills the chatter, and everyone sets their sights on the small stage erected especially for tonight.

It's Judge Peterson, ready to publicly jerk off Walter. "Ladies and gentlemen and Bobby Turlington," he says with a laugh as he looks at the hotshot councilman.

The crowd erupts into laughter while I try not to gag. These people are fucking lame.

"Thank you for coming tonight. We honor a great man. A man who has done everything in his power to protect this town."

I snort while Darcie elbows me in the ribs to can it.

"Put your hands together in welcoming my friend, Walter Beckett!"

Walter, Theresa, and Carson take the stage, appearing coy and thankful for such an introduction. The sight only sets my plan into motion.

I didn't have a plan, per se. But I suppose this was always my plan B. I always knew I would go down for the shit I'd done. But Darcie, no fucking way. I want her to live a normal, happy life and she can't do that with me in it.

We are toxic for one another, and it's time I did something right for once.

"Move," I say to her under my breath.

She looks at me, eyes wide when I gesture she's to walk toward the stage. But she complies because she trusts me.

She shouldn't.

"I have no words, no words to express my gratitude. This town has been in my blood since I was born…"

Blah fucking blah… Walter continues his dribble as Darcie and I get closer to the stage.

No one is paying attention to us, too enamored by the DA and his cookie-cutter family—a family of which I could have been a part of. I wonder how I would have turned out if I had.

I use patrons as shields to hide us from the view of security who suck at their job, but like I said, no one would suspect a public attack from two wanted fugitives, especially at a party where anyone of importance is in attendance.

Which is exactly the reason I reach for the gun Darcie has hidden in her handbag and shove it into her back.

"What the fuck, Rev?" she whispers when she feels the piece in the small of her back.

"Sorry, baby, but this never ended with us riding off together into the sunset."

It takes her a second, but she soon understands what I have planned. "This is the reason you didn't tell me what was going on because you knew I'd tell you what a fucking stupid idea it is. Don't be a martyr!"

But it's too late. My mind is made up.

"Hate me all you want, but hate me outside a prison cell because I promised to protect you and this is the only way how."

"I owe everything to my family. To my wife. To my son—"

And just like that, the lights go out, and the visions inside my head become real life.

I shove a protesting Darcie up the three steps that lead onto the stage and before Carson knows what's happening, I have my gun, which I remove from the small of my back, pressed to his temple.

"Hello, buttercup. Don't you look dashing, playing the part of the perfect son when we all know you're far from perfect, you motherfucking fuck."

The lights come back on, and when they do, the crowd's panic is silenced when they see two new members have joined the Beckett family.

Security runs for the stage, guns raised, but I simply shove the gun deeper into Carson's temple.

"Stand down!" Walter screams, waving his hands at them to stop in their tracks.

They do as ordered, like the good little dogs that they are.

I wink at Theresa. "Hello, darling. Miss me?"

She blanches, tugging at the string of pearls around her neck.

"Oh, peaches, don't act coy. I know you blush that pretty pink all over." I lick my lips with intent, and Walter reads it for what it is.

Theresa bursts into hysterical sobs. The perfect wife act has been ruined.

When Darcie asked why I wouldn't kill Walter and Carson, the answer is, death is easy, living with what I'm about to deliver is far more of a punishment than death.

The Becketts pride themselves on their status, on being better than everyone else, so I'm going to show them what it's like being an outsider; just like I've been my entire life, thanks to Daddy dearest.

"Son, let him go. We can talk about it."

He could have used any other phrase, but son? Fuck him. That is just another blow.

"The time for talking has come and gone," I reply, taking my gun off Darcie and aiming it at Walter.

I have both guns trained on the Beckett men—my brother and father.

"Do you want to confess your sins to the good people?" I ask Carson, who suddenly pales.

"You're fucking crazy! Shoot him!" he bellows at the security flanking the stage. But they don't have a clear shot.

"No!" Walter screams, and I know the men will listen to him.

He knows I'm not bluffing. "Augustine, we'll work something out. Now, please put the gun down."

"How about no? Something your wife clearly doesn't know how to say."

Theresa howls while I grin.

"You're angry. I can see that. Let me help you."

"What gave it away?" I quip, but the question is rhetorical as I pistol-whip Carson. "I don't want your help, fuck you very much."

"Please, don't hurt him. Take me instead." He pats his chest, like a hero, swooping in to save the day.

But he's missed the memo.

"Don't you get it?" I question, rolling my eyes theatrically. "Hurting him hurts you. Win-win."

"What did I ever do to you?" Carson has the gall to ask.

Darcie is about to slap him, but God strike me down, she can't. She needs to look like the victim for this to work.

So swallowing my disgust, I slap her cheek—hard, so hard she stumbles back, cradling her reddening cheek.

"Oh, that poor girl," someone in the crowd says. "She was brainwashed."

"He held her against her will."

"He made her do it."

"Is it Stockholm syndrome?"

These are all the mutterings I hear amongst the crowd. Darcie hears them too and shakes her head. She pleads I stop this, but she knows I'll shoot her in the kneecap if she takes another step.

So she stays put—for now.

"You did nothing to me other than being an annoying fuckass," I reply with a shrug. "But what you did to others —" And I whistle. "The worse thing, however, is what your *father* did."

The interest of the crowd is piqued because, who doesn't love a scandal?

I don't have time to dally, so I nod at Gunter, the AV nerd I paid one thousand dollars to, to fuck shit up. And it's time to fuck shit up to biblical proportions.

Behind me, the screen flashes with the first piece of incriminating evidence I found in Walter's office. The guests read it, and it takes a minute, but when they read over the crimes Carson committed and was never held accountable for, they soon understand where this is headed.

Page after page flashes before them as I air the DA's dirty laundry.

"Eileen's son is in jail for that crime, but it was Carson all along? And the DA knew?" I hear someone utter in disgust.

Walter gasps, but that soon turns to horror when he realizes I found what else was hidden away in his secret stash.

"Hello...Daddy." I smirk because as far as family reunions go, this is fucking stellar.

The guests' adoration turns to disgust when it's revealed what a dirty player Walter Beckett truly is. The hometown hero and his son are seen for the vile bastards that they are.

Not only have I shamed the Becketts, but half the town's judges, councilmen, and whoever else had a hand in protecting a sociopath.

My job here is done.

"I would love to stay and chat, but I've got places to be. Move, golden boy."

Carson's gaze is rooted on his father, pleading he help him, but he is shit out of luck.

Walter appears stunned he's been outplayed by someone like me. But little does he know, he made this monster. "You follow me, and I swear to fuck, I will kill him. You owe me."

Walter stands arrogantly, never wavering, because I know this isn't the end...this is just the beginning as Carson suddenly grows a pair and elbows me in the stomach, catching me unawares.

He wrestles me for the gun, while the other I have trained on Darcie, warning her if she moves, I'll shoot her. There's no way this will be for nothing. If she so much as hints that she's a willing participant, then she's going to go down with me.

But not on my watch.

Carson and I wrestle with the gun, and I hate to admit the asshole has the upper hand, thanks to me being stabbed, beaten, and hit in the knee with a torch, but there's no way this ends with Carson being the hero.

We fight desperately, and the hysteria of the crowd grows. I know I have seconds to overpower him before security shoots up this stage. Carson reads my injuries, and when he punches me in the shoulder, I loosen my grip on the gun but don't let go.

However, I sag on impact, which results in Carson's finger pulling the trigger and firing blindly into the crowd. The crowd screams in absolute terror as their fancy attire is now showered in blood.

"Holy mother of fuck," I pant, tears in my eyes. "I think I can see his wisdom teeth in that woman's hat."

The woman's trembling fingers search the brim of her hideous hat and when her hands come away red, she faints beside a headless Blake because Carson shot his fucking head off.

I can't take it any longer and holler in hysterics while Carson peers down at the oozing pile of meat that used to be his "bro."

"At least he's safe from Coach Anderson giving him a facial 'cause ya know...he has no face."

A single sob gets caught in Carson's throat as he looks at Blake—or rather, what's left of him.

"Killer aim."

"It was an accident!" he screams, shaking his head.

At least he has a head to shake...

Party time is over, however, when bullets begin zipping around the room. I've created mayhem and panic, and I've also just pinned a murder on Carson.

Let's see his daddy try to bail him out this time.

This is perfect. The list of crimes keeps growing, and I don't even have to try. Go me.

I grip Darcie by the crease of the elbow, and she struggles, which merely reinforces my whole kidnapping ploy. The crowd runs for cover, which inhibits a clear shot for security. I lead my victims out the back door by gunpoint to the garage, where I head for the hotted-up truck.

Carson appears to be in shock, but just for good measure, I shove him into the back seat and cuff him to the seat.

"Do you have any idea what you've done?" Darcie screams, ready to rip out my throat.

But I ignore her and tap the front leather seat with the gun. "Get in."

Darcie folds her arms across her chest in defiance. "Fuck you, Rev. Fuck you and your self-sacrifice bullshit!"

"Baby..." I coo, stepping close.

I wrap my arms around her, and before she has a chance to fight, I shove her arms behind her and snap on a pair of handcuffs of her own and toss her into the car. I buckle her in. She tries to bite my face.

Carson is sobbing in the back seat. The sound is music to my ears. I aimed to destroy the Beckett empire—what a way to start.

I speed out of the garage, leaving the carnage behind with a smile. When I pull onto the road, I'm surprised a SWAT team isn't waiting for us. But I know they won't be far behind, which is why we need a plan.

Darcie isn't talking to me right now, so I peer at Carson in the back seat, sniveling. I can't help but laugh. "Oh, stop being such a whiny little bitch. You know, for a murderer, I expected a little more balls."

"It was an accident!" he screams, teeth bared. "I didn't mean it."

"Shame that, because killing Blake is the best thing you've ever done. You've got one up on me."

Carson sniffs, and his tears are soon replaced with the

asshole we've come to love. "What are you talking about? You killed Buckets! You both did!"

That comment finally snaps Darcie from her vow of silence. "He's not dead," she states firmly. "He may be missing a hand, but he's fine."

"No, he's not fine! I went to his house, and his grandma told me what you two did. What did you think would happen? You shoved his hand down a garbage disposal! There's no coming back from that."

I peer at him in the rearview mirror, expecting to see his deceit, but when I see he's actually telling the truth for once, I know we're screwed. I then wonder about Foss.

"She's got to go," Darcie says to me, her guilt clear when she reads my thoughts.

Killing little old ladies isn't our modus operandi, but she's a witness who can fuck this entire thing up for us. She will identify me *and* Darcie, which throws out my whole plan that Darcie was an unwilling participant in all of this.

Fuck!

Seems like our location chose itself as I pull a U turn and head for Buckets's family farm.

The truck is quiet as Carson has finally shut up with his sniveling. He's now no doubt planning ways on fucking us up because he knows it's him or us.

My stolen cell rings, and although it's hardly the time for chitchat, I answer when I see it's June. I wonder how she got this number because I haven't spoken to her since I left her in the hospital.

She doesn't let me speak, however.

"What have you done?" she cries, her panic clear. "Walter told me you kidnapped Carson."

"I didn't realize you and the DA were on a first-name

basis," I quip, curling my lip in disgust. "But I guess I didn't realize a lot of things...like him being my fucking father!"

A gasp leaves Carson as he clearly missed the memo. I meet his eyes in the mirror and know the war has begun.

"Rev, please, don't hurt him. He's your brother."

"I know what he is, June. I don't need you to remind me. I'm not sure why *his* safety is your concern, however."

Silence...

This can't be good.

"Because...because you have an older brother...and that's Carson. I'm his m-mother. Both of you are my sons."

I slam on the brakes, stopping in the middle of the road, because what in the ever-living fuck did she say?

"Are you high?" I ask, and for the first time in my life, I hope she is.

"No. I've never been more sober in my life."

Funny, I wish I was wasted right now because fuck!

"When your father left, he took Carson with him. I begged that he left you both, but he always favored Carson."

"You're fucking lying. How is this possible? We're in the same class!"

"No, I'm not. This is the reason I never wanted to tell you any of this. And this is the reason I...lost my mind. Not only did Walter take my firstborn, but he took my heart and my sanity as well. You're in the same class because Carson had to repeat a year. His behavioral issues got too much."

I think back to all the times June sat in front of the window, staring vacantly out of it. I always thought she expected to see my father, but now I know she was waiting for Carson to return.

This can't be happening.

This asshole fucker cannot be my full brother.

Carson glares at me because he can't hear what June is

saying, but he can read my expression for what it is. We're cut from the same fucked-up cloth.

"Please, don't hurt him. Please do this not just for your father, but for me as well. If you kill him, I won't survive. Please."

And this day just keeps getting better.

I look at Darcie and sigh. I've fucking let her down in every possible way because I will do as June asks...but that doesn't mean I'm not going to beat Carson within an inch of his life for what he did.

I hang up, hearing enough.

Taking a deep breath, I continue driving, a million thoughts racing around my head.

My entire life, I just wanted to know who I was, but now that I've uncovered my family secrets, I wish I had remained in the dark.

When we arrive at Buckets's family farm, I kill the engine and unfasten Darcie's cuffs. The moment she's free, she slaps my cheek.

I was expecting worse. I seem to be collecting injuries like some weirdo collecting spoons.

There's no way Carson is getting the same treatment, however. He's remaining cuffed.

When I get out of the car, Darcie jumps out and stands in front of me, demanding answers. "I thought we were in this together? Talk to me!"

Talking is the last thing I want to do right now.

"Rev! Don't you dare shut me out. This is the end, right?"

Cupping her cheek, I draw us nose to nose, inhaling her into me. I want to consume her whole. "No, my little firecracker, this is just the beginning. Walter is my father. He's both our fathers. And June...she is Carson's mother too."

CHAPTER TWENTY TWO

Darcie

I can't quite comprehend what I'm hearing.

Rev is speaking words to me that sound like echoes underwater, and my brain is fighting to block it out.

I know that Rev won't let me take action against Carson for the hell he orchestrated on me. He is the reason I'm broken; he is the reason I'll never feel the same way when a man touches me again. He is the reason I hate myself, and every time I think about what they did to me, all I see is his lying face.

He watched it all happen and did nothing.

He came to me, pretending to protect me after instructing his goons to destroy every fiber in my body.

Carson is the most disgusting human on the planet, and I want him to pay for every second I endured with his crew.

I'm glad he shot off Blake's head. I only wish he'd shot himself too. Maybe I'll play Russian roulette with him and watch him cry and beg me to stop? Just like I did that night.

How can he and Rev share the same bloodline? It makes me sick to my stomach, and I feel bile creep up into my throat.

"What the fuck, Rev? No. No, this can't be happening!" I yell through tears, and the porch light comes on.

"Is that you, Harold?" a small voice says. Buckets's grandmother.

Rev looks at me, and I know what he's thinking—we cannot kill her. But killing her is the only way to save this man I love.

I know who I'd choose to keep in this world. She's had a good life. Maybe we'd be doing her a favor? Dying from whatever ailments old people end up with can't be fun.

"What then? You want to go to jail? I don't!" I cry, almost talking to myself as he just stares back at me.

He knows we've gone too far now. And I know it too, but once you start telling lies, deceiving people, and shooting heads off, you've gotta see it to the end.

"Let's just drive her to another state and leave her at a bus stop, then?" I offer as a compromise.

I picture her sitting at a dark bus stop, holding a bag, a stranger coming up and ripping it off her, hoping to steal cash. Her starving to death in the middle of nowhere and getting her eyes pecked out by crows. I swear it would be nicer to just shove a pillow on her face in her own bed.

Rev smirks back at me. "Let's find out where the one-armed fuckhole went and then decide, okay?"

We look over at the truck, and Carson is booting the back door with his legs and hollering like a banshee.

That's right, scream harder, you sick fuck. This isn't even a pinch on what I'm going to do to you later.

"We better bring fuckface inside, or he will rouse attention with all that shit he's doing in there."

Rev sighs and calmly walks to the car while I go to greet Granny. She's not smiling like she did the first time. Instead, she whips the wire door closed, trying to lock herself inside, and starts screaming for Harold.

I just kick that damn door in, and my foot slides through the lazy mesh easily. I tear it open to the handle and unsnap the useless door.

"No dinner tonight, Gran?" I ask, trying to pretend she's my bitch of an aunt so I can stay focused, but it's not working.

She's off, and I'm not sure where she went, but I doubt it's far. I race around the house to see who else is home but don't find anyone.

But I can hear moaning—like those zombies from Michael Jackson's "Thriller" music video. Not even my era, but I'm well versed in the '80s.

I start humming the tune and searching for the rogue zombie. I think I've lost all ability to feel afraid after everything I've been through. I just don't care anymore, and the numbness is great.

I pounce upstairs with my hands gripping the rickety wooden railing. The moaning is getting louder as I make my way down a musty corridor, and fucking hell, it stinks. I have to hold my nose, and for anyone who's ever said to me, it's okay, just breathe through your mouth—like that's gonna work; they're lying.

I swear, I can smell it through my mouth, and I'm gagging. It smells like dead pigs down a well.

I find the sound and push open the door. Buckets's father is balled up in the corner of a teenager's bedroom covered in posters, just rocking and moaning. This is a new one. He can't be freaking out over us, surely?

These farmers are brutal on a regular day. I would expect him to have a shotgun out and...holy fuck, look who has gone nigh-nighs.

Lying in the bed next to the rocking lunatic is Buckets. His mouth and eyes are wide open, and he's so dead that the flies are doing a sermon around his missing arm stump.

The moaning continues like a tribal ritual, and Granny bursts in, telling the boys dinner is ready. I've come to the conclusion that everyone has lost their minds, and nothing they say would stand up in court anyway.

What the fuck is Buckets doing in bed?

I really need Rev to see this.

"Go get Harold!" I yell at Granny.

"Is he coming?" she beams and suddenly looks delighted.

"Yes! Go set another spot!" I say, rushing past her to race back downstairs to find Rev.

Carson and Rev are outside having a fistfight in the dirt. Why the fuck are his cuffs off?

"Hey!" I yell and search around for a hose to cool down the dogs.

They keep fighting, and watching them, I can see how similar they actually are. One might be dark and the other blond, but they have almost the same movements and build.

Rev is a dirty fighter, though, and ends up pinning him to the ground in a headlock within his legs and punches him with all his might in the dick. Even I flinch at the sight.

"That's just about enough!" Granny bellows from behind me, clapping her hands in authority.

"Hey! Harold's waiting in the car for you!" I say, coaxing her over to the truck and then shoving her in like Hansel and Gretel did to that bone-collecting bitch when they pushed her in the oven.

I jam the door shut and lock her in from the outside, and figure she can stay there until we take her to the bus stop in Cartagena, Colombia.

But now, we must get Sleeping Beauty out of that bed and hide the body.

Bury it. And fast.

We drag Carson inside, handcuffs reinstated, which

Rev cleverly secured during the tussle. He puts up a fight, and I endure a few kicks and headbutts to the face along the way. I receive it with relish, however, as I just want to return the favor with every ounce of pain I'm feeling.

I know there are important matters to attend to with Buckets's body still in that bed, but I have some serious business to address with Carson. Rev knows it, and I'll be damned if he's going to stop me.

We throw Carson onto the living room floor, where then Rev grabs an old phone off the wall—circa '80s edition —and whacks him in the head with it. He then winds the curly cable tightly around his ankles.

He's one pissed-off piece of work.

"Go get Buckets," I say to Rev, never taking my eyes off Carson's squirming body.

Rev looks at me for a moment because he knows what I want. He eventually concedes, and I watch him disappear up the stairs.

The moment he's gone, I smile.

"You piece of shit." I'm shaking as my body responds to the reason I feel so much internal anguish.

He's right there, lying before me on the floor—the reason I can't find the heart in my chest anymore.

"This is bullshit, Darcie! I tried to help you. I tried to take you home, and now my best friend is dead. What the fuck?"

"Oh, boo-hoo, Carson," I quip, sitting on the floor next to him.

"Why? Why did you do this to me?" I question, gently brushing a lock of hair from his brow.

He's confused as I've gone from wanting to rip out his spleen to tending to him, but this is just another way to get into his head—just as he's gotten into mine.

"Do what? You're fucking insane!"

Lying piece of shit that he is, he's still trying to stick to a story that even a child would see through.

Coming to a stand, I peer down at him. "They took my body and raped me, over and over again. You told them to. *You* did. Which makes you the worst of them all," I say and kick him with everything I've got in the mouth.

He bleeds through the cracks in his teeth.

"Fuck you, princess," he snarls, spitting blood over me.

This is what I want, for him to show his true colors so I can smash that pretty face into ground beef.

"Oh no, darling, fuck *you*." I kick him again in the mouth, but this time, a tooth comes free, and he gags on it before vomiting it out on the floor.

It rolls along the flooring gracefully, and I smile. Carson looks at it in horror.

"It's just a tooth," I say, rolling my eyes. "Grow some balls. Buckets lost an arm. This is a gentle walk in the park." I pick up the tooth and examine it closely before throwing it across the room.

"Buckets is dead!" he screams, gurgling on the blood collecting in his throat.

"Yes, I know. He's dead in his bed," I singsong, suddenly laughing at my little rhyme.

I hear loud banging and look up to see Rev dragging a very large, very dead body down the stairs, banging the head on each step.

"Oh, look, here's your date now!" I exclaim with a smile.

Carson pivots to see Buckets's stiff body being steered by the ankles toward him. Rev lumps him over Carson's legs, which helps to pin him down.

"Aw, look at the sweet couple. I should make *you* choke on his dead dick for what you did to me!"

Carson looks at me in horror and madly wriggles to get himself free of the rancid corpse.

"Don't treat your friends like that," I mock, and Rev looks down at me, frowning.

He sees how I've lost my mind. But he doesn't judge. Another reason I love him.

"It's time to bounce." He's got a look on his face that says we have no time to waste on torture tactics.

I've always hated funerals. Ever since my parents had one. All my tears just stayed trapped in my brain. Cry, dammit. Everyone wants you to cry. Everyone stared at me because I didn't. Sometimes, the greatest pain can't be released. It stays trapped in your system to fester and rot away at your organs, turning itself into cancer and cysts. Turning itself into murderous tendencies.

Those boys had no idea who they were dealing with when they picked me. Carson had no idea. But now, he's going to find out.

We drag the assholes outside one at a time until my arms feel like they may break off. I suddenly have sympathy for Buckets losing his arm. Must've sucked dying like that. I do wonder what happened.

Maybe if we'd let Granny out, she could've called an ambulance. So really, it's her fault.

Who am I kidding? This is all on us.

"Dig," Rev says, pointing the borrowed shotgun at Carson's head. "Time to bury your BFF."

I love that in the face of something so fucked up, he's making jokes. It doesn't make me feel so messed up.

Carson struggles to his feet and attempts to dig into the

hard dirt with cuffs on his hands. "Fuck you," he mutters under his breath.

"Take 'em off," I say to Rev and take the shotgun off him to hold it on Carson while he removes the cuffs.

The moment he's free, he punches Rev in the face. The crunch is intense, and when blood begins to pour from his mouth, it's evident the punch was as brutal as it looked.

"Motherfucker!" I yell and spin around quickly, shooting the gun right through the windshield of the truck Granny is locked in.

Carson ducks down and puts his hands over his ears.

"I'll shoot all of you if I have to!" I warn and point the gun back at Carson.

Rev wipes his mouth with the back of his hand, it coming away with blood. "Well, look who grew a pair. You still hit like a little bitch, though."

Carson jumps to his feet, ready to rip off Rev's head, but I wave the shotgun in warning. He bares his teeth, and Rev bursts into laughter.

"My, my, what big teeth you have," Rev mocks, placing the back of his hand over his forehead, faking horror. "Although, I think you're missing one."

Rev turns to me and nods proudly. "That's my girl."

"You're both fucking crazy," Carson says, looking back and forth between us.

Rev deadpans him. "Thanks, Dr. Phil, but no one asked for your opinion. The lady told you to dig...so, mother-fucker, start digging."

Carson knows he's fucked.

He starts digging like a good boy, but my God, it feels like an eternity. If only Buckets could help. Although, with one arm, that would be a shit-fest too.

Rev whistles "Patience" by Guns N' Roses while I yawn because this is taking all fucking day.

By the time the grave is long enough and deep enough for a body, we decide to just roll the ole boy in there.

"Take a photo for his dad," I say to Rev. I hate myself. But everyone is entitled to a viewing.

Rev searches his pockets and comes up empty. He stares at me with his hands open, and we look back at the truck.

Fucking left the phone in the car with Mrs. Doubtfire. I throw the shotgun back at Rev and race over to the truck. Granny is shaking like a madwoman. Poor love, she's had a really shit time. I reach through the broken windshield, scraping my skin along the cut glass, and reach for the cell off the dash.

Immediately, I toss it in the dirt and stomp on it until it shatters.

Rev is talking to Carson, but I can't see what's going on. There's an argument, of course, but Carson suddenly falls to his knees and hangs his head.

"Just fucking shoot me!" he yells, arms out wide.

Rev is torn, and his teeth are mashed together, but tears build in his eyes.

I storm over, and this is it. It's time to show me where his loyalties lie. Honestly, he's done enough, and if he wants to spare Carson's life, then I will think about it. I understand in the span of a couple of days, he's just found out who his father and brother are.

So I wait... I give him a choice and will accept whatever that is.

And the choice he makes warms my dead heart.

"Get in," Rev orders, pointing toward the fresh grave

Buckets rests in. There's barely enough room, but it's possible if he lies on top.

Carson pales when he realizes Rev isn't playing. Family or not, he's going to...bury his brother alive.

I feel sick, but at the same time, I hate him with everything in my body. I think about Foss, Buckets, and Blake. How Carson was the puppet master. They could've killed me that night, and instead, he would be burying me.

I can't let this happen to another soul.

I just can't.

"No!" Carson screams, the fight in him never dying, and if I didn't hate his fucking face, I would admire his tenacity.

"He said get in!" I scream, shoving his large back with two hands, using as much force as I can. He hardly moves a muscle and turns to look at me.

"You asked why, darling...well, the answer is...why the fuck not?" he says, smirking, showing me his true colors.

Everyone wants answers to their questions, and most feel comforted when told the truth, but not me. He did this just because? Just because I was there? Just because I rejected him? Just because he could?

This suddenly makes everything so much worse. If there was a legit reason, I could attempt to process it. But there isn't.

He did it because he wanted to...and that's it. There is no light at the end of the tunnel. No epiphany other than Carson Beckett deserves to die.

I don't even have time to think before a whack rocks me to the core. One minute, Carson is standing, and the next, he's slumped onto the ground, thanks to the shovel Rev's holding—the shovel he just smacked across Carson's head.

"Do you want to say a few words?"

My mouth is hanging open because this was not the ending I expected.

Rev has chosen...and he chose me.

"Don't look so surprised, baby. It's always you."

I don't know what to say, so I stand on tippy-toes and press my mouth against Rev's, our kisses entwined in a blood-soaked union.

With one final kiss, Rev pulls away and uses his boot to kick Carson into the grave. He rolls onto Buckets's body, and I stand transfixed as Rev commences covering both boys with dirt.

It's over.

We did it.

I don't know how I thought I would feel, but I don't think something like this ever ends. Yes, the people who hurt me got their karma, but this doesn't make the pain go away. This just shows the world that I was stronger than whatever tried to beat me.

I survived.

They didn't.

So the question is, what happens now?

Rev

I want a smoke.

That's the only thing racing through my mind as I peer down at the mound of dirt covering a dead Buckets and a very alive Carson.

Burying someone alive *is* as brutal as it sounds. But so is what he did to Darcie. He was the maestro in all of this, so it seems fitting it ends with him being worm food.

"Burying these dickwads is fucking exhausting," I casually say, wiping the sweat from my brow with the back of my arm.

I'm covered in dirt and blood, but I never expected anything less.

Do I feel bad for burying my brother alive?

Sure, I mean, it was only an hour or so ago that I found out he was my full brother.

I thought that fact would have played a part in me not being able to kill him, but when I look at Darcie and see the girl I first met re-appear, I don't regret a thing.

She'll never be the same person, though. None of us will.

We've done some fucked-up things and left a trail of mayhem behind, but we fucking survived. The underdogs won.

Hoo-fucking-ray. The question is, what do we do now?

I honestly never thought we'd get here, as I was convinced I would be doing time, giving Darcie a real chance at life.

But here we both are.

"Where to now?" she asks, reading my mind.

"I'd go anywhere with you, baby," I reply, interlacing our mud-covered fingers. "I heard Mexico is nice this time of year."

"Ooh, did you say margaritas?"

I chuckle, my gaze still riveted on the pile of dirt which buries our secrets.

"Let's bounce."

I can't believe we did it. Does this end with the bad guys

actually riding off into the sunset and living happily ever after?

Darcie takes one last look at the grave, and I think she might want to say a few words.

She doesn't.

She walks over to the truck and yanks Granny out. "Today's your lucky day."

There's no reason to hurt her now. She can grieve her grandson at a proper burial site—everyone's happy.

Tipping my face to the heavens, I inhale deeply because everything feels different. This feels like the first breath I've taken in years...but I soon discover...it's to be my last.

"What did you do?" Darcie screams, and when I hear the unmistakable wails of sirens, I know that there's one last plot twist for us yet.

A cell drops from Granny's hand, and I'll give it to the old fox. She outplayed us. This is what we get for underestimating an eighty-year-old batshit crazy grandma who knows how to work an iPhone, which was probably hidden in the pocket of her frilly apron. But when I see black SWAT vans follow the convoy of cop cars, I know it wasn't just her.

Walter probably sent in the troops to save his son when he got the call from the cops—Carson, that is. So we got screwed over by a little old lady, and my dad, who knew what calling the cops would do to me.

It fucking stings, but I'm not about to cry about it.

We literally have nowhere to run because the property is surrounded by the cops.

We run.

We die.

"Hands in the air!"

Darcie looks at me, pleading that I don't surrender.

She'd rather this be a Bonnie and Clyde ending than be captured alive. "No! This is not the end."

"I love you," I mouth before reaching into the small of my back for my gun.

This is not the end of the line for her...but for me, it is.

Just as I'm about to fire this place up like a Fourth of July barbecue, an earsplitting boom rattles us to our cores. It takes a moment, but I see the shot came from Buckets's dad, who stumbles down the porch stairs, shotgun in hand.

"My son will be home soon. You're parked in his spot!" he screams, clearly delirious, but it's the derail I need.

"Run!" I scream to Darcie, and when the police shout at Buckets's dad to drop his weapon, she stubbornly shakes her head.

"Not without you!"

"Chuck, drop the gun. Now!" the police shout, which is answered with another shot.

Mayhem erupts in the form of gunfire, and we all duck for cover. Darcie uses the truck as a shield while I dive for a tractor. Cocking my gun, I peer around it, prepared to fight to the death to get to Darcie because *this* is the ending I was preparing for.

Shots zip through the air, and I fire back when some asshole in full SWAT gear shoots at Darcie.

We lock eyes from across the field, and she too knows this is the end, in one way or another. As far as the cops know, she's still an unwilling participant in all of this. I'm the one with the gun.

I stand and begin shooting at anything that moves. I can hear Darcie's screams, but if they focus on me, she has a chance at running.

I duck and weave, using anything I can as a shield. The cops shoot, but I won't stop until Darcie is free. She, however, won't surrender and starts fighting, using the shovel we buried Carson with as a weapon. I need to think fast, which is why I aim and shoot a young rookie in the stomach.

"Officer down!"

All attention is riveted my way, and I hope for once in her fucking life, she does as she's told. I'm taken down by a bulldozer of a cop who almost breaks my wrist while disarming me.

With his knee in the middle of my back, I lift my chin and look at my little firecracker who set my world on fire, and for that, I'll thank her until the day I die.

With tears in her eyes, she wrestles with her emotions, her inner turmoil clear. But good sense prevails in the end because she can't save me—no one can.

She takes off into the woods, reminding me of the first night we met. My little rabbit is finally free. It's finally over.

I give up because my reason for fighting has gone.

I'm yanked up, punched in the guts, and handcuffed while being read my rights. I simply laugh in response as I look at the chaos I've created. I'm thrown into the back seat of a cop car.

I wonder what the holdup is, but when I hear the unmistakable sound of dirt being shifted, I know that it's not fucking over—shit has only just begun.

I watch as they pull a limp Carson from the ground, desperate for air as he drops to his hands and knees, gulping in breaths.

How can this motherfucker still be alive?

I'm expecting them to wrap him in a fluffy little blanket and offer him some refreshments because, you know, he was buried alive. But none of that happens.

Instead, he's yanked to his feet and cuffs are placed

around his wrists. Looks like blowing off your best friend's head in a room full of people has come back to bite him in the ass.

The door is ripped open, and they toss Carson's ass into the back seat.

I look over my shoulder at him and do the only thing that feels natural—I burst into hysterical laughter.

"You've got a little something on your face," I say between breaths, looking at his dirt-covered appearance.

"Oh, fuck you."

"That's what your mom said...but it was more of an *oh, fuck me, Rev, harder...hmm...just like that. Just like that*," I quip, poorly mimicking his mom as I bite my bottom lip theatrically.

But more laughter spills free when I realize that Theresa isn't his mom, after all.

"Your jokes are lame, cheap, and overused...just like your mom," Carson says, surprising me because that was pretty good.

But I've got an even better joke.

"Well, my mom is your mom...so you just insulted your own momma. Shame on you."

Carson's mouth hangs open, and it takes him three seconds to realize what I said. "Motherfucker!"

"That's what they call me, baby! The best in town." I sigh, resting my head against the headrest, reminiscing.

Carson shoves me in the shoulder, showing off like the lame all-star footballer that he is, and squashes me hard against the passenger window. My face is mushed against the glass, but it doesn't quash my laughter.

Maybe we could have gotten along well if we'd grown up together.

"Hey! Knock it off!" demands an officer as he gets into the driver's seat and revs the engine.

But we don't listen because, what's the worst they can do?

Carson and I continue nudging each other because we can't do jack shit cuffed, but I shift and headbutt him in the nose.

"My bad, I didn't see you there," I quip while blood pours from Carson's nose.

He screams and launches on top of me, biting my neck like fucking Edward from *Twilight*.

"Oh my God," I pant, laughing hard. "Did you just *bite* me, you fucking pussy? Did Coach teach you that?"

"Enough!" one of the cops barks, pulling over to the side of the road with a cloud of dust.

Both officers quickly jump out of the car like it's an emergency and rip open my door, hauling me out. One of them plants his ass in the middle seat next to Carson while the other cop shoves me back into the car on the opposite side, bashing my forehead on the doorframe.

Once buckled up tightly, I lean forward and wink at Carson.

He simply mouths, "Fuck off," and stares out his window like a sulky little bitch.

The cop jumps back in the driver's seat, slamming his door closed. We take off with the sirens sounding as the bad guys are driven away. The good people can sleep soundly once more.

Suddenly, I see a flash of blonde zipping through the trees. I don't know if it was a mirage or my little rabbit. But I close my eyes, knowing I'll find her again. Even if I have to dig my way out of a goddamn jail cell with a spoon.

All is well again in this fucking town.
But surely, they didn't think this was the end, did they?
See you soon, fuckers...

ABOUT THE AUTHOR

Monica and Michelle are best friends who have combined their love for dark comedy, crime documentaries, and bad boys to write dark romance that will steal your heart and haunt your mind.
Follow the white rabbit...

CONNECT WITH MONICA JAMES

Facebook: facebook.com/authormonicajames
Goodreads: goodreads.com/MonicaJames
Instagram: @authormonicajames
TikTok: @authormonicajames
BookBub: http://bit.ly/2E3eCIw
Amazon: https://amzn.to/2EWZSyS
Reader Group: http://bit.ly/2nUaRyi
Newsletter: https://tinyurl.com/mvjjk6k2
Patreon: https://www.patreon.com/c/
AuthorMonicaJames
Shopify: https://authormonicajames.store/